ANGELS FOR ALL

Nancy Powell

Book Two of the Ollie's Angels™ Series

TotalRecall Publications, Inc.

ISBN: 978-1-59095-589-5
UPC: 6-43977-45897-1
Copyright © 2013 by: Nancy Powell
Edited by: Jessica D. Caruso and Elizabeth Easter

TotalRecall Publications, Inc.
1103 Middlecreek, Friendswood, Texas 77546
281-992-3131 281 - 482-5390 Fax
6 Precedent Drive Rooksley, Milton Keynes, MK13 8PR, UK
1385 Woodroffe Av, Ottawa, ON K2G 1V8

Printed in the United States of America with simultaneous printings in Australia, Canada, and United Kingdom.

1 2 3 4 5 6 7 8 9 10

FIRST EDITION

TO MY FAMILY

Acknowledgement

I want to thank my family for their love and support, and my writing friends for their help and encouragement.

About the Book

In *ANGELS FOR ALL* Ollie believes in premonitions sent by guardian angels, but has no warning of hardships to come with drought and The Great Depression.

Roy and Ollie start married life striving for a better future and a place of their own. Each chapter is an episode that illustrates different difficulties imposed by farm life.

Almost every year, Roy goes away to other states working to earn money to pay the mortgage on a home they buy. Ollie stays on the farm to harvest crops and care for the children. She struggles against wild animals, foraging pigs, sickness, storms, hunger, and neighbors that prowl night and day stealing everything they can, including diapers, garden vegetables, harness, and cottonseed.

Ollie offers thanks for blessings she receives, giving credit to guardian angels for helping, but berates herself when she discounts premonitions of impending danger.

Book two in the Ollie's Angels Series.

List of Main Characters

Ollie McNew, born in 1908, (POV Character), light brown hair, blue eyes, **olive** complexion, slim, smart, helpful, competitive, strong willed, loves children and animals, skilled with a pistol, competent horseback rider, and has premonitions that alert her of dangers..

Roy Glenn, Ollie's husband, tall, dark hair, blue eyes, olive skin, excellent horseman, a farmer.

Robert McNew, Ollie's papa, dark curly hair, dark eyes, olive skin.

Artie McNew, Ollie's mama, small and thin, dark hair, blue eyes, olive skin.

Bertha McNew, Ollie's older sister, light brown hair, blue eyes, olive skin, plays the organ.

Earl McNew, Ollie's oldest brother, brown hair, blue eyes, olive skin.

Herbert McNew, younger brother, died as a baby.

Eldridge McNew, brother four years younger than Ollie, brown hair, blue eyes, olive skin.

Bronnie McNew, Ollie's youngest sister, black hair, dark eyes, darker olive skin.

Sherrill McNew, brother nine years younger than Ollie, black hair, dark eyes, olive skin.

Eugene McNew, asthmatic brother, eleven years younger than Ollie, brown hair, blue eyes, olive skin.

John McNew, Ollie's youngest brother, black hair, blue eyes, olive skin, winning smile.

John Lane, Grandpa, Artie's father.

Ann Lane, Grandma, Artie's mother.

Ma Glenn, Roy's mother.

Pa Glenn, Roy's father.

Morene Glenn, daughter born 1928, brown hair, blue eyes, olive skin.

Syble Glenn, daughter born 1930, brown hair, blue eyes, olive skin

Mary Ann Glenn, daughter born 1935, called Ann, brown hair, blue eyes, fair skin.

Doctor Hart, the community doctor and good friend of the family.

Kay Hart, Ollie's best friend.

Table of Contents

Chapter 1
The Wedding

Ollie pulls back the bedroom curtain. It is a typical February day in central Arkansas, the sky changes from sunshine to snow-spitting gray clouds. She slides her arms into a warm coat.

Mama taps on the door and enters. "Surely you're not going to work on that house again today. You'll catch cold and be sick for your wedding."

Ollie raises her chin and tightens her jaw. "I'll start a fire in the fireplace." Noticing worry lines on Mama's face, she softens her voice. "I have to get it ready."

Mama sighs and exclaims, "Ollie, you need a wedding dress. Tomorrow your Papa has business in Conway. We can go with him, and buy the material."

"Mama, I don't want a fancy white dress and a big wedding. I just want to go to a justice of the peace. If you're buying material, get something for a nice Sunday dress."

"No. People will whisper questions if you don't have a church wedding."

"Let them. I don't care." She lowers her head and twists her ring. "Remember how Grandpa always teased about dancing at my wedding?"

"You know Pa wouldn't want you to sacrifice your special day."

Tears fill Ollie's eyes. "I always promised he could have the first dance."

"That was only teasing."

"No, it wasn't. It was a promise. I won't have dancing."

"At least agree to let the preacher marry you. No dancing, I promise."

Ollie takes a deep breath. "All right, set it up. But a white dress is a waste of money. I'll never wear it again. If I have a colored one, I could wear it for Easter."

"I have white piqué that I bought on sale last fall. It's enough to make a dress and jacket. You can wear white for the wedding, and then we can dye the dress."

"I don't have white shoes."

"I'll buy you some. White gloves, a hat, and stockings too."

"That's an awful lot of trouble for such a small wedding."

"We'll always have the memories."

"Will you help me sew it? I've never made a jacket."

"Certainly. We can buy accessories tomorrow, and while in town, your dishes."

Ollie sighs. "Getting married sure takes a lot of planning and work."

"This is the start of a new life. After marriage, the two of you will plan things together."

"I hope Roy can get used to the way I want things."

Mama grins. "Things will not always be done the way you want."

Ollie laughs, and tosses her coat on the bed. "His mama needs to tell him that."

That afternoon, Ollie stands while Mama marks the hem in a white piqué dress.

"I was hoping roses would be in bloom." Mama folds the fabric and secures it with a pin. "Will daffodils work for a bridal bouquet?"

"Any flower is fine, providing they don't drip. I'm worried about housewares."

"Eldridge said he's going. I know you've always been closer to him, but you can't invite one brother and ignore your older brother and sister. If you don't invite Bertha and Earl, they'll have their feelings hurt."

Ollie makes a face. "Pretty soon the church will be full. I wanted it to be private."

"Think about how a sister and brother will feel—and Roy's parents. You'll regret it if you don't include them. An angry mother-in-law is not good for a marriage."

"Oh, go ahead; Ask them. Plan and invite anyone you want, as long as I don't have to worry with it. I'm still trying to get my house ready."

The next morning Papa waits in the buggy, impatiently tapping his fingers. Ollie steps up and pulls her coat tight around her legs. "Mama will be out soon. She's giving Bronnie instructions on what to do after school."

"Your sister knows all that. I told Artie I wanted to leave before daybreak. The sky's already getting light."

On the long trip, Ollie keeps thinking of things she needs to do before the wedding. *I could be making curtains.*

Papa leaves Mama and Ollie in front of the general mercantile and hurries away.

"Ollie, first let's look at hats and gloves inside the millinery."

Ollie glances at the mercantile. Dishes and housewares decorate the window. She would rather be over there.

A bell dings when Mama opens the door. Instead of the customary scent of fabric and glue, a sweet perfume hangs in the air. Mama picks up a small white hat with a short veil. "This will be perfect, don't you think? Especially for an afternoon wedding." She sets it on Ollie's head. "It's simple yet festive, and these gloves will go well with it."

"It's fine with me. So are the gloves. But I thought the wedding was at night."

Mama ignores Ollie's statement, and moves to another table. "I'm enjoying this."

"I noticed." Ollie smiles. It's good to see her happy. The winter was rough for Mama, with Grandpa's death and Eugene being sick most of the time. Ollie worries about her frail little brother almost as much as Mama does.

It will be harder to leave Eugene than John and the others. John is fat, healthy, and a bundle of mischief. Bronnie and Sherrill are good to help so Mama can care for Eugene when he has trouble breathing, but they are in school and cannot cook and do all the household chores. *What if Mama can't care for Eugene's every need after I leave, or what if she gets sick from overwork?* A wave of fear and guilt causes Ollie to shiver.

Mama leans close and whispers, "It's not every day that I get to dabble in finery."

The clerk finishes helping another customer and hurries over. "May I help you?"

Mama is stroking a roll of white satin ribbon. "We need to look a bit more."

"Certainly. Take all the time you want." She adjusts a hat ribbon before turning back to them. "Be sure to take note of this perfume, a real import from Paris. It came in last week. Men keep peeking in and telling me how good my store smells." She lifts, points it toward her neck, and squeezes the atomizer bulb. "I just love it."

"The fragrance is very nice." Mama picks up another hat.

She goes along every aisle, looking at elegant accessories. Ollie follows while glancing at the shopkeeper. She was right about the men: the banker, mayor, and several other well-dressed gentlemen enter one at a time to whisper in the lady's ear.

While passing the perfume counter, Mama generously sprays the perfume toward her wrist and inside the hat. She pays for the chosen items, Ollie gathers the packages, and the two women cross the street.

"Mama, why did you spray perfume inside my hat?"

"Do you not like the fragrance?"

"Yes, but why spray it on the hat?"

"You'll have that scent, a memory of your wedding, each time you pick up the hat."

Ollie knows Mama spent more than she should have. Papa frowns and shakes his head at the bags and boxes she has for him to load into the buggy.

On the way home, long shadows stretch across the road from the west, still Mama insists that Ollie stop and invite Roy's ma and pa to the wedding. Mrs. Glenn meets them at the door. "Come in. Come in and have a seat. Roy and his pa have gone to look at farm equipment, but they should be home soon. Will you stay for supper? I have plenty cooked, and I made a peach cobbler."

"No, thank you. We can't. Papa's in a hurry to get home and feed the animals. I stopped to invite you to the wedding, in case Roy forgot."

Mama reaches for her hand. "It's good to see you again Mrs. Glenn. We can step in for a minute. You'll freeze out here without a coat."

Mrs. Glenn and Mama find a lot to discuss; minutes stretch toward twilight. Ollie watches Papa through the window and marvels at his patience. He has repeatedly taken off his hat, combed fingers through his hair, and jammed the hat back on. He has checked the hooves of the horses three times—finally he gets in the buggy and sits tapping gloved fingers on the seat. Before Mama says goodbye, Ollie is again having regrets about agreeing to a church wedding.

The day before the wedding, Roy and Ollie move their few belongings into the little unpainted house. They have a bed, a chest of drawers, a table and four chairs, a kitchen cabinet from Ollie's grandma Lane, and a cook stove left by previous tenants, but they have no curtains for the windows.

Saturday afternoon, Eldridge brings the buggy to drive Ollie to the church. Before leaving, Ollie walks around the bedroom she shared with Bertha and then Bronnie. She touches curtains, pats the bed, opens the chifforobe where she kept her clothes, takes a journal from a dresser drawer and writes: *Wedding Day, February 26, 1927.*

Ollie and Eldridge ride in silence until they approach the McNew Cemetery. Ollie looks across rows of gravestones. "You know, I always thought I would be buried out there, but a woman has to be laid to rest next to her husband and his family. I don't even know where that will be."

"Well, big sister, you'll soon be married, but you're not dying. Forget about the cemetery." They laugh, and look down the road at a stream of wagons and buggies. "I'm surprised you didn't run away," Eldridge adds. "A big wedding doesn't seem like your style."

"What do you mean *a big wedding*? Do you think those folks are coming here? It's supposed to be only family!"

Eldridge turns his face toward her. "You mean you don't know? Bertha and Mama have been cooking for two days. I think every acquaintance Papa and Mama have will be here, and they know *everyone*."

"I told Mama I wanted a simple family affair."

"It got way past simple when Papa started inviting."

She takes a deep breath. "No use whining. It'll be over soon."

"I wouldn't count on it. I overheard talk of a shivaree."

Ollie jerks her head toward him. "Who's planning that?"

"I can't tell you. I'll get killed if they find out I told. So don't you dare let on that you know, or I'll never tell you anything else."

A short time later, Ollie peeps from a small room while waiting for the music to start. Every seat in the church is full. Plates and bowls of food cover two long tables at the back of the auditorium.

She opens the door enough to see Roy talking to the preacher at the front of the church. Handsome in a dark suit and tie, he smiles and shakes hands with people passing. Mama and Eugene, on the second seat from the front, try their best to keep John quiet.

Papa's voice is jovial as he greets people entering the church. Sherrill, usually so shy that he is overlooked, stands beside Papa welcoming people with a smile and even a few handshakes. "Bronnie, will you go tell Papa to come in so we can start. This will take all night if he hinders everyone trying to come through the door."

The ceremony passes in a blur. People laugh, talk, and eat. At last, Roy asks if she is almost ready to throw her bouquet.

She nods, and leans close to whisper, "Is the buggy ready?"

"It was, but I asked Pa to make sure someone hasn't tied a load of cans to it. That horse is high-spirited. We don't want to wind up in another county with a runaway."

Pausing at the door, Ollie tosses the bouquet over her head and runs. With no concern for poise and grace, she scrambles into the buggy. Roy jumps in, and they trot away.

They are barely out of the driveway when cans drop to the ground, clanging and banging. The horse leaps forward.

"Hold on, Ollie!"

She grabs a handrail seconds before one wheel hits a rock and bounces the buggy into the air. Ollie stifles a scream.

At last, Roy stops the frightened animal. He wraps the lines around the brake and gets out to calm the horse.

Ollie climbs down, borrows Roy's pocketknife, and cuts the string holding the cans. "I could kick myself for letting Mama talk me into a church wedding."

"Ah, she enjoyed it, and it's over now."

"No, it's not over. We can expect a shivaree tonight."

"Are you sure?"

"I got it from a reliable source."

They rush to the little two-room sharecropper house that they have repaired and scrubbed clean. Roy parks Pa's buggy behind the barn, unhitches the horse, and fastens him in a stall. Once Roy is inside the house, they lock the doors, blow out the lamps, wrap themselves in blankets, and crawl under the bed.

Within an hour, they hear shouts, and banging on the door. Lanterns are held close to curtainless windows. "Come out and celebrate! This is a shivaree!"

Roy and Ollie lie motionless without a word.

"I don't believe they're in there. I can see with the lantern that the bed's empty and still made up with a smooth quilt. Tell Charlie to get the skunk and throw it under the house. At least they'll know we've been here when they come back."

The crowd leaves with as much noise as when it came. A pungent scent creeps into the house. Ollie buries her head in the blanket until she has to gasp for air.

"Try to hold on for a little longer, Ollie. That skunk smells as if it's been dead for a few days. I bet Charlie caught it in one of his traps and shot it so he wouldn't get sprayed. We'll wait a while to make sure they're gone, before I look under the house with a lantern. If the skunk's dead, and I'm sure it is, I'll drag it off and bury it."

"I'll stay in here, unless you need me to help."

Roy eases the door open and listens before going outside. The lantern flickers, and the musty scent of kerosene mingles with the stench of the decaying skunk. "It's been dead for a long time. Can you come hold the lantern while I try to hook a wire on it?"

She holds her nose with one hand, and the lantern with the other. "This is not exactly the kind of wedding night that people dream about."

"What did you say, Ollie?"

"Nothing important. I was just trying to breathe."

Chapter 2
Giving and Taking

Roy and Ollie step into the cool air. "Look at the sky, Ollie. The whole world seems to have a warm glow."

She brushes a strand of hair from her cheek. With one arm around him, she looks up. "This is the best time of day. I'd like to sit down with you, right here on the ground, and watch the sky turn from morning rose to midday blue, but we better get to work. It could rain this afternoon."

He kisses her forehead. "With a wife like you, how can a man fail?"

Rain clouds threaten and sprinkle off and on for several days. More than once Ollie leaves the garden and retreats to the house to cook or clean until she is warm and dry. Roy stays in the field, driving the mules to break the ground.

On the fifth day, sprinkles turn to drizzle, but Roy refuses to come inside at noon. Ollie takes a quart of hot soup to him. "Roy, stop and drink this. You're wet, and cold."

He takes the jar and drinks quickly. "Ollie, that was the best soup I ever tasted." He wipes his mouth with the back of his hand. "I have to get to work. Unless this drizzle starts causing mud to collect on my plow, I'm gonna finish this field." He winks at her, and clicks his tongue at the mules. "Get up. Get up, boys."

The mules jerk their weight against the chains, and the sharp plow unzips the damp grass to reveal a deep furrow of dry earth. Roy stumbles over rough clods. His shoulders slightly bent above the handles, elbows out to each side, he lifts the back of the plow so the mules can pull the point deeper. With her heart full of love, Ollie wants to run and hug him. Instead, she smiles and turns toward the house.

A pail of seed potatoes, cut for planting, waits on the porch. Ollie places the empty soup jar inside the door and starts for the garden with the bucket.

By mid-afternoon, Ollie has planted potatoes, carrots, radishes, and early green peas. Mud clinging to her hands and shoes, she sets out a row of cabbage. As she packs the damp soil around the last plant, the sky opens, pouring rain in torrents. She can barely see Roy following the mules to the barn. She hurries to the house, dragging her shoes on wet grass to remove the mud.

Ollie pushes a chair toward Roy when he comes in the back door. "Sit here and pull off your shoes. There's dry clothes and a tub of warm water in front of the fireplace. I hope you don't get sick from being in this rain."

"You either. I saw you in the garden. How did you get clean so fast?"

"Before noon, I put the tub in front of the fireplace, and heated buckets of water. There was enough wood in the stove to keep it warm all afternoon. And I hurried so I wouldn't be the one to get second-hand water." She grins and takes his wet socks.

"It's a good thing you did. It'll be like a mud pie when I get out, but I finished the field. I was at the end of the last row when, all at once, I could hardly see. I'm glad the mules knew where to go. I unhooked the plow, and they led me to the barn."

"The rain master must have been waiting for us before tipping his bucket. I was setting my last plant when the downpour began."

"Well, I'm thankful for the blessing."

"Me, too."

"Ollie, that was a good idea to hang a covered milk pail in the barn. Now the work is done, and I don't have to go outside again. Too bad I had to milk with dirty hands."

She frowns, turns her head sideways to look at him, and grins. "You better not have. I left a bucket of soapy water and a clean towel for your hands. I would have milked, but I couldn't have got to the bath first." She giggles, wiggles her hips, and bursts into laughter.

"I figured that much."

"Are you hungry? I cooked cornbread, fried potatoes, and beans with ham hock."

"I could eat a pot of that, but I hate to get out of this water. Bring me a plate?"

Ollie grins. "You don't look very comfortable with your long legs hanging over the tub, toward the fire."

"You're right. The ridge on this tub is cutting my back. I'll come to the table."

Days turn into weeks before the fields dry enough for plowing. Roy and Ollie are not idle. While it rains, he sits beside the fireplace sharpening a saw, and whittling new handles for a rusted ax and a grubbing hoe given to him by relatives. When winds whisper, with no rain, he cuts and burns brush. While winds howl, he shovels manure from the barnyard and puts it on the garden. Ollie sews curtains from flour sacks, cuts donated scraps into quilt pieces, and bakes.

"Ollie, I love all the good things you've been cooking. But if the fields don't dry pretty soon, I'll be too fat to work."

"You don't need to worry. I bet you haven't gained a pound."

When the weather clears and the *Farmer's Almanac* indicates the signs are right for gardening, Ollie has healthy tomato plants waiting on the south side of the house. She covers them with feed sacks on cold nights to guard against frost.

On a warm evening in April, she and Roy sit on the porch, talking and looking at the stars. "Ollie, if it stays dry until Monday, I'll start planting. The fields are broken and ready, and the whippoorwills have been calling for several nights, saying it's time."

"I've been listening. It seems longer than a year since you first walked me home. The whippoorwills were calling that night, and you talked about wanting land of your own."

"A lot has happened in a year. We're working for ourselves, and eventually we'll get our own land with a herd of cattle to graze the hillsides."

Ollie scoots closer. He puts an arm around her.

"If this is a good season, we'll be busy from planting until winter. So, I'd like to go to Ma's for Sunday dinner. We can stop by your mama's on the way home."

"Oh, Roy, that sounds good. I'm eager to tell them about our garden. I think every seed came up, even though the ground was a little too wet when I planted some of them. If they continue to grow, maybe we'll have leftovers to fatten our pig."

"Not counting early ones that tolerate frost, what kind of seeds did you plant?"

"Tomatoes, lettuce, cucumbers, squash, peppers, cantaloupe, and melon."

"I don't remember you buying all those."

"Our mamas gave them to me. I'll save seeds from everything for next year."

Sunday morning, they get on the road early. Ollie wants to see Mama and Papa before church. About a mile down the road, they meet two riders. When they are out of hearing range, Ollie whispers, "Roy, one of those guys is the one that went to prison for stealing a cow. Let's turn around and go home."

"Why?"

"They've seen us leaving. They'll steal anything they want while we're gone."

"Ollie, we can't stay home all the time."

"I know, but I have a bad feeling about today. I'd like to go home."

He grasps her hand. "Don't worry so much. We need to visit our families."

The day is like a holiday. When they arrive, Ma has mashed potatoes, green peas, pickled peaches, green onions, hot biscuits, gravy, and fried chicken on the table.

It is late afternoon when they get back to Mama and Papa's. Eugene slips cookies into Ollie's pocket and whispers, "Two for you, and two for Roy."

"Oh, Eugene, you're so nice, but keep them for you, Bronnie and Sherrill."

"No. They ate their share. These were mine. They're a present from me."

Ollie hates to take the cookies, yet it is evident that the giving brings him great pleasure.

Leaving the yard, Roy whips the mules into a trot. "We'll have to hurry to get the animals fed and the milking finished before dark."

Ollie rushes to unlock the door and get the milk pail ready. Roy takes the team and wagon to the barn. She has kindled a fire under the kettle, changed out of her Sunday dress, and is pouring boiling water over the bucket when Roy comes in. "I was starting to worry about you. It never takes long to unhitch the mules."

She glances at him and slams the kettle down. "What's wrong Roy? You look sick. Ease into one of those chairs. I'll go milk the cow."

"I should have listened to you. Someone stole my new harness and plow lines while we were gone—the only things I didn't get around to marking with my name."

"Oh no! Should we go call the sheriff?"

Roy slumps into a chair. "It wouldn't do any good. Even if he found extras in their barn, I have no way of proving one set is mine." He props his left elbow on his knee and combs through his hair with the other hand. "I'll just have to do more patching on the old harness and buy new lines."

Ollie sighs, and shakes her head. "Is that all they got?"

"No. They took the cottonseeds we stored in the loft. Unless one of my brothers has more than he can use, we'll have to buy some."

Roy walks around the room, constantly slamming a fist into his palm. "I should have listened. Ma told me to respect a woman's intuition. She said some have a special sense for hearing angels whisper warnings."

Ollie pauses. "I believe angels can bring notice of danger."

She grabs the milk pail. "But I don't believe we should wait for them to tell us what to do. We have to deal with worldly evidence." She opens the door. "Especially if it passes you on the road." She yanks on the knob, the latch clicks, and she heads for the barn.

The garden produced well. Since early morning, Ollie has been picking, shelling, peeling, chopping, and canning vegetable soup. She takes the last jar from the pressure cooker and places it under a towel for it to cool and the seal to click.

Through the window, Ollie sees Roy coming up the path from the barn. Immediately, she removes bowls of peas, squash, stewed potatoes, and a plate of cornbread from the warming oven.

The kitchen door slams. "Good gracious, it's hot in here." Roy looks at her, and takes her hand. "We're going to the well. You need to wash your face in cold water before you faint. Sit on the step while I draw a fresh bucket." He holds the wash pan while she splashes her face.

"That breeze feels good. I got too hot while rushing to finish the canning and cook supper." She smiles and takes a towel from Roy's outstretched hand.

"I could see that. Go on to the porch. I'll fill our plates and bring them out. Next time you use a cooker, open the windows."

She jerks her head up and starts to speak.

He raises his hand. "I know, flies come in open windows. Someday we'll have screens. In the meantime, take a few breaks outside. I don't want you cooking your brain."

"I was afraid the pressure might go too high if I left the

cooker. I worked hard preparing those vegetables. I didn't want to take a chance on it exploding."

"Your face is red, but your eyes don't look glassy like they did when I came in."

"I was feeling a little faint, but I'm fine now. I was rushing to get finished."

Roy shakes his head. "Don't do that again."

"It wasn't only the hot kitchen making me feel sick."

Roy puts down his bread and turns to her. "Do you think you might have caught something? I heard that woman in front of us at church saying her kid was sick."

"No. It's not that." She pauses while he takes a drink of tea. "I'm expecting."

Roy stops chewing and stabs a chunk of potato with his fork. "Expecting what?"

Ollie grins, and leans against a post. "A little girl. Or a boy."

"What?" Shock turns into a grin spreading across his face. "Are you sure?"

"Pretty sure. I think it should be born next April."

He stands and pulls her to him. With his arms wrapped gently around her, he kisses her forehead. "You'll have to take it easier from now on. Don't try to can the whole garden harvest in one day. We want a healthy mama, too."

"It's only the last six weeks that I'll have to be careful."

"You've been working harder than most men. I don't want you doing that now. I'll gather the crops by myself."

"As long as I'm feeling well, I'm gonna help. Today, I noticed the cotton. It's ready for the first picking, and the corn is almost dry enough to gather. We'll work together, so we can get it all harvested before cold weather sets in."

"I can get it done. I'll start early and stay late."

"We'll both start early and stay late. By the way, I mended those old cotton sacks your pa gave us. I rushed to can soup so I can start picking tomorrow."

"All right, but promise you'll stop if you have any doubts about working."

"I will." She hugs him tight. "Hey, let's rest while we can."

They sit on the porch. Roy wraps one arm around her waist, and starts planning. "There's been no dew the last few mornings, so I can start picking early while you're washing the breakfast dishes." He pulls a pipe from his pocket, lights it, takes a long draw, and blows smoke into the twilight. "In a few years we'll have a little boy to help."

Ollie lays her head against his shoulder. "Or a little girl."

The next morning, by the time Roy puts sideboards on the wagon, parks it, and gets the scales set up to weigh the cotton, Ollie is in the field ready to start.

Long canvas bags, coated on the bottom with tar, trail behind them, getting plump and heavy. Ollie stops to shake the weight down in her sack. Before hooking the strap over her shoulder, she arches her back and slings her arms from side to side.

"Ollie, I think bending over these stalks is one of the hardest jobs I've ever done, much harder than herding cattle. Let's get a drink of water and rest for a few minutes."

"I know you're saying that so *I'll* rest, but I'm fine. This will be miserable if we get an early cold spell, and we're out here with our hands freezing."

He rubs a shoulder and flexes his neck before bending to

continue grabbing handfuls of the white fluff spilling from inside sharp barbs of dry brown bolls. When Ollie's sack gets heavy and hard for her to pull, Roy takes it to the scales. Sometimes, she walks with him to the wagon to get a drink and write down the weight. Other times, she slips behind his strap and continues picking until he returns to weigh and empty his own.

It is late October before all the corn is gathered and the last load of cotton from the second picking is ready to haul to the gin. Roy stops the wagon near the porch. Ollie comes out of the house, locks the door, and climbs up to sit beside him.

Roy clicks the leather lines against the mules. "We did it, and you were right—I couldn't have done it by myself. I expect we'll have freezing weather any day now."

"It's been a good year. We're ready for winter with canned vegetables, a fat pig, and we'll still have a little money in the bank after you pay for use of the property."

"You didn't count all our blessings. We have a little boy on the way."

Ollie shakes her head and laughs. "Maybe one of each."

"It's possible. I'm a twin. Two healthy babies would be great."

Ollie raises her eyebrows. "I prefer one at a time."

He chuckles and pats her leg. "Bronnie and your brothers will be home from school before I get back. After I get the cotton baled and sold, I'm going to Pa's. He said he'd go with me to the bank, and to pay the landlord. It could be after dark, so don't get worried."

"What about the cow?"

"Milking late won't hurt her. Her calf is weaned, and she'll soon go dry."

"I hope she has the new calf before we get ice and snow."

"Ollie, don't fret about things we have no control over. There's plenty of hay in the barn. I'll put them in the dry if she has it in bad weather."

Roy stops the wagon. "Remember, I may be late if there are long lines at the gin."

From the porch, Mama waves to Roy, and holds the door open for Ollie. "I'm so glad you're here. I dug out a few baby things, and found blue and yellow flannel scraps. Each piece is big enough for a baby gown. If you can stay awhile, I'll help sew them."

"I have all day. It may be dark before Roy gets back."

Mama and Ollie finish the sewing before school is out. Bronnie and Eugene rush to hug Ollie. Sherrill sticks out his hand for a quick handshake, but pulls away before she can wrap her arms around him. Eldridge slaps her on the shoulder. "I hear you're gonna need bigger dresses."

"Yes, and I'll need a babysitter. Do you want to volunteer?"

Eugene has gone into the kitchen, but Bronnie squeals, "I do! I do!"

Eldridge grins. "I'll take him hunting when he's big enough."

Ollie laughs. "What if it's a girl?"

"I'll teach her to shoot."

Before dark, Ollie starts peeping out the window, watching for Roy. She can hardly wait to show the little blue and yellow gowns to him. When the hour grows late, Mama sends the younger children to bed. Papa says he's tired from a long hard day and needs to say goodnight. Mama sits dozing in her rocker. Eldridge is full of stories, and keeps Ollie laughing until Roy pulls into the yard.

In a flurry, Ollie says goodnight and hurries out the door with the gowns and bag of baby clothes Mama gave her. "Roy, I know you said not to worry, but I couldn't help it. It's so late. Did you have trouble?"

He chuckles. "Not yet. Not unless you don't like the news I have for you."

"What news?

"I bought us something."

Ollie catches her breath. "What did you buy?"

"When I went to pay our yearly dues, the old man asked if I wanted the property. He said his health is not good. He wanted to sell, and gave me a price to consider, but only until next week when he has someone else coming to look at it."

Roy clears his throat. "I knew we'd have no place to go if he sold it to someone else. Pa was waiting outside, so I talked it over with him. He thought it was a fair price. We went to the bank, and I applied for a loan."

"Just like that! Did you have enough for the down payment?"

"Barely. Money will be tight for the next year. I'm glad you have all those vegetables stored away. Maybe I can find some odd jobs around the community. Pa told me about a man who needs help clearing a field."

"I'm excited, but scared. Did you save a little money for emergencies?"

"I couldn't. Don't worry. Now, it's a home of our own."

"I can't help worrying. I won't be able to help much in the spring. The baby's due at planting time."

Winter descends in early November with howling winds from the northwest. Each day for a week, Ollie keeps a pot of beans or soup bubbling on the stove, and she bakes fresh bread. When not in the kitchen, she sits near the fireplace, hovering over her sewing basket, cutting and stitching baby quilts.

Roy sharpens every farm tool he owns, and cleans and oils all the harness. "I hate this weather. My mules stand useless in the barn, eating the winter's hay. If this blasted freezing wind would stop blowing, I could hitch them and pull stumps from the new ground. Or I could look for work, and maybe earn some wages."

"I know, Roy, but you can't argue with the weather. It'll change soon."

He tosses another log into the fireplace. "Snow would be better than this. I can burn brush piles with snow on the ground. But I can't do anything in a wind storm."

"Why don't you crack and shell a basket of black walnuts? Then, I'll bake us a pie sweetened with sorghum molasses."

"I'll do that. Last week I put a flat rock in the corncrib for that purpose. I'll crack them, and come in by the fire to pick them out." By suppertime, Roy has a basket full of hulls and a bowl of shelled walnuts.

He stands and stretches his back. "If this wind is still blowing tomorrow, you may have to teach me how to make baby clothes. I don't like being idle."

The next morning when they wake, the room seems unusually bright. Roy rises on one elbow and looks outside. "Did I wish for snow?"

"I think you did."

"In the future, remind me to be more careful with my

wishing." He jumps from the bed and runs to the fireplace. Working in a frenzy, he shovels ashes off the hot coals, tosses on kindling, followed by small sticks of split oak, and then races back to bed.

"The way you were dancing on your toes would make a good vaudeville show."

"Really." He turns his head sideways and grins at her. "Do you want to do the entertaining tomorrow?"

"No." She rolls onto her side and giggles. "I couldn't top your show."

Propped on his pillow, he stares at her. "To make up for laughing, you better make me two pies. I'll come in every hour for a slice. Pie will give me lots of pep for dancing."

"I'll do it." She starts to giggle again, but buries her face in a quilt.

"The wind's not screaming around the eaves, but the floor is like ice." He shivers, and touches a foot to Ollie's ankle. "See?"

"Oh! Stay on your side." She pulls her feet underneath her long flannel gown. "I need to make you some wool slippers to wear when you build the morning fire."

"I didn't do much building this morning. I merely threw wood on last night's coals." He shivers. "In spite of the cold, I still want to burn those brush piles. Make a big breakfast. It'll take lots of energy to keep two of them going."

Ollie moves to the edge of the bed. "Yes, it will. I'll get started right away."

"Not so fast. Stay in bed until the house gets warm."

"But I need to start a fire in the cook stove."

"I'll start it when this room gets warm. Ollie, promise me you won't go outside today. You might slip and fall. I'll bring in extra water, and wood from the porch."

"I'm not getting clumsy yet. I'm only about four months pregnant. The only thing I plan to do outside is to get sweet potatoes from the barn."

"You don't have to be clumsy to slip on snow and hurt yourself. I'll get your potatoes. Now, promise you'll stay inside."

She pulls the quilt tighter. "All right. Should I simply sit by the fire eating bonbons?"

Roy chuckles. "If you'll save me some." He swings his legs over the side of the bed, and takes a deep breath before touching his feet to the floor.

From a nail on the wall, Roy snatches a heavy blue shirt darned at the elbows. He jerks the shirt on over his long johns, jams his legs into patched overalls, and drags a frayed gallus over one shoulder. In three long strides, he reaches the chair where Ollie has left his clean wool socks. He pulls on the socks, slips his feet into high-top shoes, scraped and skinned from rough work. Dragging the laces, he plods into the kitchen to start a fire in the cook stove.

November and December seem to creep along. When he can, Roy hires out to work for anyone needing help. He cuts wood, hauls manure, cleans a chicken house, builds fence, and helps repair a barn.

Ollie wonders if Roy will have a Christmas gift for her. He has been working every day and has not been to town, although he has been to the general store. The store sells useful items for the home, and carries a few bolts of fabric.

If he bought me something, how did he pay for it? Each time he is paid, he brings the money home. They count it together and store it away for emergencies. None of the money is missing.

She tries to tell herself it does not matter, but deep inside she wonders how she can hide the disappointment if he does not care enough to bring her some kind of present. Still, they did agree not to spend the emergency money on anything but a dire need.

With scraps of heavy wool, that Grandma gave her, Ollie sews a saddle blanket. The leftover pieces she fashions into a pair of warm slippers. She hides the gifts in a box, under the bed, until Christmas.

Chapter 3
Gifts

On Thursday before Christmas, Eldridge drives down with eggs. "Mama said eggs are healthy for you and the baby. She intends for you to eat all you want."

"I'm glad you came. It's so good to see you. I get lonesome when Roy's off working." She laughs. "And we were out of eggs."

"I bet you *do* get lonesome. What keeps you busy all day?"

"Cooking. Sewing baby things. Come in, and I'll show you what I've made."

"Show me the food first. Oh, before I forget, Mama wants you to know she's having her big dinner on Saturday, Christmas Eve. She said it'll be too hectic to have it on Sunday. She wants to know if you and Roy will be there."

"Yes, we will." She pauses. "Unless Roy has told his ma we'll be at her house."

On Friday night, Roy comes home after dark. He is covered with dirt, and his face is black with soot. "I don't think I've ever been so tired. I've been clearing ground and burning brush for one of Pa's neighbors."

"No wonder you're so dirty. Your bath water's in front of the fire."

"I'll have to wait until I milk the cow. Is the pail scalded?"

"Better than that. The milk is already strained."

They linger over supper, Roy's head nodding while Ollie

talks. He stands as she starts to clear the dishes. "I'll bring in fresh water."

"Sit and rest. We don't need water. I brought in an extra bucket."

"I have to get something from the barn." He is gone before she can comment.

Ollie takes her sewing and sits by the fire with her back to the kitchen. When Roy comes in, the door slams. "Is the wind starting to blow again?"

"No. I kicked the door closed. My hands are full."

"What are you bringing in to work on now? You won't have much time in the morning. I want to leave early so I can help Mama cook."

"Is it all right if you get your Christmas present now?"

Ollie jumps when Roy drops something beside her. "A rocking chair! Oh, you don't know how I've been wishing for one." Tears fill her eyes. She reaches to touch it and run her hand over the seat. "It's so pretty."

Roy grasps the rocker to hold it still. "Sit in it."

She gets up, places her sewing in a strait-back chair, and gives Roy a kiss, "Thank you." She sits with her left elbow on the armrest, and curls her hand around as if holding something. "All I need now is a baby."

"It won't be long. I can hardly wait to take the little guy fishing."

"I bet our little *girl* will like fishing." She smiles at him. "Oh, your present is under the bed."

"Keep rocking. I'll get it." He lifts the box, sits, and removes a piece of tightly woven red cloth. "I've never seen such a pretty saddle blanket. Where did you find it?"

"I made it from an old piece of wool that Grandma gave me."

"The color is bright. It doesn't look like it's made from old material."

"It's dyed. The piece shrank in the hot dye, but I cut it afterward."

Roy turns it over, rubbing each side. "It's pretty enough for one of those fancy parade horses. The one I've been using is so shabby; it can hardly be called a blanket."

Roy bends to kiss her. "Thanks for going to so much trouble."

"I wanted to make you something nice."

He is still rubbing the blanket as if it is a live pet.

"Did you see what else is in the box?"

"Something else?" He rushes to the bed, and lifts a piece of tissue from the box. "Oh, I need these, too, and they match my saddle blanket." He grins. "I'm not supposed to wear these slippers when—?"

Ollie laughs. "No, they're not meant for wearing when you're riding."

"Good. I doubt such a fashion would catch on." He turns them over and runs his fingers along the stitches. "This double-thick material must have been hard to sew."

"It was. Even with using a thimble, my fingers got sore."

He pulls off his shoes and slides his toes between the soft layers of wool. "Thanks. These are warm." He walks back and forth in front of the fireplace. "You've eliminated the morning vaudeville act. There'll be no more dances on the cold floor."

Ollie continues to smile and rock. "This is a wonderful Christmas. I'm wondering, though, how did you buy my rocker? All your wages are still in the jar."

"Except for yesterday and today. I got more money the last two days because I used the mules. That guy's pretty horses couldn't budge those stumps."

"When did you ever have time to go shopping? You've been working every day."

"Ma and Pa bought it for me last week when they went to town. I paid them today. Ma told me to get it. She said a new mama needs a rocker."

"Your ma is a thoughtful lady."

The next day is wonderful. Ollie enjoys helping Mama cook, hearing Papa tell funny stories, visiting with family, and seeing the children.

Bronnie and Sherrill run in and out of the house, playing with nieces, nephews and cousins. Because of his breathing problems, Eugene is not allowed outside in the cool December air. He stays beside Ollie, offering to peel, mix and stir.

Eugene, intelligent beyond his years, tells her of books he has read. He explains reasons for the Great War, its end, and for the fighting going on now in other countries. "Ollie, do you worry about things in Europe?"

"We don't get a newspaper. I worry if we'll have money to pay the bank next year when our loan payment comes due, and I worry if my baby will be healthy."

"Do you ever worry about dying?"

Ollie takes a deep breath, and drops into a chair. "Yes, sometimes."

"Don't. You're a Christian. I'm not afraid of dying."

Mama takes one look at Ollie, and sends Eugene to get a wet cloth. "He didn't mean to upset you. Some things he doesn't understand, but he knows far more than most children his age. He reads the Bible, the newspaper, and magazines the doctor saves for him. His questions leave me stuttering. Some, I can't answer."

Mama rushes to a boiling pot on the stove. Eugene pats the cold cloth to Ollie's face. "Ollie, you're not going to die when your baby comes, and neither will the baby. You'll live to be an old, old woman."

Ollie smiles. "Is my brother a fortune teller? What's the charge for predictions?"

Eugene scowls. "I know some things. I knew when Grandpa was going to die."

Later, Ollie follows Mama into the kitchen with a stack of plates. "Mama why did you take Eugene to visit Grandma and Grandpa the week before Grandpa died?"

"Eugene insisted. He rarely asks anything for himself, but he couldn't be talked out of going to visit them that week. I'm so glad we went. Why do you ask?"

"I was only wondering."

Ollie has a lot of time to think about Eugene's prediction. Roy usually works from dawn until near dark. To occupy her time, she tries new recipes from a well-worn cookbook given to her by Grandma Lane.

Roy stops near the door. "I smell spices. Does your cake have frosting?"

Ollie giggles, hoping she has stumped Roy at the guessing game evolved from her daily baking. "I didn't make a cake. Guess again. And remember, you only get two more tries if you want a taste before supper."

"Give me some hints. I'm so hungry I could eat a whole

cake by myself."

She folds her arms, tilts her head back, and smiles. "I started making it early this morning. I used yeast. It's spicy, and bubbly when it's hot."

"It can't be pie. It must be cinnamon bread with syrup on top."

"You're getting close. Only one more chance."

Roy jumps down from the wagon. "I need another hint." In two long strides, he is on the step. Ollie stands in the doorway, holding onto the facing. He puts his hands under her arms, and tries to move her.

"No fair! You're cheating." She laughs so hard that she can barely hold on.

"I'm hungry! When Esau sold his birthright to Jacob for a bowl of stew, he must have felt like this." He tickles her ribs. She turns loose, and backs away from the door.

Ollie, still laughing, plops into a chair. Roy mumbles something she cannot understand. His mouth is full of warm cinnamon roll.

"Slow down, and breathe. You already ate one almost as big as a plate." She grins. *"Man chokes to death on cinnamon rolls* would sound awful bad as a news headline. I'd be a widow forever."

"Yeah, it *would* make a man think twice." Roy grins and takes a deep breath. "Ma never made these. I've got to have another one."

"You didn't even stop to wash your hands, did you?"

"I washed a little, when I quit work. It only takes three fingers to hold one." He takes another bite, and mumbles, "I didn't swallow much dirt."

Ollie wrinkles her nose, and shakes her head as he wipes his hands on the dishtowel. "Well, if you want more, you'll need to go by the store tomorrow. I used the last of my cinnamon, and I'm almost out of flour and sugar."

"I doubt it'll be open that late. We're trying to finish clearing a field before it rains. Mr. Snow wants to plant it in the spring. If you can hold off until Saturday, we'll both go. Maybe some of your friends will be there."

On Saturday morning, Ollie has scarcely finished washing the breakfast dishes when Roy comes inside. "Will you be ready to go pretty soon?"

"I can be, but I thought we were going this afternoon."

"I'd like to get home in time to do some work around here."

Ollie reaches to untie her apron, and quickly turns toward the nail where she hangs it. She does not want Roy to see her disappointment. "I need to change my dress and put on my good shoes. Hitch up the wagon, and bring it to the porch."

"I've already caught the mules. I'll be back in a few minutes."

Ollie knows that none of her friends will be at the store this early. Mostly older people shop before ten o'clock.

Trace chains rattle as the wagon stops. Ollie puts on her coat and goes out. On the way, Roy starts recalling things he wants to do before dark.

"I can go to the store by myself." Ollie says. "Stay home and start on your work."

"No. You're good with horses, but these mules are temperamental and stubborn. They might get spooked and run away, or balk in the road. I have time to take you."

In front of the store, Roy stops to talk to some men. Ollie

goes inside to gather supplies. Old Miss White listens while Ollie tells the storekeeper that she will need a sack of flour and a sack of sugar. "Girl, you ought to forget about all that sweet baking until after your baby gets here. Extra fat makes it harder to give birth."

Ollie starts backing away when the old woman lifts her hand as if to pat Ollie's stomach. "When's it due?"

"The middle of April."

"That's a bad time for the first. In the wintertime, new mamas spend too much time eating and sitting around. Weak muscles can't push a baby into the world. I've midwifed for lots of women. Only ones I lost were in late winter, or spring." The old lady shakes her head. "Sad thing to lose a life. I'm telling this for your own good." She leans close to Ollie's face, her dark eyes squinting. "Eat vegetables, lean meat when you can get it, stay away from sweet food, and get up, move about."

She steps back and looks at Ollie's stomach. "Have you got an iron bed?"

Ollie nods.

"Hold to the foot rail and squat twenty-five or thirty times a day, but not so many at first. You need to strengthen your pushing muscles."

Ollie glances from side to side. She has backed into a corner; the broad-shouldered woman is in front of her. Ollie stands motionless, except for an occasional nod. Before leaving, Miss White reaches to wrap strong hands around Ollie's fingers, bends her head crowned with gray-white braids, and kisses the top of Ollie's right hand.

"God bless you, child. If you need me, call any time, day or night. Tell Roy, if your time comes when White Oak Creek is out of its banks, I can go where the doctor's buggy can't. My mule's a good swimmer."

Ollie holds onto a shelf and turns slow, staring into space. Passing the spices, she makes her way to a bench. The floor seems to rise and fall and the bell on the door jingles muffled and unclear as Miss White leaves the store.

The bell chimes clearer and Roy approaches. "Did you find all you want to get?"

"I think so. It's on the counter."

Ollie continues to sit while Roy pays. When he lifts the flour and sugar, she waves to the storekeeper, and goes to the wagon.

Before stepping up, Roy asks, "Are you sure this is all you want? I thought you were going to buy spices for pies and cakes."

"Get them, if you want. I'll make desserts for you, but I won't eat them."

Roy turns to stare at her.

"Miss White said I shouldn't eat sweets. Getting fat will make it hard for me to have the baby." She turns her head to look across the fields.

He clicks the lines against the mules. The wagon jerks and moves along the road. "I'll wait until the baby gets here. But I sure hope *he's* not late."

Ollie twists to see his grin.

That afternoon, while Roy is working, Ollie starts the squatting suggested by Miss White. Later, she goes to the garden to rake and mark rows for onions and cabbage.

When Roy comes inside, Ollie is sitting in her rocker with a warm fire burning in the fireplace. "Your supper's in the warming oven, but I haven't milked the cow. I nearly overdid myself with raking the garden. My legs hurt. So does my back."

"Should I go get your mama?"

Ollie shakes her head. "No. I'll be fine. I've got soft and fat while sitting around all winter. I'll have to build some muscles."

"I noticed the garden. All that raking was unnecessary. You need to remember you can't work like you did last spring."

"I discovered that."

The next day, Ollie is so sore she can hardly walk. It is days before she can do the squat activity. In the following weeks, she slowly increases the exercises.

Poke greens can be seen along fencerows toward the last of March. Ollie enjoys searching for the plants more than the eating, but they are healthy. She cooks them often.

At night, she dreams of new mothers dying in childbirth. During the day, she worries that April rains will flood the creek, preventing Mama and Dr. Hart from getting across when her labor pains start. She walks farther and farther searching for poke greens, does all the squat exercises her strength will allow, and repeats Eugene's prediction that she will live to be an old woman.

In March, whenever Roy leaves the farm, he insists that Ollie stay at Mama's. In April, he does not leave the farm to work for other people, and comes to the house in mid-morning and afternoon for water, a snack, or something. Ollie knows he is checking to make sure she is all right.

People keep telling Ollie sad stories about women having babies. Most of the time, the baby was turned backward or it was too big. She dreads going to church on the last Sunday in

April, and tells Roy she wants to leave as soon as the service is over.

They sit in the back row, and stand to leave during the last song. Roy is helping her into the wagon when a woman rushes toward them. "Ollie, don't wait until your baby gets too big. Take a dose of castor oil. It'll start the pains."

Roy steps up and taps the lines against the mules. As they drive away, the woman yells, "Don't wait too long."

Tuesday is the first day of May. The weather is nice for planting. Ollie knows Roy needs to get the crops started. All day the same thoughts keep reoccurring. *If this baby keeps delaying, the rains may start again so he can't plant. Or the creek might flood, and the baby keeps growing bigger.*

When Roy goes to milk on Wednesday morning, Ollie takes a full tablespoon of castor oil. She gags, shivers, shakes, and keeps swallowing until she is able to keep it down. She starts to pour another spoonful, but the scent of the oil almost causes her to lose what she has already swallowed. She tosses the spoon into a dishpan of water, tightens the bottle's lid, and gulps a cup of black coffee.

Ollie's stomach starts cramping as she cooks the noon meal. The pains continue into evening, she wonders if it is the medicine, or if the baby is finally ready to be born.

Near midnight, Roy states, "I'm going for your mama. I've helped with calving, but I don't want to deliver a baby."

When Mama comes in the door, Ollie has an urge to grab onto her and cry. Instead, she takes a deep breath, and clenches her teeth against another contraction.

Near daybreak, Ollie's pains get closer and more intense. Mama sends Roy to get the doctor. "Tell him not to delay. I want him here when this baby comes."

The doctor gets Ollie up and forces her to walk back and forth around the bed. Her hair is wet with perspiration, and she is trembling before he lets her lie down again.

"Ollie, I wish this baby was born—two weeks ago would have been good."

"Yes, it would." she whimpers, gripping the side of the bed as another pain hits.

"You'll be fine. I could give you something to ease the pain, but it might make the baby stop moving." He listens with his stethoscope. "The heartbeat sounds weaker. We can't let it keep struggling. We have to help it."

Ollie is vaguely aware of Roy praying and walking the floor. At last, the doctor stops pushing on her stomach. A baby cries, but Ollie is too tired for questions.

When she opens her eyes, Roy is rocking a small bundle. "Honey, we've got a pretty little girl."

"Lay her beside me. I want to look at her. Is she all right?"

"She's perfect."

Chapter 4
Guardians

The crops grow well with the right amount of sun and rain—so do weeds. Roy stays busy plowing, but plowing does not separate weeds from corn and cotton in the rows. Morene is five weeks old when Ollie decides it is time to help.

Ollie walks to the cornfield with a quilt, a piece of mosquito netting, a hoe, and the baby. The only good shade for Morene is near the creek. Before putting her down, Ollie checks to make sure there are no snakes, hornet's nests, or animals nearby.

She picks up the hoe and starts chopping weeds and grass as fast as she can. When she gets to the middle of the row, she cannot stand not knowing if something might be bothering the baby. She runs to check. Finding Morene safe, Ollie rushes back to the spot where she stopped, hoes to the far end of her row, and again runs to check on the baby before starting another row.

All day long, day after day, she repeats the same half-row process until grass and weeds disappear from the corn rows. The same is repeated in the cotton field.

The first Saturday in July, Roy and Ollie take Morene to Hart's store in Centerville. Roy stops the wagon in front and takes the baby while Ollie climbs down. An old man tips his hat when she steps onto the porch. "Ollie, you've lost a lot of weight since I last saw you. How much do you weigh now?"

"I don't know. I haven't weighed lately."

"I've been entertained this morning by that weight machine the doctor put on the porch. Step up. I'll put a penny in, and hold the baby for you."

A woman rushes forward and takes Morene. "I want to hold her. I love babies."

Ollie steps onto the scale. The old man's coin clinks through the shaft. "Ninety-five pounds. Well, I declare, I didn't think you'd weigh that much. How tall are you?"

"Almost five-foot six."

He shakes his graying head, "Muscle and bone. While you're nursing, you better start sopping an extra biscuit in the morning gravy. You need some meat on those bones."

She looks down at herself. "Do I look too skinny?"

"It's not how you look. A little fat is reserve to carry you through a sick spell." He grins and looks at Morene. "I don't think your baby's missed any meals."

Ollie reaches for Morene. "Do you want me to take her now?"

"Shucks, no. I'm enjoying this. My kids are too big to cuddle." The woman kisses the baby's fat cheek. "Go do your shopping. I'm waiting on Tom to play another game of checkers. We'll be here a while."

Ollie places a folded diaper on the woman's shoulder before going into the store. "This will protect your dress in case she spits-up."

Dr. Hart comes in from the storage room. "Ollie, I have some iron tonic that you should take to improve your appetite."

Roy hears the doctor. "There's nothing wrong with her appetite. She eats more than most men. It's all the running and work she's been doing. She's hoed all our corn and cotton. Every half-row, she ran back to check on the baby."

The doctor grins and shakes his head. "Ollie's always been a worker. I knew she'd be a good mother."

Roy places a sack of sugar on the counter and chooses cinnamon, cloves, and cocoa from the spice rack before turning to Ollie. "Now that the hoeing is done, and you don't have to worry about getting fat, can we have more pies and cakes?"

Ollie smiles. "Look in my basket. I picked up spices."

He raises his eyebrows and grins. "We'll have enough to last awhile."

Gardens and crops do well in 1928. Roy makes the loan payment in early fall, and deposits money into a savings account for buying seed and fertilizer next spring. Still, the cotton field nearest the creek has not been picked the second time. Ollie wants to help, but the weather is turning cold. They are afraid to take Morene out in the chilly air.

It is midmorning by the time sun burns away fog hanging thick around the creek, and dries the drooping cotton on stalks almost as tall as Roy's head. When the haze lifts, mosquitoes buzz and bite. He buttons his shirt at the neck and cuffs, rubs kerosene on his hands, face, neck, and ears. Still they bite.

The field produces well. A short time before rains start, Roy drives the last load into the gin. It is a hard rain, the kind that keeps coming until stalks sag onto the soggy ground. The following morning, after milking, Roy plods through the downpour, his head hot with fever, and he shakes with chills.

"Roy, get in the rocker in front of the fireplace. I'll bring you a quilt."

All day he sits by the fire or lies wrapped in a quilt. When

Ollie tries to bring his fever down by washing him with a cool towel, he starts shaking again and begs her to stop.

She forces him to take aspirin, water, and a few bites of potato soup. Roy moans and talks in his sleep all through the rainy night. The next morning, with thunder and flashes of lightning, the downpour is still drumming against windows and the tin roof.

Ollie holds a wet cloth in front of the fire until it is lukewarm, kneels on the floor beside Roy, and begins washing his face.

"Keep the baby away from me. She couldn't survive a fever like this." He moans and rolls back and forth. "My head hurts so bad, it feels like it could crack open. Do you have any more aspirin?"

Ollie opens the tin box that Mama gave her for a medicine chest. She finds a small bottle marked 'Quinine-for mosquito fever.'

She takes a yellow pill from the bottle, carries it and a glass of water to Roy. "Take this. It's quinine. It'll be bitter; don't bite or chew it. Swallow it whole."

Roy shivers again. "Do you think those mosquito bites gave me this fever?"

"Yes, I do. They bit all around your hat and cuffs. Papa got it one time, with chills and fever like what you're having. Open your mouth. Swallow it, quick."

He gulps the pill and makes an awful face. "I hope you and the baby don't get this."

"I barely remember Mama saying she was putting quinine in the medicine box. She was worried about us working so near the creek. I'm glad she was mindful of such a thing."

When the rain stops, Ollie dresses the baby in warm clothes and lets the fire burn out. She hopes a cool house will help in keeping Roy's fever down. As the house cools past comfortable, she pulls on a jacket, and puts a sweater on the baby. Several times, she goes to the wood box for kindling to restart the fire. Each time, a voice seems to whisper, *"Don't."*

In late afternoon, while working in the kitchen, Ollie hears a loud thud. Roy has rocked forward and is face down in the fireplace. She pulls him from the ashes, rolls him away from the hearth, washes his face, and looks for bruises. His chin has a small cut.

He is mumbling and trying to sit up when she returns from rinsing the cloth. "Did I fall out of the rocker?"

"Yes. You were face down in the ashes."

"My chin hurts. But I don't feel any burns."

"Men have angels, too. Yours warned me to not put wood on the fire."

For several days, Roy continues to take the quinine pills. At last, the fever disappears, but he is weak. During his illness, Ollie does all the farm chores.

One cold morning, while cutting a piece of sugar-cured bacon hanging from a rafter in the barn loft, the butcher knife slips and slices into the heel of Ollie's left hand. Blood pours from the cut. She jerks the cotton scarf from her head and wraps it tightly from wrist to palm.

Before she can get down the ladder, blood is dripping through the bandanna. She rushes to the house without the bacon and milk pail. The kerosene can sits behind the kitchen door. Ollie grabs it, and pours some into the wash pan. When she removes the scarf, releasing pressure, blood flows into the pan.

Roy calls from his bed, "Ollie what are you doing in there? I smell kerosene."

"The knife slipped and I cut my hand."

He comes to the kitchen. "That's bad. You need sti-tch-es."

Ollie, trying to deal with her own queasy stomach, turns to look at Roy. His eyes look hazy and he is staggering backward. As his legs begin to buckle, Ollie shoves a chair under him. She pulls a dishtowel from its hook and down onto the cabinet. With her right hand, she dumps a dipper of water on the towel, before slinging it over Roy's face. He is conscious enough to sit in the chair.

Rushing to the wash pan, she slips in the blood dribbled across the floor, but regains her balance before falling. Dipping her hand once more in the kerosene, she pats it dry with a clean towel, presses the cut flesh together and wraps a flour sack tightly around it.

Roy tries to stand, but falls back into the chair wiping his face with the towel. "Ollie, we have to take you to get stitches. That cut is deep."

"It'll be fine as long as I keep it bound tight." She looks around at the red-drizzled floor. "We'll skip having bacon this morning, but as soon as I clean up this mess, I've got to go to the barn and get the pail of milk."

"Such a deep cut might get infection if you don't get it sewn up."

"I washed and wrapped it with a clean cloth. When it stops bleeding, the cut will stick together and grow back, but it'll be hard changing diapers, milking, and cooking for the next few days."

"I'll have to help more." He tries to stand.

"No. Sit down. You can help by getting well. That's what we need most.

In January, many in the community have flu symptoms. Ollie keeps the baby home from church, and only goes to see Mama and Papa late on Sunday afternoon when she thinks other visitors will be gone.

"Mama, how was Bertha and her family?"

"They were fine. I suggested she and the little one stay close to home until the weather gets warmer, and there is not so much danger from the flu." Mama shakes her head. "She smiled and walked away."

"I hate that we missed them. Maybe we'll see them before long."

Eugene is rocking the baby. "I'm glad they're gone. Now, I can play with Morene without someone taking her away from me."

Mama frowns at him. "Eugene, that's not a nice thing to say."

"I know, but it's how I feel. I won't get to play with her much longer."

"Babies grow fast."

"That's not what I meant."

Mama stares at him—her forehead wrinkling.

Before Eugene can explain, Papa comes in. "I'm ready for more pumpkin pie. Do you still have whipped cream for the top?"

Mama's face is expressionless when she answers. "The pie is on the table. Cream is in the icebox. You and Roy can help yourselves. I want to show Ollie my new quilt top."

Mama leads the way into the bedroom and spreads the patchwork across the bed. "I've been so afraid that Eugene will get the flu. I send him to the kitchen to play when someone comes to the door, and I'm keeping him home from school. I know he won't fall behind. He's always ahead of children his age." Mama rubs her hand over the bright material. "Eugene picked these colors."

"It reminds me of a rainbow."

"There have been so many times when I doubted Eugene would live another day. Now he's nine years old." Mama sighs, and sits on the bed. Dr. Hart has pulled him through numerous bouts with pneumonia, but since he's a state legislator, he'll be in Little Rock much of the time. I can't help worrying that he won't be here when we need him."

Within a few days, Eugene is sick with flu-like symptoms. Mama calls the doctor at Quitman, the nearest town. He cannot come until the next day.

Eugene is having trouble breathing. The family knows the diagnosis before the doctor tells them: pneumonia. The prescribed medicine does not help. Mama tries every treatment that worked before. He shows no improvement.

News of Eugene's illness spreads. Friends and family begin to stop by the house. Usually Mama enjoys visitors, now she ignores them and sits at Eugene's side, wiping his face with a cool cloth, or rubbing his chest with ointment. His breathing becomes more and more labored.

Papa is not joking today. He sits quietly listening to people offer prayers. Bronnie keeps Morene at Bertha's house so Ollie and Bertha can help Mama.

With people coming and going through the front door and letting in gusts of cold wind, the fireplace requires stacks of wood to keep the house warm. Men circle in front of the crackling fire, puffing on pipes or rolling cigarettes with Prince Albert tobacco.

Ollie keeps a kettle of water boiling in the kitchen. Yet, the air inside is extremely dry, and hazy with smoke. Mama dabs the wet cloth to Eugene's lips. Between gasps for air, he sucks at the cloth to wet his throat.

The wind rolls dry weeds across the yard, the house trembles, and windows rattle. Ollie glances outside; dark clouds cover the moon, leaving the yard veiled in black. The frail little boy gasps once more, closes his eyes, and relaxes against the pillow. He stops breathing on Monday night, January 21, 1929.

Mama holds him in her arms, rocking slow. Following a long silence, she speaks with profound bitterness. "I wish Dr. Hart had never won the election. If he had been here, I believe he could have saved Eugene."

Chapter 5
Taking Chances

Through a window of the two-room home that last year was their sharecropper cabin, Roy and Ollie watch two mules and a cow eagerly munching sprigs of tender grass pushing through the sun-warmed soil. Roy wraps an arm around Ollie's waist and pulls her close. "I can almost see rows of cotton and corn spread over the hillside and along the creek. I'm ready for warm days. I'm eager to plant crops that belong to *us*."

Looking at his face, she smiles. "Then you're not sorry we bought this farm?"

"Not a bit." He grins. "We made it through the winter on thin soup and prayers. Harvest is still a long way off, but with hard work and God's help, we'll make ends meet. I'm counting on our venture as an opportunity." His voice drops to a whisper, "But no doubt there'll be rough spots in our path."

Spring finally arrives and flies faster than honeybees rushing over clover blossoms in the yard. Ollie watches Roy plowing the chest-high corn. This is the last working before fields will be laid-by to wait for harvest.

Glancing up at the cloudless blue sky, she mouths a prayer asking God to water the thirsty soil. She tries to tell herself that dark clouds from the southwest will deliver the blessing, but too many times, she has seen farmers despairing over drought. It is not easy to have the faith she needs.

With ground moisture and sparse early morning fog, cotton along the creek continues to develop, although the stalks are shorter and the bolls smaller than in wetter seasons. Roy searches the community for jobs to help make the mortgage payment, but every able-bodied man is hunting work. Very little is available.

One hot July night Ollie sits next to Roy on the porch, listening to crickets and wishing for a cool breeze. "Roy, what will we do if we don't get enough for the cotton to make the land payment?"

"I haven't given up yet. Keep saying your prayers. We'll make it somehow." He reaches for her hand. "I may have to go away to find work."

She swallows, and bites her lip.

"I don't want to go. I'll be home as soon as I can."

"I know you will. It's just that—" Ollie starts to sob.

Roy puts his arm around her and pulls her close. "You know I won't stay away from you and Morene a day longer than I have to."

"But I'm gonna have another baby, and I want you here."

"What!" He draws her tighter. "When?"

"Late February, or early March."

"Before planting time. Good. Maybe I won't even have to go, but if I do, I'll be home in plenty of time before the baby's due. Everything will be fine, and Morene will have a little playmate."

In 1929, harvest comes early. The last week of August, Roy and Ollie get ready for the first picking. Morene trots through the house holding a little pillowcase repeating, "Cot-ton. Cot-ton."

Roy opens the kitchen door. "Are you girls ready?" Morene runs to him with outstretched arms. He sits on the step. "Climb on my back. I'll give you a ride."

Once in the field, Morene selects long white tufts of cotton and wiggles them like worms, plays in the shade of the wagon, and rides on Roy's sack pretending it is a pony.

The following day they go to the field, but Morene is irritable. She wakes from her afternoon nap with a hoarse cry. Her face is red, and her hair is wet with perspiration. She takes one bite from a cookie, lays it on the quilt, and starts again with the raspy whimpering.

Ollie pours water from the drinking jar onto a rag and washes Morene's face. "Roy, I think she has fever. I'm going to take her to the house and give her a cool bath."

When Roy comes in from milking, he lifts the baby. She lays her head on his shoulder. "Ollie, do you think we should take her to the doctor?"

"She probably caught a cold from the cool air coming in that open window last night." Ollie walks over and puts her ear against Morene's back. "I don't know what we should do."

"Last week, I heard some men talking about diphtheria. They said a little boy over near Barney died with it. This is not a time to gamble."

Ollie's forehead creases, she hugs herself and rubs her arms as if she is cold. "Until we sell some cotton, we don't have any money in the jar. We'll have to charge it. If it's a simple sore throat, we don't need to . . . but we can't chance . . ."

"Only the doctor will know if it's more serious. I'll hitch the team."

"Do you need to unload some cotton? The wagon's full."

"The mules are strong. It won't slow them down. If you want to change your dress, hurry. I'll be back as soon as I can."

They pull onto the road as the last traces of red sunset fade, and stars begin dotting the indigo sky. In the cool evening air, Morene seems to breathe easier. She crawls into the back of the wagon to play in the cotton.

"Roy, she doesn't even act like she's sick now. Do you think we should go home?"

He stops the wagon and turns to look at her. Morene tosses cotton in the air and smiles at him. While he is watching, she frowns, grabs her throat and takes a ragged breath.

He clicks the lines against the mules. "We can't chance it."

The doctor's office is behind the community store. Several people sit on porch benches while waiting to see him. Morene alternates between playing with pop bottle caps and lying across Ollie's lap. When the doctor calls them, Morene snuggles against Roy's chest and tries not to look at the doctor.

Dr. Hart holds a small light in one hand. "Morene, see this?" He flicks it off and on several times. "And see this red candy! You can have the candy if you'll open your mouth wide, and let me shine this light in your throat. Will you do that?"

She nods, and reaches with one hand.

"Let Daddy hold the candy until I look in your throat. Then you can have it. Turn this way and open big and wide. Like this." Dr. Hart opens his own mouth and shines the light into it. "Are you ready?"

She opens her mouth.

"Good girl. Wider now, so I can see if a birdie's in there."

She grabs the bib of Roy's overalls with both hands and opens as wide as she can.

"No birdie, but you did such a good job that you get two suckers." He hands her a yellow one. While Ollie opens candy for Morene, Dr. Hart speaks to his wife. "Get a needle and some serum ready."

He turns to Roy and Ollie. "You have a very sick little girl. It's diphtheria. She'll be fine after I give her a shot, but she would not last until morning without it. This disease is like a thief to the unsuspecting. Parents go to sleep thinking their child has a simple case of croup, and within hours a fast-growing membrane fills the airway, making breathing impossible."

Ollie turns away, and tries to hide the tears streaming down her face by wiping them on her sleeve.

Roy lays his hand against the side of Morene's face and holds her close to his chest so she cannot see the doctor with the needle. She yanks the sucker from her mouth and screams as the medicine is released.

Roy kisses her face. "Did an old bee sting you? Don't cry, baby. It'll be all right. I'll kill that old bee." He slaps at the air and stomps his foot. "I got him. He's smashed. He can't sting you anymore."

Morene sniffs and looks at the floor.

Roy drags his foot back and forth. "He's gone now."

With the candy in her mouth, she lays her head against his chest and continues to sniffle for several minutes.

The next day, while Ollie keeps Morene inside, Roy picks the rest of the cotton and takes it to the gin. With money from the sale of a heifer calf, the cotton, and the remainder of last year's savings account, he makes the yearly payment on the farm loan.

When he gets home from the bank, he rushes inside. "Ollie,

I heard that a merchant in Conway will buy black walnuts, hickory nuts, and pecans. I know the location of every nut tree on Pa's farm, as well as on this place. Those near the creeks should have produced despite the drought. I'm gonna start gathering in the morning. Day after tomorrow, if I leave before sunup, I can make the trip in one long day."

"What if you go to all that trouble and he doesn't want any more?"

"I have to take a chance. We need money to live on until we make another good crop."

Two nights later, it is past midnight before Roy unhitches the mules and turns them out to pasture. Ollie stands in the kitchen doorway as he walks the path from the barn.

"You shouldn't have waited up."

"I couldn't sleep knowing how tired you must be."

"It was worth it. That man only wanted the pecans, two bushels of walnuts, and one of hickory nuts. With several full baskets left, I drove through a nice neighborhood, knocking on doors and handing out samples of cracked nuts. Some people only bought a few cents worth, others wanted a peck or a half-bushel. Before the day was over, I sold them all."

Ollie gets into bed and pulls the warm quilt over her shoulders. Her mind is drifting into dreams when Roy crawls under the covers.

He shakes her awake as he props himself up on one elbow, "You know I made more from those nuts than I could have in a week of hard labor. It's too bad we don't have another load to sell."

She yawns and turns to face him. "There's a walnut grove on the back side of my parents' place. They only gather from the trees close to the house. If Mama's not too busy, she'll watch Morene so I can go with you."

"Can we drive the wagon over there?" He eases onto his pillow. His words come soft and slow. "Walnuts get awful heavy when you have to tote them on your back."

"I think so, but it's been a long time since—" Ollie hears a faint snore. The conversation will have to wait until morning.

Breakfast is waiting when Ollie sees Roy coming up the path with the milk pail. She is eager to get away from the house for a change. Today will be like a picnic.

While he washes his hands, she begins straining the milk. "You can wake Morene while I put this away. Bring her to the table in her nightgown. I have clothes ready for her, but I'll change her while you're hitching the mules to the wagon."

Roy jerks his head around to stare at her with a puzzled look. "Why do I need to hitch them to the wagon? Where are we going?"

"Don't you remember us talking last night about looking for walnuts on Papa's place?"

"Faintly. I was so tired that I can't remember it all. You'll have to tell me again, but I can't go today. I heard some scary talk in town yesterday, and I need to ride over and talk to Pa."

"Talk about what?"

"People were saying that banks across the country are failing and going broke. I want to warn him so he can withdraw his savings before it's too late."

"How awful. Will it affect our mortgage?"

"I don't see how it could, but Pa might lose his life's savings."

"Well, hurry and get on your way. We'll go scouting for nuts another day."

It is late afternoon before Roy returns. He stomps his shoes on the rock doorstep, and lets the door slam behind him. "Pa wouldn't listen. He said he's already talked to the banker and was told his bank has nothing to worry about."

He sighs and drops into a chair. "I hope he's right, but I don't think so. Ma doesn't, either." He shakes his head. "Do you know what his answer was? He said anyone who draws out their money will have to sit and guard it night and day, and maybe get killed by robbers."

"He might be right about the robbers."

"Sure he is, but I'd certainly fight for my life's savings."

"You did your best. Let's get ready to go pick up walnuts tomorrow, so we can have a little savings for winter."

A few days later, Roy gathers pumpkins that Ollie planted near the creek. He peddles them in Conway, along with turnips from the fall garden, and the nuts they gathered from Papa's farm.

It is late when Ollie hears him stop in the yard. She opens the door.

He steps inside. "I need a drink before going to the barn." He gulps from the water dipper. "The wagon's empty. Every item sold."

"That's good. Do you think we'll have enough cash to last through the winter?"

"I hope so." He shakes his head. "We sure can't go to Pa for help. On the way home, I stopped and ate supper with them. Ma told me that when he finally went to the bank, it was too late to withdraw any money. He's too old to work now, and they have nothing to sell but the home place." Roy takes off his hat and slumps into a chair.

Morene stumbles across the room in her nightgown, crawls into Roy's lap, and begins searching the bib pockets of his overalls. "Candy?"

He pulls a small bag from his shirt pocket, and kisses her cheek. "I didn't forget about you, but it's too late to eat candy. Put it on the table for now, and get under your quilt." Roy watches as she peeks in the sack, smiles, and scampers to her bed.

Ollie begins to rub his neck. "How will your folks get along without money?"

"Ma said she has a few dollars left from her inheritance, and she'll still raise a garden, chickens, and a pig." Roy straightens his back and leans his head forward as Ollie massages tense neck muscles. "Pa is always warning me to be careful. It's hard to believe he took such a risk."

"He counted his banker as a friend."

"Sure, but he always taught me to put my family's interests first."

"We're barely surviving, but if there's any way we can help, I'm willing. Do you know how much he lost?"

"I didn't ask, though it must be thousands. It was a lifetime of work—money from the sale of his cattle, horses, and some land. He didn't say much tonight, only sat in his chair looking pale and sick."

Roy hands her a canvas bag of change, and reaches into his pocket for his wallet. "We'll count it after I unhitch the mules."

He pauses. "Ollie, we're gonna have to watch every penny. From the talk I've heard in town, hard times wait ahead. Factories are closing, and there are no jobs available in most cities. The stock market crashed, and some men that lost their savings have gone crazy and killed themselves. Hungry people will be flocking to the country, stealing from smokehouses, gardens, and cellars, like many did during the Civil War."

She nods as if trying to convince herself. "Somehow, we'll make it."

They sit silent for a moment. When Ollie speaks again, her voice has lost its soothing tone—it reflects panic. "What about spring? We don't have money for seed and fertilizer. If banks go broke, where can we borrow?"

He shakes his head, draws in a deep breath, gets up and starts for the barn.

Chapter 6
Syble Marie

When the weather is too cold or rainy to work outside, Roy whittles ax and grubbing-hoe handles. Most farmers whittle for pleasure, but very few can finish a piece of hard hickory into a smooth handle that will not crack and splinter. Roy takes the handles along as he travels the countryside looking for work. He sells them at half the store price and, even with the depressed economy, rarely brings any back home.

Squint lines around Roy's eyes show he is tired after a day of working in the December wind. He sits by the fire with his knife and another piece of wood. This time the hardwood will not emerge as a handle, but a toy for Morene.

"Ollie, I'd like to go to Ma's for Christmas dinner. She's been saving a big gray turkey for the occasion. That bird keeps raising his wings at me as if he wants to fight. He'll taste extra good with a little gravy. We can stop at your mama's on the way home, or go there on Christmas Eve."

"That's fine. Your folks haven't seen Morene in a while. I bet they'll be surprised at how she's grown, and how well she can talk."

On Christmas morning, while Morene plays with the pony Roy whittled for her, Ollie takes extra care to make a jam cake look pretty. Roy is busy tying a wagon sheet over the wagon's sideboards so Morene can play underneath, out of the wind.

When the food box is packed, and a quilt spread for Morene in the wagon bed, they start on their way.

"Roy, I'm dreading this."

He jerks his head around to look at her. "Why?"

"For some reason, your sisters make me nervous. They're nice, but I feel like I'm an outsider, and they're all watching to see if I make a mistake."

"No, they're not. They like you." Roy looks at her and winks. "There's just so many of them. Did I ever tell you that Ma gave birth to fifteen babies? One set of twins died at birth, another little boy died when he was very young, but twelve of us lived."

"I can't imagine trying to take care of so many children."

"We weren't all little at the same time. Some of my nephews are older than I am."

A young man races by on a horse. He waves and glances back with a big smile.

"He's one of them. Stay clear of him. He's always full of pranks."

When they top the last hill before reaching the house, Ollie sees a yard full of buggies, hacks, and wagons. She takes off her bonnet and pats at her hair. "Morene, look at all those little girls that you can play with."

Morene stands, giggling and bouncing, until Roy sets her down in front of the smiling children. "Roy, can you keep an eye on her while I go inside to help with dinner?"

"Sure. Go on. I'll watch her."

In the kitchen, cabinets and tables are covered with rolls, pies, cakes, and vegetables. On a huge oak dining table is the biggest roast turkey that Ollie has ever seen. Roy's ma, a slim woman with gray streaks in her hair is stirring a pot of gravy. One look around the house tells how she has stayed slim. Wood floors are bleached white from scrubbing, starched and ironed curtains frame clear windows, and on an earlier visit, Ollie marveled at her pantry full of canned fruit and vegetables.

With a pleading look, Ollie hands her basket to Roy's youngest sister. "Do you mind setting my food in the proper places? I don't know where to put it."

"I don't mind at all." Elzie peeps under the cloth covering the basket. "But I may find a dark corner and sample your pretty cake while no one's watching. It looks delicious."

Ollie blushes, "Thank you. It's a jam cake. Mama makes them for holidays."

Ollie approaches her mother-in-law. "I'll stir the gravy if you want. I'm sure there are other things you'd rather be doing."

"Thanks, Ollie, as soon as it gets done, I think we'll be ready to eat." Mrs. Glenn turns and starts giving directions. "Fronnie, will you tell some of those men to set up sawhorse tables on the porch for the big kids? It's warm enough for the little ones to sit on the steps, in sweaters and jackets. You girls with babies, fix their plates and help them before the older group gets in here. Lottie and Doshie, will you set out some coffee cups and glasses? Ellen, you're doing a fine job of carving that bird."

When the gravy starts to boil in the large cast iron pot, and appears thick enough, Ollie removes it from the heat. "Mrs. Glenn, do you want me to pour this in a bowl or leave it in the pot?"

"There's a blue clay pitcher in the cabinet on your right. Fill it, and leave the rest in the pan."

Ollie follows the lead of other mothers with babies, and uses a pie tin instead of a plate for Morene's food. One bite of turkey, and few bites of sweet potatoes, is all she will eat before wiggling free of Ollie's grasp.

Ollie stands. "All this good food and she wants to run off."

Fanny, Roy's oldest sister, pats Ollie's arm. "Let her go. On holidays, we leave the food under a tablecloth, so the kids can come around nibbling. She'll eat when they do. Right now, she wants to play."

Ollie glances at the water bucket and wash pan.

"Don't worry. The bigger kids will help her wash. Ma scolds the older ones if she catches a toddler with dirty hands."

"I guess you're right. Morene would rather play than eat. She's never seen this many little kids at one time."

"Be glad she's playing with them. Maybe she won't be as timid as her daddy was as a child."

"Roy! Was he really timid?"

"Lands, yes. One time he was helping chop cotton on my husband's home place, when he got sick with a fever. I told him to go up to the house and tell my mother-in-law he was sick, and that I said to put him to bed. She was a good woman. I knew she'd take care of him." She pauses to wipe her mouth and take a breath. "I guess he was a little afraid of Mrs. Woodrum, so he started walking home. We took our lunches to the field that morning, and it was late afternoon before I discovered what he'd done."

"Was it a hot day?"

"It was terribly hot, especially for a child with fever, and without any water. He spent the whole day trying to get home and even said he hid in the bushes when a wagon or rider came by, because he didn't want to tell anyone he was sick. It's a true wonder he didn't die. He finally staggered into Ma's yard a little while before I came looking for him."

"How old was he?"

"Oh, ten or eleven."

"Ollie grins. "I was probably bolder at ten than I am now."

Fanny shakes her head and chuckles. "When he got well, I scolded him good. From then on, he never seemed bashful. His twin brother Coy is a different card. He wasn't so shy."

On the way back to Mama's, Ollie comments, "Roy, your family has a lot of good cooks. I feel like a stuffed turkey myself."

He reaches over to pat her stomach.

"Don't you dare say I look like one."

He grins. "I'm smarter than that."

"The only good thing about money being so tight is that I'm not making desserts.

Sugar is a luxury for us now, but I still need to exercise. The new baby will be here in a little over two months."

"You get lots of exercise while taking care of Morene. I don't think you have to worry."

Weeks pass quickly, and on Saturday, the twenty-second-day of March the labor pains start. Roy goes to pick up Mama, and takes Morene along to stay with Bronnie.

Mama shakes her head and wrings her hands. "Dr. Hart's in Little Rock. We'll have to call the doctor from another town."

It is early Sunday morning before the doctor comes rushing in. "When did she start into hard labor?"

Mama's gaze is cold. "Over four hours ago."

"That's too long. We'll have to help her."

At last, Ollie rests next to a little girl they name Syble Marie, and listens to the doctor talking to Mama. "This was a difficult birth. She'll never carry another baby to full term, unless she has surgery to repair the damage caused by having such large babies. She needs stitches inside. I can't do surgery in the home, only at the hospital."

In the dimly lit room, no one sees Ollie's silent tears. *How can I have surgery? We barely have money to buy necessities for two little girls and ourselves.*

The next day Ollie gets an awful headache, and terrible cramps. As the day progresses, she begins to cry with pain.

Mama lays her hand on Ollie's forehead, "Roy, you need to go to my house, get on the phone, and ask that doctor to come back. She has a high fever."

When Roy returns, he ties the mule near the porch and hurries inside. "The doctor said he doesn't have time to come out again. He said to give her aspirin."

Mama slams her hand against the door facing. "Aspirin! Did you tell him how much pain she's having, and that she has fever?"

"Yes. Yes, I did, but he didn't seem to listen. He said most young mothers have headaches and cramps. Is there any other doctor we can call?"

"No. I doubt we could get one to come from Conway. You stay with Ollie. I'll go home and call him again."

"I'll hitch the mules to the wagon."

"No. I don't want to waste any more time. I can ride a mule."

"He's stubborn. What if he balks with you?"

"Do you have a whip?"

"In the barn, but I don't think my mule's ever been ridden by a woman. Your skirts could scare him, and cause him to run away."

"Get me the whip. I can ride." Her eyes are squinted and she speaks through clenched teeth. "That doctor better listen this time."

While Roy rushes to the barn, Mama slips off her skirt and pulls on Roy's khaki pants that he hangs behind the door. She rolls the pant cuffs to the top of her shoes, hangs her long coat on the nail, and puts on his work jacket.

Roy is breathing hard from running. "Here's the whip. When he balks with me, I hit him hard across the nose with the handle, and then across the right hip with the lash end. Hold on tight. Sometimes he acts like he wants to buck."

"Back him up, so his left side is next to the porch."

Ollie starts to protest, but the door closes. They are outside.

It seems like hours before Mama returns from making the phone call. When they hear the mule trot into the yard, Roy dashes out, letting the door blow open behind him. "Is the doctor coming?"

"As soon as he can get here."

Once inside, Mama glances at the sleeping baby, and touches her cold hand to Ollie's forehead.

Roy comes in the kitchen door after taking the mule to the barn. "What did the doctor say?"

"I didn't let him say much until I told him my daughter's not a complaining young mother, she's very sick with a high temperature, and he needs to get here quick. I told him that besides having nine children of my own, I've assisted Dr. Hart with several births, and I know the difference between whiny and sick. He said he'll be here as soon as possible."

"Thank God!" He rubs his hands through his hair, turns toward the window, takes a handkerchief from his pocket and blows his nose.

Mama is giving the baby a bottle of sugar water when the doctor arrives. He checks Ollie's temperature and starts giving orders. "Mrs. McNew, give the baby to Roy. I need you to help with the examination."

After the exam, he gives Ollie a shot, glances at Roy, but turns to Mama. "You were right to insist that I come back." He looks at the floor and rubs his hand across his chin. "I removed a small piece of afterbirth lodged in one of the lacerations. It could not be extracted normally, and decay was causing infection. She'll be fine now, but many new mothers have died from the same thing."

Mama and Roy, with solemn faces, silently stare at him until he starts packing his bag. Mama speaks first. "Should I feed the baby on canned milk for a few days?"

"Mix it weak; don't add sugar. Tomorrow, her milk should be all right for the baby."

He glances again at Roy. "I apologize for the manner in which I spoke to you over the phone. I was in the clinic with a patient, a dear friend. He's hovering close to death. I must get back to him right away."

Roy drops his gaze to the floor and pauses a moment before looking at the doctor's face. "Thank you for coming. I hope your friend recovers."

The doctor nods and reaches for the doorknob. Before opening the door, he turns to Roy. "She'll be fine, but she needs to come see me at the office in six weeks. Like I told you earlier, she'll not carry another baby to full term without reparative surgery."

"Doctor, these are hard times. We want more children, but we don't have money for surgery and a hospital stay. If the crops are good this year, maybe she can come see you after the harvest."

"That will be fine."

When the doctor leaves, Mama starts gathering her things. Ollie still has fever and a headache. She wants Mama to stay, but will not ask.

Mama sets her bag in a corner, and looks at Roy. "I know it's late, but if you'll ride up to the house and tell Robert, I'll spend the night here so I can help with Ollie and the baby. Missing school tomorrow to take care of Morene won't hurt Bronnie."

"I'll go tell him. Gladly, I will. I appreciate your help. I could take care of the baby, but I think Ollie will rest better knowing you're here. The doctor said rest is what she needs most of all."

"Yes, she needs a good night's sleep. Oh, while you're there, tell Robert I said get you two quarts of peaches, and to wrap them so they won't break on the way back. Ollie loves peaches. I think they'll be good for her."

Ollie's eyes are closed; still she hears the conversation between Mama and Roy. She relaxes knowing Mama will be near to take care of Syble. Roy would do his best, but Mama knows the answer to almost everything about babies.

Chapter 7
Calamity

Syble is a month old when Ollie decides she needs to make some extra-gentle soap for washing diapers. While the baby naps, Ollie props the window open so she can hear any cries. She takes Morene and the soap-making supplies into the backyard. Morene runs and hops, chasing a moth drifting out of reach in the April sunshine.

Ollie stirs Mary War Lye into the cold water measured in her large black washpot. She places the red can of caustic white granules on top of a tall fence post before adding lard and a bowl of unsalted butter to the pot. While the mixture heats, she stirs it with a long paddle, listens for the baby, and watches Morene play.

Ollie's eyelids flutter as she fights to stay focused on her chores. Syble's birth, and getting up for nightly feedings, has drained her strength. A loud blowing sound startles her from oblivion.

She spins around in time to see granules of lye spewing from Morene's mouth. Ollie grabs her from atop the fence, turns her upside down, and runs to the house with the child tucked under one arm, all the while yelling, "Spit! Morene, spit!"

Once inside the house, Ollie grabs the vinegar jug, jerks the cork out with her teeth, pours some into Morene's cheek, shifts her to the other arm and pours vinegar into the second cheek. Morene continues to spit and blow as Ollie pours a little vinegar into a glass of water. "Take this in your mouth, and swish it. Like a frog puffs his jaws." She proceeds to show her how to rinse with the liquid. "Like you and Daddy were doing yesterday while watching that frog."

Morene holds the vinegar water in her mouth, and whines.

Ollie yells at her, "Swish it like a frog, or I'll spank you for getting my lye can!" Ollie is still holding her with Morene's head tilted toward the floor.

The liquid dribbles onto Ollie's feet as Morene tries to imitate a frog by expanding her cheeks. Ollie makes her repeat the process once, stands her on the floor, adds a spoonful of sugar to the glass and forces her to drink several sips.

Morene whimpers and starts to gag.

"Does your throat hurt?"

"No. My yip." She pulls at her bottom lip.

Ollie examines the inside of Morene's mouth and only finds burn spots on the front of her tongue, and on her lips.

Syble whimpers, and wiggles on her pallet. Ollie glances at her, and whirls toward the window. "My soap!" She runs out the door, and grabs the paddle to stir, but the soap is past the stirring stage. With a long stick of wood, Ollie rakes coals from underneath the pot. She sloshes water across the ground toward the coals. It runs under the pot, but does not splash on it. Cold water, hitting the hot cast iron, could cause it to crack.

She leaves the soap to cool and rushes inside to check on the girls.

That night when Roy comes in from work, Ollie tells him what happened with the lye.

"It's a good thing you knew what to do."

"The instant I heard her blow, I realized what she'd done.

And, just as quick, a voice inside my head was telling me to pour vinegar in her mouth."

"You must have heard that before."

"I've been studying on this all afternoon, and I don't remember ever hearing anyone say vinegar would kill lye."

They sit quiet for a while and watch Morene dancing her rag doll in front of Syble.

"I believe her guardian angel gave me that knowledge."

He stares at Ollie for a moment before looking at the children. "Do you think we should have the doctor check her?"

"No. I've looked in her throat and mouth. She didn't swallow any of it, or her throat and stomach would have been hurting long before now."

"Thank God for all blessings." He reaches for the milk pail. "I got most of the corn planted on the north side. If it grows and we get rain at the right time, then I'll try to borrow money to side dress it with fertilizer. But if it turns dry, fertilizing would be a waste of money."

"I'm glad you saved those cotton seed, instead of selling, or having them ground into cow feed."

"Yes, it's lucky we have them. Seed are twice that price now."

"I'm getting eager to plant my vegetables. As soon as you're finished putting in the crops, I'd like for you to break the garden."

"I need to spread a wagonload of manure on it first." He starts out the door, but stops to look at her. "Don't you think it's a little soon after the baby for you to be digging?"

"A little, but I don't want to wait too long and miss the spring rains."

"I know, but—"

"Most people dropped Irish potatoes over two months ago. I hope it's not too late for them. One year, Papa planted potatoes in May. The summer heat made them rot in the ground before they were big enough to dig."

"Yes, Pa did that one year when there was too much rain to plant early. Root crops start to rot when the weather gets hot. Sweet potatoes do better than most because they have low-growing foliage to shade the ground and keep it cool."

"Do you think those little sweet potato roots would grow into a crop if I plant them down by the creek?"

"They might. Then again, it might be a waste of time."

I've got a basket full of them, and I hate to spend money on slips if those will make."

"At the least, they should grow enough to feed a few opossums and raccoons." She shakes her head and jams her hands down on top of her hips. "You know how I hate those critters. I'll never be able to keep chickens if they move onto our farm. Have you seen any around?"

"I've seen tracks. Ollie, they're in every wooded area across the country, especially opossums. They scavenge at night, so you're not likely to see one, unless it's sick. If you see one during the day, keep away from it, because they carry rabies."

"I remember Papa telling me that. I'll probably never be able to keep chickens this close to a creek."

"Yes, you will. When we can afford to build them a little house with a good wire fence around it. I'll keep the promise I made before we got married–we'll have a home with lots of chickens and children playing in the yard. Although, at the rate we're going, the kids in the yard will be barefoot and ragged with chicken poop between their toes."

Ollie grins and squints. "The picture you describe is dazzling. I'll need a horse trough instead of a bathtub, so I can run them down a line."

"Ma didn't use a horse trough, but in the summer when we ran barefoot, she kept tubs of water warming in the sun all day. Before bedtime, the boys lined up. Coy and I were first, because we were the youngest. To begin with we washed our feet in a small tub, and then got in the big tub to wash with soap."

"What about the girls?"

"They bathed in the smokehouse."

"I hope we don't have fifteen kids like your ma and pa. A couple of girls and two or three boys will do."

"We'll take what the Good Lord gives us."

She raises her eyebrows. "Now what do you think I should do about those sweet potato roots?"

"Put them in water. If they're any good, they'll sprout in a few days, and then I'll mud them in around the creek bank." Again, he opens the door, but turns toward her with a heavy sigh. "If you'll take it easy until Saturday, we'll go to the store for the supplies you need, and plant your garden in the afternoon."

Saturday morning, Syble is fussy and has a runny nose.

"Roy, the baby's getting a cold. I better keep her at home."

"That's too bad. I know you were looking forward to getting out. If Morene's not getting sick, I'll take her with me." He stoops to look into the little girl's eyes. "Morene, do you want to go to the store with me?"

She nods her head. "Go to store. Get candy." She giggles and dances around swinging her doll.

Ollie bathes Syble in the warm kitchen, mixes a tiny bit of Vick's salve with a dab of lard and rubs the mixture on the baby's chest, back, and under her nose. After dressing her, she sits in the rocker to cuddle and nurse the baby. When Syble falls asleep, Ollie puts her on a pallet where she can see her from the kitchen.

Ollie would like to lie down on the quilt and take a nap with the baby, but Roy will expect dinner when he gets home. Soon she has pinto beans, turnips, greens, and fried potatoes on the table. While the cornbread is baking, she opens the last jar of blackberries on the shelf and makes a cobbler pie with a thin biscuit top drizzled with melted butter. She has taken bread from the oven and put in the pie when Morene comes bouncing through the back door.

"Look, Mama. Look at my issil." She pops a little red whistle into her mouth and begins to blow.

"Did Daddy buy that instead of candy?"

She shakes her head. "Man gave it to me."

The wind catches the door and bangs it before Roy pulls it closed. The noise wakes the baby, and she starts to cry.

Morene runs to the quilt, drops to her knees, and starts blowing the new toy as fast as she can. Syble stops crying and stares at her.

"Roy, where did she get a whistle?"

"A salesman in the store gave it to her."

"It looks awful small. Do you think she could choke on it?"

Roy raises his eyebrows and nods his head. "I've already thought about that, and I cautioned her to only put one end in her mouth." In a low voice he states, "It's destined to disappear as soon as she puts it down."

Syble is waving her arms and kicking as Morene continues to blast the repeating sounds. Morene begins to giggle as she blows faster and faster. In an attempt to catch her breath, she sucks the whistle into her throat.

Roy runs to her, turns her upside down, and beats on her back with the flat of his hand. When the toy does not come out, he shakes her and pounds harder on her back. Ollie, paralyzed with fear, grips the edge of the table. Morene's face turns blue.

"Help me, God! Help me! Please, God! Please!" Jumping around with her, he nears the bed. He has her by the feet, still shaking her, when he yells, "Jesus, help us!" He slams her across the bed. The whistle bounces onto the floor. Morene takes a gasping breath. Roy lifts and hugs her to his chest.

Ollie collapses into a chair, shaking uncontrollably, tears trailing down her face.

Morene does not cry, merely sits on Roy's knee, taking deep breaths. In a few minutes, she runs to wipe at Ollie's tears. She points to the little red toy. "Bad issil."

Roy goes to the whistle and stomps it. Morene pats one foot over the pieces. "Bad issil." She helps Roy gather the broken bits and toss them into the yard.

After they eat, Roy plows the garden and lays off rows for planting. "Ollie, if you'll hand me the seeds and point to the rows where you want them planted, I'll drop and cover them while you cut the potato eyes."

"That's a good idea."

Morene sits at the edge of the garden with her bare feet in the plowed ground. She covers her feet, packs dirt around them, and pulls them out making little caves. "Look, Mama. I make frog houses."

"Little frogs will like those. I have to go check on baby Syble. Stay there. Don't go near the horses and don't bother Daddy while he's planting seeds."

Ollie places her pan on the doorstep. It holds the chunks of potato with an eye on each piece that she has been cutting with a sharp paring knife.

She raises her voice. "Answer me, Morene. Will you stay there?"

"I stay."

Ollie changes Syble's diaper, and pulls the rocker near the kitchen window so she can see Morene playing while she nurses the baby. Rocking and humming a lullaby, it is not long until Ollie and the baby are dozing.

A shrill scream wakes Ollie. Clutching Syble in the crook of her left arm, she rushes out the door. The paring knife is on the ground. Blood drips from Morene's hand and down the front of her dress.

Roy runs to her. "Ollie, put the baby down and pour some kerosene in the wash pan."

Morene's hands, clasped into fists, knot together against her stomach.

Ollie plops Syble on the bed, leaves her crying, and runs outside with the kerosene and wash pan.

"Let me see your hand," Roy demands.

Morene bends forward and shakes her head.

He takes hold of her arms, but she stiffens. "Hush screaming. Let me see."

She continues to cry and hold her arms close to her body, but relaxes her fingers. He cannot see a cut; still, blood dribbles down the front of her dress. "Oh, God, did she stab her stomach?" His face pales.

Ollie kneels beside Morene. "Honey, let Mama see where you hurt, so I can make it better."

Morene leans her head against Ollie's shoulder and extends her left arm. Blood trickles from a small cut on her wrist.

Roy's asks, "Why did you touch Mama's knife?"

Morene looks up at her daddy through tear-filled eyes. "Bad knife."

Chapter 8
Two Gray Mares

Ollie untwists the curtain and lets it fall in front of the window. A gentle breeze flutters the folds. Last night, she fussed at Roy for coiling it so tight. Pulling and smoothing wrinkles made from staying twisted through the tieback, she smiles, remembering his comment: "Would you rather have a wrinkled curtain, or a husband all crinkled from sleeping in a bed of sweat?"

The air is cool as she joins Roy on the back step. He is savoring the last of his morning coffee.

"The girls remain asleep. I let the curtains down so the sun won't wake them."

Roy looks up. "There's not a cloud in the sky, and that sun will be blazing when it pops over the mountain. If we don't get rain soon, I'll have to go north to find work. I can't wait much longer. Our country's in a depression and the south is in a drought."

Ollie turns her face away, to look at the blushing pink sky. "I know. It's what has to be done."

"Bob Vaughan wants my mules for clearing land. They've helped me earn money doing jobs most horses are not strong enough to do, but they're contrary and too hard for you to handle. Bob has a couple of gentle gray horses that he'll trade. They're mares, both broke to the saddle and for pulling a wagon or plow. With them, you can gather what few crops we'll have.

I'm sure Eldridge will help if you need him."

She turns to look at his face. "I've known this was coming and hated to ask you to sell your mules. I know how much you care for them, but with gentle mares, I shouldn't need help to gather the crops. Morene is good to watch the baby. She'll call to me if anything comes near them."

He hands her the coffee cup, stands, and stretches his back. "Before I get rid of the mules, I've got a couple of stumps to pull, and some oak logs to drag into the yard for firewood. If I can get that done this morning, I'll go get the mares this evening." He starts toward the barn, stops, and turns around. "Why don't you and the girls go with me? Doshie hasn't even seen Syble."

"We'll do that. I like Doshie. She is your jolliest sister. She seems to laugh and joke about everything."

"There's a possibility it might get late, and she'll insist on us spending the night. Would you object to staying?"

"It should be fun. I'll bake cookies and pack a basket with canned food."

They eat a quick lunch before Roy starts filling the wagon. Ollie spreads quilts for the girls to play on.

"Why so much stuff? It looks like we plan to stay a week."

"It's only food, quilts, and our clothes. Babies require a lot of things."

He shakes his head and picks up a basket.

When they pull into the yard, Doshie runs to meet them. She hugs Roy as soon as he steps down. "Oh, I'm so glad you came and brought Ollie and the babies." She reaches to pat Morene, who hides her face in Ollie's skirt. "Can I hold the baby?" Syble snuggles against her, cooing and giggling as

Doshie laughs and talks to her in happy tones.

"I love little girls." She tickles Syble under the chin.

Roy and Bob exchange good points about the mules and horses. Bob turns to the women and motions with his hand. "Let's all go down to the barn and look at the mares. Ollie, I know you'll like them. I hate to get rid of Bell and Bess, because they're so gentle. But I need some tough mules to help me clean up this place."

The horses amble over to the fence. "This is Bell." Doshie pats one side of the mare's neck. "I like them both, but this is my favorite. I can put a bridle on her in the pasture, or call her to the barn. "She's never tried to shy away, and Bess will follow her."

The mare bends her head and leans closer for Ollie to pet her. "These are some of the prettiest gray horses I've ever seen. They glisten like silver in the sunshine."

"I agree, but please don't get me started bragging on them. I can hardly stand to let them go."

Doshie looks toward the sun hanging low over the hills, "Ollie, let's go cook supper. Roy, if you can grab one of those young chickens, I'll fry it for tonight."

Roy removes a piece of barbed wire from a post, straightens it, bends a hook at the end, walks close to a group of chickens, and with one quick jerk of the wire catches a young rooster by the leg. He yells to the women about to step onto the porch. "Get the grease hot. I'll have the feathers off this bird in a few minutes."

The men sit at the table talking after supper. Ollie washes and dresses the girls for bed. Doshie starts on the dishes.

With an excited fling of one hand, Doshie slings soapsuds from the dishwater across the cabinet. "Roy, do you remember that big cottonmouth snake we saw down by the creek? It stood several feet in the air, showing us the white insides of its gaping mouth. That was the biggest snake I've ever seen. I still have nightmares about one like it. It's a wonder some of us didn't get bit as we ran through the grass and leaves, to swim there every summer."

Roy chuckles. "We were a real challenge for our guardian angels. Remember the old rusty gun that stood behind the front door, and that dud shell? We must have snapped the trigger on it a hundred times. One time, Pa really got after Coy for pointing the gun at me and popping it. Of course, none of us thought it would work, until the day Coy clicked it at a stray dog. Every one of us turned white when the bullet buzzed across the yard and hit a tree."

The next morning, Roy, Ollie, and the girls leave in the wagon pulled behind two gray horses. "Roy, are you sad about leaving your mules?"

"No. They served their purpose. In days to come, they can do the same for Bob. Besides, I was beginning to worry that one of them might kick Morene if she got in the pasture. She loves horses, and she's too young to understand that those mules are not gentle."

"I'd love to go horseback riding, but we need someone to watch the girls."

"Your mama will watch them, and we'll take turns riding some in the evenings. Before I leave, I want these horses to know and recognize you as their new boss."

The next day, Roy hitches Bell and Bess to the cultivator and starts plowing the cornfield near the house. Morene runs to the window each time he passes near enough for her to hear him calling out the 'gee' and 'haw' commands to turn the horses right and left.

"Morene, you can sit on the porch and watch Daddy work while I cook dinner. Stay right there, don't leave the porch, and maybe he'll let you ride a horsey to the barn."

Ollie takes the bread from the oven, pours the beans into a brown crock, and goes to call Roy. Her eyes quickly scan the yard and field, looking for Morene. She spots her, asleep in the row, right in front of the horses. A scream freezes in her throat as Bell raises one large hoof, then another, and carefully steps over the child.

Roy, concentrating on the corn plants, does not see Morene until she is in front of the plow points. "Whoa!" he calls, and pulls back on the lines.

Bell and Bess stand still. Roy lifts Morene from between Bell's feet and the cultivator plows.

Ollie races across the field. "Is she all right?"

Morene rubs one eye and blinks.

Roy pulls her hand away from her eye. "What were you doing in the row?"

"I wait for you, Daddy." She leans her head against his shoulder.

Ollie looks at Roy and shakes her head. "I told her she could watch, and wait for you on the porch. I didn't think she would come all the way down here. I should have checked on her sooner, but I was rushing to get dinner ready."

Roy swats Morene on the bottom, and speaks in a gruff voice. "Why didn't you stay on the porch like Mama told you?"

Morene wails, "I wait for you and horsey. My eyes take a nap."

"You have to mind Mama. Since you didn't do what you were told, you can't ride the horse, and you get a spanking." He swats her again on the bottom and sets her down. "Now, walk to the porch, and wait until I put the horses in the barn."

Morene stumbles across the plowed ground, crying, "Horsey. I wanna ride horsey."

"Morene!" Roy calls. "Hush bawling, or you'll get a hard spanking."

She stops crying, except for sniffing, and goes on toward the porch.

They eat the noon meal, and Ollie washes the dishes while Roy smokes his pipe and plays with the girls. "Ollie, if you'll have supper ready a little early this evening, we'll eat, and then go to your mama's in the wagon. If she has time to watch the girls, we'll go riding for an hour or so before dark."

"That'll be fun." She smiles and smoothes her apron. "Supper will be waiting."

Roy leaves for the field. Ollie nurses the baby, and puts the girls down for naps. While they sleep, she washes all the clothes and diapers used since the day before they left to get the horses. She also washes a stack of new diapers that her mama bought for Syble.

Ollie shakes each diaper and snaps it in the air to help remove wrinkles before she pins it on the clothesline. When all are hanging smooth and tight, she stands a moment watching them. Red thread stitched across one corner of each diaper waves in the breeze like stripes on white flags.

Finished cultivating the corn nearest the house, Roy goes to another field. Since he is away from the house, Ollie locks the kitchen door, hooks the front screen, and lays on the bed to rest.

Before Syble's birth, Ollie never took naps. To compensate for sleep she loses during the night feeding, Dr. Hart tells her that every nursing mother needs to rest for at least an hour while her baby is sleeping.

Ollie wakes with a very uneasy feeling. She lays her hand on Syble's back. The baby is breathing evenly. Morene rolls over and clutches her doll: She seems to be fine.

Ollie looks out the front door. No one is in the yard or on the road, but hoofbeats echo in the distance. *The noise of someone riding by must be what woke me. Anyway, it's time I start supper.*

When Roy comes in from the field, Ollie sees him at the well washing his hands, face, and arms. He dries with a towel hanging on the post before disappearing behind the house.

Soon he elbows the screen door open. "Ollie, I gathered the clothes from the line. I'll put them on our bed."

Ollie does not look away from diapering Syble. "Good. I wouldn't want to leave them on the line while we're gone. Supper's ready, and I've already fed the girls. Go ahead and serve your plate, I'll be there in a minute."

Morene is excited about going to Grandma's and can hardly sit on her quilt as they ride along. She stands, most of the time, holding onto the straps of Roy's overalls.

Mama, Papa, Bronnie, and Ollie's youngest brother John come onto the porch to greet them. John tugs on Ollie's arm. "Did you know I'm seven years old now? I'm learning to read? Pretty soon I'll be reading the newspaper."

"I know. I wanted to come to your birthday supper, but I was afraid the baby would get the colic if I took her out in the cool night air. Now that you're older, maybe you'll help Mama watch Morene and the baby while I go riding with Roy."

"I could watch them by myself." He points to Syble. "Except I won't change her messy pants."

Mama laughs. "You won't need to. I'll rock the baby while you and Morene play with the toys."

Roy and Ollie go racing across the pasture and stop in the shade of a giant sycamore tree. Roy leans over and takes her hand. "You look like you're enjoying this ride."

"I am. I almost feel like a girl again. Do you realize the last time I went horseback riding was before our wedding?"

Roy nods. "I hate that things have been so hard, and I really hate that I have to leave you and the girls to go find work. Someday we'll have it easier."

"I wasn't complaining." Without talking, they hold hands and walk the horses under the tall trees. The fluttering leaves cast a dappled pattern on the ground. Overhead branches, rustled by the breeze, seem to whisper a love song. Ollie wants to sing along, but the appropriate words never come to her.

It is almost dark when they get home. Roy carries Morene inside. He pushes the laundry to the foot of the bed to allow room for Ollie to change Syble's diaper.

"I boiled the new diapers Mama bought for Syble. I didn't want to use them until I was sure they were germ-free. I'll fold them in the morning."

"You must have already gathered them before I got home. Only a few old ones were hanging on the line."

"What! I hung them minutes before taking a nap with the girls." She hands Syble to him and searches through the pile of laundry. "They're not here! Someone took them while I was asleep."

She plops down on the bed. "Something woke me. At first,

I thought you might be home early, and I called your name. When you didn't answer, I checked in front and didn't see anyone. But as soon as I was inside again, I heard hoofbeats on the road."

"The thief was probably still in the backyard when you opened the front door."

"It has to be our thieving neighbor. Her baby is only a few weeks older than Syble." Ollie clenches her fists, and hits them against the bed. "I'd like to beat her face."

"It was probably him. I doubt she would be out riding."

"Either way, they're both thieves."

Roy chuckles. "Wonder why he didn't steal my underwear. They only have a couple of patches on the seat."

"He probably would have if I hadn't called your name."

"Too bad I didn't catch him. He probably walked right by the window and noticed you sleeping."

"Papa said we should mark everything we own because those thieves live down the road from us. Well, I marked those diapers with red thread, but not because I thought someone might steal them. I did it so I wouldn't get them confused with Bertha's when we're at Mama's."

"You'll never see those diapers again."

"I know it's unlikely. She'll probably fold the marking inside when she takes the baby out in public, but if I ever catch her with one of them, it'll be hard to keep from punching her face."

Chapter 9
Alone

Roy starts dumping apples from his pockets. "Ollie, that apple tree by the creek is loaded. They're little, but they'll make good pies. I'll pick a bucket, if you want."

"Yes, I'd like some. Last year, the animals got them before they ripened. I'll work up all you bring home. What I don't use right away, I'll cut and spread on top of the barn to dry. Dried fruit makes delicious fried pies."

Roy takes a bucket from a nail on the wall and pauses before opening the door. "What about canning some?"

"I don't have jar lids, or enough sugar."

"That is a problem." Roy pauses and turns his head to look out the window. "I think I'll go to Conway tomorrow, and check around to see if anyone knows where I might find a paying job. If you want, I'll drop you and the girls off at your mama's."

"How early are you leaving? I want to take a load of mending to repair on her sewing machine."

"I'm taking the wagon to get supplies, so I'll need to leave before daylight if I make it home tomorrow night."

"Why don't you wait about picking apples? They'll be harder to peel if they start to shrivel."

"But I can almost taste apple pie."

Ollie grins. "You probably brought enough in your pockets for a pie, but pick a half-bucket, to make sure."

Ollie packs her mending and all the things she will need for the next day. Roy has been gone a long time. She starts to worry before he comes up the path with the bucket in one hand and a string of fish in the other. She steps outside and reaches for the apples. "I'll peel while you clean fish."

"Ollie, there's an abundant crop of sweet potato vines along the creek bank. I didn't dig to see if they've made potatoes, but the plants look healthy. Until it's cold enough for frost to drive snakes into hibernation, I don't want you to go down there to check on them. This dry weather is causing all kinds of critters to gather around the creek. I saw two copperheads and a water moccasin."

"Then it's dangerous to be picking apples."

"It is now, but as soon as I clean these fish, I'm gonna hitch the team to that old mowing machine I borrowed from Pa. I'll mow under the tree and make a good path for us." He plops the fish onto a rock near the well. "Still, it won't be safe to take the girls down there unless they're in the wagon."

The next morning, as they pull into Mama and Papa's yard, they see lights in the kitchen. Papa is on the porch, calling a greeting before they can climb down. Mama rushes out from behind him. "What a nice surprise! You're here in time for breakfast. Coffee's on the stove. It'll be ready in a few minutes."

"We ate already, but if you don't mind, the girls and I will spend the day. Roy's on his way to Conway."

"Splendid." Mama smiles as she reaches for the baby.

Papa holds out his arms to take Morene from Roy. She rubs her eyes and leans against his chest.

"Ollie, it may be late tonight before I get back, but have your

things packed and ready by dark. I'll be along as soon as I can."
Roy clicks the lines. The horses start down the road at a swift
trot.

"Mama, I brought a sack of mending. I hope you don't mind
if I use your sewing machine."

"Of course, I don't mind. I'll help."

"Both of Roy's work shirts are getting thin and ragged. He
thinks he'll have to go north into the cold country to find work,
which means he'll need warm clothing. I have some feed sacks
that I can use to make new ones. They won't be thick and warm
like denim or khaki, but we don't have money to buy material
or store-bought shirts."

"I may have an answer for your problem. Robert bought a
new kind of feed. It was in some of the heaviest sacks I've ever
seen, almost as strong as pillow ticking. They're white, but I
have blue dye. I'll trade with you, if you don't think he'll mind
wearing such heavy cloth."

"I didn't mention the shirts to him. He has enough on his
mind, but I think he'll be glad to have them. Roy's always
practical."

Papa leaves for work. Bronnie rocks and entertains the
baby, while the other children play games with Morene. Mama
and Ollie are free to work on the shirts.

By noon, both shirts are almost complete.

"Ollie, you make the buttonholes in one, I'll do the other. If
we hurry, maybe the shirts can be dyed and dry before Roy gets
back."

"I hope so. I don't know when he'll have to leave. I'll mend
his clothes while the shirts dry, and come another day to finish
the rest of my mending."

When Ollie hears Roy pull into the yard, she hurries out with the new shirts tucked inside her bag. Papa and Mama carry the sleeping children. The wagon has a crate in the back with a grunting pig inside. The rest of the wagon bed is loaded with bags and boxes.

Light from a lantern, hanging on the porch, illuminates Roy's grin. "Ollie, can we hold both of the girls on the seat? Pa gave me that runt pig. I figure she'll grow nicely when she doesn't have the other pigs pushing her away from the trough. The other things are supplies for while I'm gone."

"I can hold the baby, but Morene will get awful heavy before we get home."

"I'll wake her. She can help watch the pig." He takes her from Papa. "Wake up, Renie. Look at our new pig. She's a baby now, but she'll grow big."

Morene blinks and squints. "A pig. Can we keep it?"

"Yes. We're gonna keep her until she grows big and fat. What do you want to name her?"

She yawns and leans her head on Roy's shoulder. "I don't know."

"Wake up. You can't sleep now. You have to help me watch the pig. If she gets out of her cage, she'll run off and a wolf might get her."

She raises her head with a jerk, her eyes wide open. "A woof will eat her all-gone!"

"Yep. You can sit behind me, on this sack of feed, and tell me if she starts to get out."

"I don't want woofs to eat you, Piggy."

Papa takes Syble from Mama, hands her to Ollie, and extends his hand to Roy. "Did you have any luck in locating work?"

"Day after tomorrow, there's a truck leaving for the North Dakota wheat harvest. Pa's going to town with me tomorrow afternoon. We'll sleep in the wagon, and after I leave, he'll bring it and the team back to Ollie. I hope you'll check on Ollie and the girls often. I have no idea how long I'll be gone."

"Of course we will. Good luck, and may God be with you."

A short distance down the road, Morene slips between the supplies with her head and arms resting on a feed sack. Ollie looks back at her. "She couldn't watch the pig any longer. She played all day without a nap."

"Ollie, I wanted to talk to you first about going away, but when your Papa asked, I felt obligated to tell him."

"I don't mind. What do you know of the work?"

"I don't know much more than what I've already said, except it was the only thing available for a farmer. I'll ride up there in the back of a truck with several other men. We'll work ten-hour days, six days a week. They'll furnish our meals, and we'll sleep in a bunkhouse. We can't go to town, but we can mail and receive letters. On Sunday morning, a visiting preacher holds church. I'll write to you in the afternoon."

"They said bring durable work clothes, and a heavy jacket. I hope you patched my old work shirts today. They'll have to do, durable or not."

"I did patch your shirts, and Mama helped make two new ones from some heavy feed sacks. She dyed them dark blue. I'm anxious for you to try them on. I think you'll like them."

"I'm sure I will." He reaches over and pats her arm. "What do you think of our pig? The others in the litter were twice that big."

"It was nice of your pa to give it to us. Maybe it'll be big enough for hams and bacon by Christmas."

"Don't mention ham and bacon to Morene. It can be a pet for a little while."

"I won't. It should be a good distraction for the first few days that you're away."

"Before going, I wanted to get so many things done, but I'm lucky to have the promise of a job. Ma loaned me money to get you some canning lids and sugar for the apples. Now I won't have time to pick them. Don't worry about gathering crops. I doubt they're worth salvaging. Above everything else, take care of yourself and the girls."

"I can do what has to be done."

"There's not a woman around who is more capable, but I'll still worry. Don't take any chances with danger. Always remember that you have two babies with you alone to look out for them."

"I know."

"I bought a new box of shells for the shotgun. Keep it next to the bed at night, and don't go outside for anything after sunset. Keep the screens hooked, and don't open the door to strangers, night or day—times are bad. Scoundrels might try to take advantage of a woman. I looked at a pistol for you, but it cost more than I could pay."

"I'll be cautious."

"The wheat harvest will probably be finished before the end of October, but I think I've bought enough supplies to last through November. If you run out of anything important, ask your papa to get it for you. He won't mind. I'll pay him for it when I come home." He takes a quick breath and exhales. "There is so much I want to tell you. I'm afraid I'll forget something."

They carry the sleeping children and supplies inside. She hands him one of the new shirts. "Try this on. I can't wait to see how it looks."

"It fits, looks good, and it's heavy enough for rough work in the fields."

"Good. Mama helped me make them, and get all your clothes mended. I'll pack your bag in the morning while you're doing other things. Now, take the wagon and team to the barn. You need to get a good night's sleep."

The following day, while the girls take naps, Roy pulls the wagon onto the road going toward Conway. Ollie holds her tears inside until she can no longer see the wagon.

Chapter 10
The Stallion

From behind the window curtain, Ollie watches the mail carrier take something from his bag and place it in the mailbox. She looks down at the soiled spots on her dress, and waits until his buggy starts up the nearest hill before she rushes outside. It has been ten days since Roy left. Maybe the mailman brought a letter.

Inside the box is one solitary postcard. It is from Mama.

Clutching the card, she holds her arms against her chest, bows her head, and whispers a prayer. "Dear God, you know I was hoping for a letter from Roy. Please let him be all right."

Despite many prayers, worries dominate Ollie's thoughts. *What if they had a wreck—they must have traveled over high mountains. What if he's hurt or sick? What if he went all that way and didn't get a job?*

She turns Mama's card over and reads:

Dearest Ollie,

I'm coming to spend the day on Friday. I'll bring lunch. If you have something you need to do, I'll gladly help, or I'll watch the babies.

Love,

Mama

Morene pushes the screen door open, and stands waiting for Ollie. "Did we get mail?"

"Close the screen. You're letting flies in the house."

Morene steps aside, allowing the door to slam. Immediately, Syble starts to cry.

"Now, you've woke the baby. You're not supposed to let things slam, and make noise when someone is sleeping."

Morene looks down, and turns to go inside. Her broad smile has turned into a sad frown.

Ollie pats her on the back. "It's all right. Anyway, it's almost time for the baby to wake. Remember, close doors softly."

Morene wraps one arm around Ollie's leg, looks up smiling, and nods. "Sof-ly."

Since Roy has been gone, Ollie goes to milk the cow a little earlier in the afternoon. Today, she promises Morene a sugar cookie to stay inside and talk to the baby if she wakes. "You are a big girl to take care of Syble. I'll be back as quick as I can."

Ollie hangs the milk pail on a nail outside the corncrib, and steps into the barn to get feed for the cow. Bess shakes her silver mane, rushes from the stall, and runs into the lot. Ollie calls after her, "My goodness, girl. Why so excited? Did a horsefly get you?"

The other mare, still inside the stall, drops her head and continues to stand in the same spot when Ollie speaks to her. "Bell, are you shivering, girl? What's wrong?"

Outside, horses run. Ollie turns to look. A black stallion is chasing Bess. Ollie grabs a long stick that she keeps beside the door. She waves it in the air and yells.

The black horse whirls like a streak of lightning and runs

toward her with his ears back and his teeth bared. She barely makes it up the ladder before he is inside the barn, rearing toward the loft.

His breath smells of rancid grass, and his yellow teeth are only a few feet away from where she cowers. Ollie looks around for the pitchfork and remembers it is in the stall. She grabs a handful of hay and tosses it at his eyes. He merely blinks and paws harder at the ladder, trying to reach her.

Bell jumps from the stall, rushes past the stallion and into the barnyard. He turns to chase her.

Ollie moves to where she can see through a crack. All three horses run across the pasture. Bell turns to one side, but Bess dashes toward the woods, with the stallion biting at her shoulders and neck as they race along.

Ollie scrambles down the ladder. It has two broken steps from the pounding of the stallion's hooves. She glances around for the cow. It is nowhere in sight. *It's time for her to dry up anyway. She'll freshen soon with a new calf.*

Ollie grabs the milk pail from its hook, runs along the path to the house, and slams the kitchen door behind her. She trembles as she recalls Roy's warning, "Remember that you have two babies with you alone to look after them."

Syble cries. Morene pats her on the back and looks toward Ollie. "Mama, close doors sof-ly."

"Yes. You're right. We'll both have to remember. Won't we?"

Morene nods.

Ollie sits in the rocker and motions for Morene to come to her. "I didn't get any milk for you tonight. You'll have to drink water with your cookie. A big black horse jumped into the pasture and caused the cow to run and hide. Did you see the mean horse?"

She nods. "Mean, mean, he bites my horsey." She shows her teeth and clicks them together.

"Don't ever go into the yard when a strange horse comes around. Our horses are nice, but some are bad."

"I don't like bad horsey."

"I don't, either. Are you ready for your cookie now?"

Worried about Bess and the cow, Ollie watches the pasture while Morene munches her reward for babysitting.

The next morning, before going to check on the animals, Ollie stands on the step and listens for any sound of the stallion. The cow is waiting at the gate, and Bell is peacefully grazing. Ollie hurries down the path. Without lingering a moment longer than necessary, she completes her chores at the barn and rushes back to the girls.

Early Friday morning, Mama arrives in the buggy with two picnic baskets. "Ollie, if you don't mind, I'll coddle these babies while you put my horse in the lot."

"I'll gladly do that. Morene has been asking every day if you were coming. She was hoping to play with John. Why didn't he come?"

"He went home with Bertha yesterday. I didn't know if I'd get to come as planned. Someone's black stallion has been terrorizing the community. I've kept the children inside because I was afraid it might come by our house, but when your papa came home last night, he said someone shot it."

"It was here. It chased Bess away, and chased me into the loft. It even tried to climb up there to get at me. I couldn't sleep that night for thinking of what could have happened to the girls if I hadn't escaped."

"Ollie, you need to take a gun with you when you go away from the house. I'll see if Robert will loan you his pistol until Roy gets home."

"If he will, I'll strap it on my side. Roy's shotgun is too cumbersome. I wish I could have shot that stallion before he chased Bess away. I keep watching for her, and—and hoping. I don't know what I'll do if she doesn't come home."

"What day was the stallion here?"

"Tuesday." Ollie swallows and exhales. "Do you think that he killed Bess?"

Mama turns her face away from Ollie. "She may be hiding in the woods. She'll probably be here in a day or two."

Ollie senses the uncertainty in her voice and turns to go. "I'll park your buggy in the shade." She glances at the children. Morene has lifted the cloth covering one of the baskets. Before Ollie can protest, Mama raises her hand and shakes her head.

"Let her alone." She mouths the words for Ollie before turning to Morene. "Would you like for Grandma to show you what's in the basket?"

Morene nods. Ollie goes outside.

She focuses on Bell standing alone near the barn. The mare's ears perk up; she whinnies and prances toward the gate. Ollie releases Mama's horse in the lot, and runs toward the house. "Mama! Mama! Bess is coming across the pasture. She's limping, but she's alive."

Mama carries Syble, Ollie takes Morene's hand, and they walk down to welcome Bess home. "Oh Mama, look at the bite marks on her neck. She looks so miserable."

"I think she'll be fine in a few days. Do you have some salve to put on those cuts and bruises?"

"Roy keeps a can of Watkins salve in the corn crib." She turns to go. "I'll get it and be right back."

"Look at all the mud. If I were you, I'd get a bucket of soapy water and wash her before putting on medicine."

Except for an occasional flick of her tail to scare away a horsefly, Bess stands still while Ollie washes away the dried mud and applies the salve. "It looks like she's been kicked on the jaw. I hope she doesn't have broken teeth or a cracked bone. I'll fasten her in the stall with some of the cow's ground feed. She can lick at that, and not have to chew."

Ollie feeds and waters Bess. The other horses watch through the gate.

Mama asks, "Have you heard from Roy?"

"No, and I can't help worrying. He's been gone two weeks."

"Maybe you have a letter in the box. The postman stopped while you were taking care of Bess."

"I hope so." She runs up the path. "Come on, Morene. Let's see if we have a letter from Daddy."

Ollie rips open the envelope. "Morene, listen to what Daddy wrote:"

Dear Ollie and girls,

I know you've been expecting a letter, but we didn't get here until late Monday. That morning they took letters to town and collected mail.

My job is to pick up wheat shocks, stack them on a wagon, and drive them to the thresher.

While riding up here on the truck, I got acquainted with a man named Pete. He lives east of Conway, and has three little girls. The second day of work, he stepped in a hole and hurt his ankle. We were worried they might send him home because he was limping.

That week, after I filled my wagon, he drove it to the thresher while I finished loading for Pete. With our system, we averaged as many shocks as the other men. Trying to fill both wagons kept me running. Believe me, I was tired at the end of the day, and was almost as happy as Pete, when his ankle stopped swelling.

I'm proud of the shirts you made for me. Wheat stems don't burrow through the material. The other men have cuts and scratches on their arms and chests. The first night I could have sold them both for more than the price of store-bought shirts.

I sure miss you and the girls. Tell Morene I'm glad she's such a good girl, and I'll bring her a present when I come home.

I love you,
Roy

Grandma, stands beside the porch bouncing the baby. Morene runs to her. "Daddy will bring me a present!"

"I know, sweetie. I heard. That's because he loves you, and you're such a good helper to watch the baby for your mama."

Ollie is leaning against a post with her eyes closed. "Mama, I'm so relieved to hear he's all right. I've had some horrible nightmares since he's been gone. If something bad happened to him, how could I support two babies by myself?"

"We need to be thankful for our blessings and have faith that the Good Lord will take care of us." Mama smiles. "You know, I bet Pete's wife is reading her first letter about now and thanking God for sending Roy to help."

"Yes. To Pete, Roy must have seemed God-sent."

"Ollie, he needs restful sleep. If I were you, I wouldn't tell Roy about that stallion until he gets home."

Chapter 11
Apples

Ollie folds her letter. "Mama, Roy said that apple tree, near the creek, is loaded with green fruit. I'd like to pick some for canning. Animals will get them all if I try to wait until they ripen."

"Do you want me to go help?"

"I'd enjoy your company, but I'm afraid to take the girls down there. Roy told me snakes are gathering near the water during this drought. I *would* like to hitch your horse to the wagon alongside Bell. Bess is much too sore to be working."

"Of course. Meg should work well with your mare. Although, I hate for you to go by yourself. Are you sure those apples are worth so much work?"

"Very sure. Our early garden dried up, and we don't have much to put away for winter. I'll gladly work to save any healthy food."

Mama removes the cover from the picnic basket. "Let's eat before you leave. It's a little early, but you don't need to start a big job on an empty stomach."

They eat fried chicken and rolls, before Ollie loads baskets into the wagon. The grass is dead along the path until she nears the low section close to the creek. It is evident where Roy mowed, but under the shade of the apple tree, the grass is green and several inches tall. Half-eaten and rotting apples litter the ground. Wasp and bees, disturbed by the intrusion, buzz into the air and around the area. Crickets and black beetles crawl over the broken apples. Bell and Meg stomp, sling their heads, and swish their tails at the insects.

Ollie pulls the wagon as close to the tree as possible. From inside the wagon, she can reach the apples and drop them into the closest basket. She grabs the fruit quickly while trying to pay close attention to Meg. The nutmeg-colored mare, not used to working with Bess, seems nervous. She might spook easily.

Gradually, Ollie moves the team and wagon until they face the path going toward the house. She picks around the edges, but fruit close to the center of the tree is larger and has less damage from insects and birds.

It is almost impossible to reach the better fruit without getting among the tangled twigs. Ollie remembers the story of King David's son Absalom, when he got his hair caught in the branches of a tree. She knows she could be left hanging if the team starts to run, but apples seem to invite her hands to snatch them.

Full baskets leave little room for Ollie to walk inside the wagon. She is tempted to reach for a high limb, hanging loaded and heavy. From the front of the wagon bed, she stands on her tiptoes, leans against the sideboard, and reaches. She continues to repeat soothing words to the horses, although they have lost her attention.

Taking hold of the bough, she pulls down and begins to jerk the apples free. Without warning, the limb breaks and crashes into the wagon. Ollie screams and fights to regain her balance.

The clamor frightens the horses, causing them to jump and run. Baskets overturn, and branches catch and yank out wads of Ollie's hair. She tumbles with hundreds of apples rolling and shifting underneath her. It is impossible to stand, but at last she grabs the check lines, pulling on them with all her strength while calling, "Whoa, Bell! Whoa, Meg."

Every basket has overturned by the time the horses stop near the barn. Ollie climbs out, pets the nervous mares, and leads them until the wagon is near the back door. She ties them to the well post before going inside.

"My goodness, what happened to you?" Mama voice echoes alarm.

"I didn't set the brake or tie the lines, because I kept moving the wagon. When the horses got scared and took off running, there was nothing to slow them, except a lot of my hair and skin which is still dangling in the apple tree."

"It looks that way. Let's wash those scratches and medicate them. You don't want to get an infection."

"Oh, they'll be fine, but I'd like you to help me get these apples into the house. I'll peel and can them tomorrow. This afternoon, I want to plant a late garden while you're here to watch the girls."

"You may waste your seed. I'm afraid we're in for a long dry spell."

"Maybe so, but I have to try. Those seed potatoes Roy bought are sprouting in the sack. They'll ruin if I don't plant them, and surely turnips will grow."

"I'll help you carry these baskets inside, but at least wash those scratches with soap and water."

Ollie grins and goes to the wash pan, flinching as she rubs the soap over her arms. "The best apples are still near the middle of the tree. After birds and animals feast for a few more days, they'll all be gone."

They walk outside together, but Ollie goes to pet the horses again.

Mama looks in the wagon. "Gracious sakes, Ollie, it will take you a week to process all these tiny apples."

"They may start to shrivel before I get them peeled. Anyway, I want to dry some of them for making fried pies."

It is late before Ollie gets the fall garden planted. She has rows of purple hull peas, turnips, and potatoes. "If these and those sweet potatoes produce, we'll make it through the winter without going hungry."

"I hope they do. You are one of the few willing to gamble on wasting seed."

"I don't think it's gambling. For me, this garden is a kind of prayer."

Mama smiles and looks at the sky. Not a cloud is in sight. "I need to be on my way soon. Why don't you take care of the animals, and milk the cow before I leave?"

"The cow's gone dry. I haven't milked her since Tuesday morning. I'll be glad when she has her new calf. Morene needs milk."

"We have plenty. I'll send your papa down with a jar, more eggs, some butter, and that gun. I'd like to know you have a pistol strapped on your hip each time you leave this house."

While Ollie brings Mama's horse from the barn, Morene insists on carrying one of the empty baskets to the buggy. "Grandma, can you come again at morning?"

"No, honey. I have to stay home, but Grandpa will come to see you soon."

"Will he bring cake and chicken?"

Before Mama can answer, Ollie scolds, "Morene, don't ask

for gifts."

Morene looks down and leans her head against Grandma. Grandma pats her back. "I bet he could. We'll see."

Through the window, the moon is shining bright when Ollie puts the girls to bed, and blows out the lamp. With doors locked and the screens hooked, Ollie steps into a darkened corner to bathe and change into nightclothes.

A cool breeze rustles the curtains. She lowers the window near the girls, and rubs Syble's back. *I don't want you waking with colic.*

She stretches out on her bed and sighs. *Tomorrow will be another busy day.* Outside, katydids are chirping. In the distance, a coyote howls.

Deep in the night, a loud noise rumbles through the house. Ollie jumps and grabs the shotgun, before she realizes the noise is thunder. Rain drums against the house. *Thank You, God, for all good things.*

She closes the windows, stands looking at the silver blessings falling on the garden, and listens to drops beating against the roof.

Roy, I wish you could be here to listen with me. I remember when we put that tin over the kitchen and you said, 'Rain on this metal will be like music to our ears on some hot summer night when our crops need watering.'

Before daylight the next morning, Ollie is at the kitchen table, next to the kerosene lamp, writing a letter to Roy. *He won't get it on Monday, but he'll know I wrote as soon as I could.*

Ollie is stirring a bubbling pot when Morene wakes.

"Our house smells good. Do we eat apple for breakfast?"

"You can have some on your biscuit, if you want."

Morene nods her head. "I like apple."

Still stirring, Ollie opens the oven with her left hand, reaches for a pan of raw biscuits waiting on the table, and shoves them in to bake. "Get a washcloth from the stack, wet it in the wash-pan, and make your face clean and pretty. Your bread will be ready soon."

Morene's bare feet pad across the wood floor to the cabinet holding the washcloth. "Baby still sleep."

"But Morene's a big girl. I want you to take the cloth, go sit in my rocker, and wash your face and hands. Sit there until they dry. I've got to pour this sauce into jars." Steam rises from the gurgling pot, and beads of perspiration cling to Ollie's forehead.

"It's very hot, so don't come in the kitchen until I say you can. You might cause me to spill it. This would hurt awful bad if it got on you. Remember, stay out of the kitchen. I'll call when you can come eat. All right?"

"All right." Morene takes the cloth and leaves the room.

Ollie begins pouring hot apples into the jars. Once she has filled a quart, she washes the rim, places a hot lid on top, tightens the metal band, and sets it aside. She is almost finished when Morene knocks the wash-pan from its stand.

Ollie jumps at the sound and bumps the jar filler. Scalding liquid splashes. Screaming, she runs to plunge her left arm into the water bucket.

Morene runs to the rocker. She sits very still and solemn, watching Ollie with her arm thrust up to the elbow in the water.

Tears stream down Ollie's face. "Morene, why did you come back in the kitchen? You caused me to spill hot stuff on my arm, and it hurts." A sob chokes in her throat.

The scent of scorching fruit causes Ollie to turns her face toward the stove. "Oh no, now the pan's burning!" She runs to move it to a potholder. Pain sears from her hand to her shoulder. She returns, plunging her arm into the cool water to relieve the anguish."

"Oh, the biscuits! They'll burn!" She takes the bread from the oven, turns off the damper, and runs back to the water. She is standing over the bucket crying when someone rides into the yard.

"What a time for a visitor. Morene look out the window and see who's here."

A man's heavy steps drum across the porch. "Ollie, it's Papa. Are you decent for me to come in?"

Water drips across the floor, as she goes to unlock the door. "Papa, I burned my arm with applesauce." She dashes back to the water.

"Let me see how bad it is."

"Would you draw me a cold bucket of water first? This one seems so warm."

"Of course." The door slams as he goes to the well.

The baby wakes, crying. Ollie stands, wiping at her own tears—Morene goes to pat the baby's back.

"Here it is, Sis. Now let me take a quick look at your arm." He frowns. "It's going to cause a bad blister. Do you have any Watkins salve? It comes in a red and gold-colored can. I think it's called Petro Carbo."

"That's what Roy uses on the horses. There's a can in the corncrib."

"It's good for burns. I'll go get it."

"But we've been using it on the horses. It may not be clean."

"It'll be fine. I'll skim off the top. I don't know of anything better to put on your arm."

Syble is still crying. Morene is getting louder. "Don't cry. Don't cry, Baby."

Papa brings the salve and pats it over the blister. Tears trickle over Ollie's cheeks.

"I've heard that water's not good for burns. It softens the skin too much."

"I can't stand the pain without it. I don't know how I'll change and nurse the baby while holding my arm in this bucket."

"I'll change her diaper, and place the pail beside your chair."

"Papa, I haven't fed the cow, and she needs to be in the pasture. I always take care of the animals before the girls wake up, but I thought I could get one batch of apples canned. It took me longer than I expected."

"I'll do that while you nurse the baby."

"Before you go, will you put some butter and applesauce on a biscuit for Morene?"

"Yes, and I'll pour her a glass of milk to go with her breakfast. It was cold from the spring when I left home."

By the time Papa feeds Morene, takes care of the animals, and cleans the messy kitchen, Ollie can keep her arm out of the water long enough to change the baby.

"Ollie, I think it would be a good idea if Morene goes home with me. She can sleep with Bronnie tonight. We'll bring her home tomorrow. One baby is enough for you to take care of today."

"Morene, do you want to go home with Grandpa, and sleep in Bronnie's bed tonight?"

Morene nods. "I wanna go with Grandpa."

Ollie, still holding the baby, leans her head back against the rocker. "All right. Will you be a big girl and not cry?"

"I'll not cry."

Papa squints and stares at Ollie. "Sis, you haven't eaten anything today, have you?"

"No. Breakfast wasn't important after getting my arm burned."

"Your mama sent some fried chicken and a cake. She said a pretty little girl asked for it."

They look at Morene. She is putting her nightgown in a bag to take with her to Grandpa's, and is not listening.

"Let's eat some chicken before you get sick."

Papa and Morene leave, Ollie locks the doors, and stretches out next to Syble with her arm in a bucket of cold water beside the bed. It is mid-afternoon when she wakes. Her arm is no longer burning so badly that she has to keep it in cold water.

Before morning, Ollie cans thirty-five quarts of apples.

Chapter 12
Snakes

Syble whines and stirs. Ollie gets up, and pulls the sheet over the sleeping baby's exposed legs. She looks at Morene's empty bed. *I hope she didn't cry last night.*

The wrap on Ollie's arm is twisted, the blister broken. She adds salve, ties on a new bandage, and goes to check the canned apples. Every jar is sealed.

The sky is getting lighter. It will be daylight in less than an hour. *Should I leave the baby and go feed the animals? She'll be safer in bed than in the barn with dust, and spiders. I'll rush down, feed the cow, and be back before Syble wakes.*

Ollie loads the pistol her Papa left on the mantle, straps it to her side, and steps into the gray dawning. She waits for her eyes to become accustomed to the dim light, before stepping onto the trail. *Papa must have dropped a stick in the path. I'll toss it into the pasture.*

Something, warns her to stop. She is staring at the object when it moves. With a slow, steady motion, she takes the gun from its holster, aims, and shoots.

A large snake coils, and strikes at the air.

Ollie shoots again.

It jerks, and begins to roll in a continuous spiral. Its movement slows. Now she can see that one of the shots hit its head.

She turns and goes back to the house. *Cow, you need to find yourself some grass. There is no ground feed for you until broad daylight.*

In the afternoon, Mama and Papa bring Morene home. She runs to Ollie, and grabs hold of her outstretched arms.

Ollie drops to her knees as one little hand grips the blister. "Let go Morene! That's my sore arm."

"Sorry. Sorry, Mama."

Ollie hugs her. "It'll be well in a few days, but now we have to be careful."

Morene is bubbling with stories of playing with John, helping Grandma cook, and sleeping in Bronnie's bed. She talks for a few minutes before Ollie interrupts.

"Papa, come see what I shot this morning."

Mama moves to take a closer look. "I've seen enough. I'll go in the house and check on the baby." She starts toward the house, stops, and turns, "Make sure Morene knows what snakes can do."

Papa turns the snake over with a stick. "That's an awful big copperhead. It's a good thing you didn't step on it."

"I'll be watching closer from now on."

"I wish you'd wait until daylight before going out in the mornings. I've always heard that if you find one snake, another is nearby."

"I plan to, until the weather turns cold. Now that the cow is dry, I won't have to go for a while, but I like to give her and the horses a little feed to keep them coming to the barn every day. Roy said feeding and petting keeps them tame."

Papa points toward the pasture. "Your cow's not dry anymore. In three days, you can start saving her milk again. Look, Morene. It's a new baby calf. The mama cow is trying to make it get up and walk."

Morene jerks her hand free from Ollie, and runs toward the gate. "I wanna pet it."

Papa grabs her dress as she tries to pass. "No. You don't pet a new calf. A Jersey cow would stomp you into the ground."

"Why?"

"She's afraid you might hurt her baby." He puts Morene down and points. "Ollie do you still keep the milk in that dug-well?"

"The rest of the jar you brought yesterday is in there. I didn't worry much about those weeds around it then. Now, I'm afraid a snake might be in them."

Papa grins. "Have the gun ready. I'll get the scythe from the barn, and cut around the well, but don't shoot near me if you see one slithering away."

He clears the weeds, and stands looking into the well. "Ollie, I've heard of snakes getting into these old dug-wells, and some shoddy masonry work went into this one. Don't let Roy get inside to clean it unless he has several men around. The sides don't look stable to me; they might cave in. You don't drink water from here do you?"

"No. We only use it to water the pig, or other stock when an animal needs to be kept in the corral, and I lower the milk jar down in a bucket."

"It's fine for that, but don't lean on the rocks, and you should watch for a snake in your bucket."

Ollie jerks around to look at his face.

He is smiling. Before she can ask if he is teasing, Morene runs into his outstretched arms. Papa tosses her into the air.

"Slow down, little one, before you fall and skin your knees."

"Papa, let's go to the house," Ollie says with a smile. "I want you to see the apples I canned after you left yesterday."

"With your sore arm?"

"It hurt no matter what I did, and I figured it was safer to work with scalding hot sauce while Morene was at your house."

"Well, I'm glad you've got them canned. Before I come in, I believe I'll take the buggy down and pick a few apples for a pie."

Papa returns within a short time. "It's a good thing you picked day-before-yesterday. There's not an apple left, and it looks like hogs have been rooting under the tree. Is your shoat in a secure pen? An old boar, might try to steal her when she gets a little older."

"It looks secure to me."

"I'll walk down and take a look. Let me carry that bucket of peels and apple cores as I go. She'll think she has a Sunday dinner with these."

Mama and Papa leave, and Morene falls asleep. Ollie sits at the kitchen table to begin another letter to Roy. Writing each day helps her to tell what the girls do, and it makes a longer letter for him. She wants to tell about the stallion, the horses running away, her burned arm, and the snake, but she writes of canned apples, rain on the fall garden, the new calf, and cute things the girls have done.

Within a few days, Ollie can see green leaves where peas and turnip greens are coming up. The potatoes will take longer to break through. Carefully, she hoes away the grass from every row. "Morene, look at these little baby plants. If we touch or step on them, they'll die, and they can't grow big and make good peas for us to eat. So don't walk in the garden."

Morene squats to look at the plants. "They'll die? Like the snake died?"

"Yes, but that snake was mean and poison. We wanted him to die, because he would try to bite us. Garden plants are good. They help us grow strong."

Since the calf's birth, Ollie has only allowed it to get part of the cow's milk. The pig enjoyed the rest. On Thursday morning, Ollie keeps all but the calf's portion.

"Sorry, Piggy." Ollie tosses a basket of acorns from the yard into the pen. "These won't taste as good as rich milk, but they'll help you grow."

Friday morning, Ollie puts a clean apron over her dress. She and Morene wait on the porch for the mail carrier.

Morene begins to jump. "Here he comes, Mama."

He stops his horse and stretches his arm toward Morene, so she is not near the buggy wheel. "Here's a letter from your daddy. You look mighty pretty today."

Morene smiles, ducks her head, and runs to Ollie with the letter. The mailman waves. His horse trots down the road. Ollie rips the envelope:

Dear Ollie and girls,

I don't have much to write about except work. A bell rings for us at five each morning. We barely have time to get dressed, eat, hitch our team, and be in the field by seven. At eleven forty-five, we go to the barns, feed our animals, eat dinner, listen to complaints or new instructions from the boss, and head back to the fields.

My first Sunday here, the minister was an old man—a real fire-and-brimstone preacher. Today a younger parson came; he spoke a while, and then asked if anyone had questions. He said he would stay all day and all night to teach if anyone wants to learn. Some of the men are still talking with him. I'll go listen when I finish this letter.

The food is good. They serve meat and some kind of potatoes three times a day, plus many other things. I wish that I knew you and Morene were eating this good.

Every night before I fall asleep, I wonder if you've got rain, if the pig is growing, if you gathered the apples, if you've planted a late garden, if the cow has a new calf, if the mares are still doing good, if grass in the pasture will be enough, and on and on.

I worry a lot about you and the girls. You are in my prayers, and I'm counting on those guardian angels to keep all of you safe.

I love you,
Roy

"Will Daddy still bring me a present?"

"Yes, honey. I'm sure he will. You'll just have to wait until he can earn some money and come home." She reads the letter again while Morene pokes a stick at a fuzzy worm.

Ollie looks across the brown pasture. The only bright spots are patches of yellow bitterweed that will make the cow's milk unfit to drink. "I wish I could tell him the crops are better than we expected, and the meadow grass is thick and lush enough to feed our animals through a bad winter."

"What, Mama?"

"Nothing, honey. I was only thinking out loud."

Morene smacks the worm with the stick, and stomps it with her foot.

"Why did you kill the worm?"

"He eats baby peas."

"Yes, he might." She folds the letter and puts it in her pocket. Until she gets another, she will read this one over and over.

"I need to go give Piggy some water. She'll get thirsty today with this awful heat. I want you to play here in the yard until I get back."

Morene nods and tosses a little red ball into the air.

Ollie walks down the path to the well, draws up the bucket, sets it on a flat rock nearby, and removes a jar of milk. Morene calls before Ollie lets down the bucket to draw water. Glancing over her shoulder, there is no time to yell before Morene slams against her.

Ollie is falling. She grabs at the air—at anything. Her right hand lands on a protruding rock. She clasps it tight. Her toes, inside leather shoes, hook over the top edge of the well's stone wall. She gropes with her left hand for another rock, touches something soft, and jerks back. A frog splashes into the water. Reaching again, she finds the rope attached to the well bucket. She pulls; it tightens against the post.

Morene is looking into the well, screaming, "Mama! Mama!"

"Morene, step away from the well, before you fall in. Listen to me. If I can't get out, you go to the road and stop anyone that comes by. Bring them to help me." Little feet patter away.

"Please, God let this rope be secure."

With her left hand, she pulls as hard as she can. The rope is tight. *Lord, help me.* She lets go of the rock with her right hand and grabs the rope. Hand over hand, she climbs the rope until her head is higher than her feet.

Her shoes still hang on the edge of the wall. Cautiously, she turns one foot and slides it up until she can brace it against a rock that feels firm. She does the same with the other. Hanging onto the rope with both hands and straddling the well, she tries to slide one shoe along the wall. A pebble plunks. Ollie looks down. Something from the side slithers into the water.

She pushes hard against the well with one foot, swings on the rope, and pulls herself higher. The old well post creaks with her weight. *Will it hold me?* Again, she pushes a foot against the wall, swinging closer to the edge. The post creaks louder and seems to bend. She kicks with all the strength she has left, propelling herself over the edge, turns loose of the rope, drops onto the ground, and rolls away from the well.

"Thank You, God!"

Chapter 13
Stew

Ollie sets the jar of strained milk on the table, glances at the clock, and goes to wake Morene. "Are you ready for breakfast? Your biscuits are done."

Morene blinks, slides from the bed, and wraps her arms around Ollie.

"Would you like to go to the store with me today? Our Bess is well now. She can help Bell pull the wagon." Morene nods as Ollie continues. "We can stop at Grandma's on the way back."

"I can play with John's toys, and sleep in Bronnie's bed?"

"No, you can't sleep in Bronnie's bed. We're not staying the night, but if you're nice, John will let you play with his toys."

"I'll be nice."

Ollie puts an ironed dress on Morene and brushes her hair. "Hold your head still, so I can make a bow." Morene whines and pulls away.

Ollie's hand is quick to leave a red print on a small tanned leg. "Don't jerk away from me." Morene's chin quivers, but the rest of her body stands rigid while Ollie ties the ribbon.

Ollie is soon lifting the girls into the wagon. She steps up to join them, clicks the lines, and pulls onto the road. "Morene, would you like to stay at Grandma's while I go to the store? I'll bring you some candy."

"No. I pick candy."

"All right, but you won't get to stay long."

Morene ignores Ollie's statement, and shakes her finger at Syble. "You a baby. Babies not eat candy. I get red sucker."

Ollie walks into the store with her purse under one arm. She holds Syble with the other. "Morene, remember, walk beside me and don't let your hands touch anything or you won't get a prize."

Mrs. Hart is busy with another customer. Ollie smiles and nods to her before walking toward the rack holding thread and buttons. Morene has her hands clenched tight. She walks behind Ollie without saying a word.

Ollie walks by a pretty doll sitting on a table. She glances back to make sure Morene is behaving. Morene's hands are still clasped in front, but she stands on her tiptoes and leans her cheek against the doll's dress.

"Come on, Morene." They pass some pink material with bright flowers on it. Morene's elbow comes up and drags across the fabric.

Ollie pauses near a shelf holding a basket of yellow apples. Morene sticks her nose close to an apple and sniffs several times. She looks at Ollie. "Mama, can—"

"No. Follow behind me, like I told you."

Ollie is quick to choose her thread and walk toward the counter. Her neighbor is sitting on the bench at the front of the store, changing a baby's wet diaper. Instantly, Ollie sees the red thread stitched across the corner of the clean diaper she is folding to put on the child.

Ollie's voice echoes through the store. "That's one of the diapers stolen from my clothesline. Bertha and I marked our diapers so we wouldn't get them confused. Mine are marked with red thread."

The woman looks up with a grin. "Well, ain't that a fluke. That's the way I mark my diapers."

Mrs. Hart grasps Ollie by the arm and whispers. "Walk away. You have two babies to look after. I know what you want to do, but you'll only cause yourself more grief. You have no way to prove she didn't mark the diapers."

Hands shaking, Ollie pays for the spool of thread and card of buttons. She looks down into Morene's big blue eyes. Her little fingers entwine. "Morene, have you decided on the candy you want?"

"I want red."

"A red sucker?"

She nods and points to a red sucker in the candy case.

Ollie digs in her purse for a coin. Papa's gun falls onto the counter.

Mrs. Hart takes a step back. "You're carrying a gun?"

Ollie's face tingles. She picks up the gun, lips forming a tight line, eyes narrowing, and with the gun in her hand, she turns to stare at the neighbor. Her voice emphasizes disgust. "There are a lot of snakes around. I shot a copperhead a few days ago." Ollie's words get louder. "My neighbors have stolen cottonseed, harness, and even diapers from my clothesline. In my mind, a thief is as low as a snake and needs the same treatment. They won't always escape justice."

A gentle hand touches Ollie's arm. "Don't let Satan tempt you."

Ollie tucks the gun in her purse and leaves the store.

While loading the girls, Ollie hears laughter inside. It is not Mrs. Hart. Her fingers fold into fists. She turns to go back, but remembers Roy's words. *Ollie, you have two babies with you alone to look out for them.*

She steps up into the wagon.

Morene holds her lollipop with both hands.

"You better lick fast, or you'll have to leave it in the wagon while we're at Grandma's. I was so mad at that woman that I forgot to buy candy for John."

"Why you mad at woman?"

"She's mean. Hurry and eat. We'll be at Grandma's in a few minutes."

Ollie pulls the brake and wraps the check lines around the wagon seat. She leaves Morene on the porch with John and takes the baby inside. "Mama, I can't stay long. My thieving neighbor was at the store. If she goes by and sees I'm here, she'll steal everything she can before I get home."

Mama reaches for Syble. "Are you still getting plenty of sweet milk? If not, we have extra."

"We do, but Morene won't drink it. The cow's been eating bitterweeds."

"Let me get you a jar. Robert has been keeping our cows in that meadow near the creek. They have plenty of grass so they're leaving the weeds alone." She starts toward the kitchen, bouncing Syble on her hip.

"Mama, I have to hurry."

"I saw you pass by earlier, so I have the milk ready."

John comes rushing inside. "Morene's leaving in your wagon!"

Ollie runs. The horses have left the yard and are starting down the hill. She grabs onto a sideboard and climbs inside a moment before Morene rustles the lines across the mares and yells, "Oh, horsey. Oh."

The horses jerk the wagon, and begin trotting. Morene swishes the lines and shouts louder, "Oh! Horsey. Oh!"

Bouncing on the rough dirt road, Ollie clasps the right sideboard and then the left as she makes her way to the front of the wagon. She grabs the lines. "Whoa! Whoa, Bell! Whoa, Bess!" She turns the wagon and returns to her mama's yard.

Morene crawls under the seat and burrows her face in the baby's quilt. "Mama, I told the horsie to Oh."

"Morene, what were you doing in the wagon by yourself?"

She sniffles. "I get candy."

"I told you not to eat it in front of John."

"He lick it, too."

"Who untied the lines from the wagon seat?"

"John do it."

Ollie stops in the yard. "Don't get out, Morene. We are not staying. You were a bad girl for getting in the wagon without me." She looks at John. He turns his face toward the ground.

Mama kisses the baby before handing her to Ollie. "Wait a minute; I'll get the milk." She rushes away.

"John." Ollie calls in a stern voice.

He turns toward her with his head bowed.

"Look at me, John."

His head sideways, he looks through hair hanging across his forehead.

"Morene is still little. You need to help me keep her safe. Neither of you should have gotten in the wagon without a grown-up, and you should never have bothered the lines or the brake. Undoing the lines and moving them told the horses it was all right to leave."

He looks down and nods as Mama comes outside.

"Ollie, you need to have your Papa take a look at that brake. It shouldn't have popped loose."

"I will, the next time he comes by."

"And don't you do something foolish, if that woman comes around. She'll get her reward someday."

Ollie grits her teeth. "She would have got part of it today, but with a baby on one hip and another on your dress tail it's hard to kick somebody's—"

"Ollie! Ollie! Stop it. I raised you to be a lady and a Christian.

"Bertha's your perfect lady. I've always been rough around the edges. I try to be Christian, though today I'm having an awful time with Leviticus 19:18. Loving a neighbor that steals every time you turn your back does not seem right."

"Our reasoning is but folly to God. Now remember, you have these babies depending on you."

"These girls—and Mrs. Hart pulling on my arm—are what kept the teeth in her mouth. You don't know how much I wanted to knock that smirking grin off her face."

"I can imagine, but she has a baby that needs her too. Don't do something rash."

"That kid will grow up to be a thief, like its parents."

"You're stewing too much over this. Go home, count your blessings, and remember the Bible says we're not to return evil for evil or reviling for reviling."

She stares at Mama. "You've got a Bible verse for everything." Ollie grins. "I don't want to return evil for evil. I'd never steal from her. I just want to kick her—"

"Ollie!"

"Morene, sit down on the quilt. We have to go." Ollie looks at Mama. "Don't worry. I won't go looking for trouble, and thanks for the verses. I'll try to remember them."

In the afternoon, Ollie walks through the garden, checking on the new plants. Something has nibbled off several of the peas. Animal tracks are visible beside the row. *If I watch, maybe I can shoot it tonight.*

Once the children fall asleep in their beds, Ollie pulls her rocker close to the back window and unhooks the screen. She loads Roy's shotgun and places it on the table. Moonlight illuminates the garden. *On a night like this, I should get a good shot at that critter.*

Ollie's head rests against the rocker's back, with thoughts drifting far away. Her eyelids begin to droop, before a shadow blocks the moonlight. Ollie grabs the gun. *Was I dreaming? Did someone pass by the window?* Her heart beats fast as she tiptoes through the house, looking out every window, assessing every weed, bush, and tree. Wide-awake, she returns to the rocker, still holding the gun.

It seems like an hour before her heart stops pounding, and she feels sleepy again. Ready to stand, she leans forward, but something moves in the garden. She kneels in front of the window. Pushing her head against the screen to raise it high on the hinges, she aims the gun, and pulls the trigger. The animal flops over.

Ollie hears someone running on the other side of the house. She pops another shell in the gun, runs to the front, and flips up the screen-door latch in time to see a man disappear into the brush. She shoots toward where she last saw him. The shot echoes in her ears. She listens for more footsteps, but only hears the cries of two frightened little girls.

She closes and locks the front door before going to comfort the children. "Don't cry, Morene. I shot a mean old animal that was eating our peas."

"Is it dead?" Morene sobs.

"Yes, now he can't eat our garden. Go back to sleep so I can take care of Syble, and in the morning I'll make pancakes for you."

"All right." She hugs her rag doll and snuggles under the sheet.

Ollie did not light a lamp, but she has no trouble finding Syble. The baby is crying hard and gasping for breath between screams.

"Now, now, don't cry." Ollie cuddles her close, and wipes the perspiration from the baby's face with a diaper. She walks around the room, bouncing and singing, "Hush, little baby, don't say a word, Daddy's gonna buy you a mocking bird. If that mocking bird don't sing, Daddy's gonna buy you a diamond ring." Syble falls asleep, and Ollie puts her in bed.

She stands at the window, looking at the bushes where she shot toward the man, and tries to estimate the distance the lead traveled. *If I hit him, he's mighty uncomfortable, but not dead.* She lifts the clock and holds it so the moonlight shines on the face. The time is one o'clock.

She loads the gun again, hooks the kitchen window screen, and stands in the kitchen, remembering Roy's words. "Don't go outside for anything after sunset." *I didn't promise him I would stay inside after dark.*

A hoe is standing beside the back door. Ollie takes it along. She looks down at the animal—a rabbit—rolls it over with the hoe, and tosses the hoe between two rows. A large stain darkens the dirt.

She turns, looking in every direction, before stooping to pick up the rabbit, and is almost back to the house before remembering to watch for snakes. She stops, and looks at the ground before rushing on.

A board Roy prepared for skinning small animals hangs on the back of the house. Ollie drops the rabbit in front of it before going inside to kindle a fire in the cook stove. In the moonlit kitchen, with a flickering fire showing through the stove grates, she scrubs her hands with lye soap.

Ollie listens to each child's soft breathing as she goes from window to window looking for any sign of an intruder in the yard. Holding a match near the kitchen lamp, she changes her mind and lights the lantern instead. With Roy's whetstone, she sharpens a knife, puts a pot of water on to boil, takes the lantern and goes outside to skin the rabbit. Papa's pistol is on her hip.

Many times as a girl, Ollie helped Eldridge hunt rabbits and squirrels. It was mostly sport, but provided some good meals. This is necessity. Since Roy left, the only meat on the table has been the fried chicken from Mama's house.

The rabbit skinned and washed, she drops it into the pot of boiling water. *Tomorrow, I'll make rabbit stew.* She grits her teeth. *My neighbors may be stewing a bit while picking out lead. It's too bad I couldn't give her some of it.*

She puts water, the skinning knife, and soap in the dishpan where she washed the rabbit, and puts the pan on to boil. To kill germs, the water must boil for several minutes.

Ollie remembers the time Mama and Eldridge got tularemia from handling raw rabbit meat. They were sick for a long time, with swollen glands, headaches, and sore muscles. Dr. Hart said the disease is transferred through contact with the raw meat of a diseased animal, but well-cooked meat is safe to eat.

A small red can with a pour spout sits in a corner near the back door. Ollie pours kerosene from it into the wash pan, and bathes her hands and arms up to the elbows before tossing the oily liquid into the yard. Again, she washes with soap and water.

Bubbles roll inside the dishpan and in the pot. Ollie closes the damper and the grate at the front of the stove, and puts a heavy lid over the rabbit. Blowing out the light, she looks outside again and listens. An owl hoots in the distance and dry leaves rustle. *I wonder what sounds can be heard in the fields of North Dakota.*

Chapter 14
Predators

A bird in the oak tree wakes Ollie with a shrill call. It sounds as if it is saying, "Whit whew. Whit whew." She listens trying to determine what bird makes such a noise. *Maybe a sick whippoorwill?* It's not the joyful echo they make in the spring.

She slides her feet off the bed and sits at the edge. Her nightdress is damp. *Bird, I know why you're making such a pitiful sound. You're burning up like we are.*

In the kitchen, she pours water from the bucket into the wash pan to wash her hands and face. The water is warm. *I hope my garden can survive this heat.*

Yesterday, she plowed to cover the roots deeper and help distribute ground moisture. It is barely light enough to see the well when Ollie goes to draw water. She fills two buckets, and uses the dipper to drizzles the center of each plant as she walks beside the rows. She will repeat this every day until rain comes. This garden is essential.

Ollie has completed the early morning chores when Morene wakes with a loud whine. Rushing to her, Ollie asks, "What's wrong?"

"My bed's wet."

Ollie runs her hand over the sheets. "Honey, your bed's damp with sweat."

Morene smiles. "Sweat?"

Ollie nods and hugs her. "I made pancakes, and we still have a little sorghum syrup for you."

"Pancakes!" She runs to the kitchen and starts to crawl into a chair.

"Wash your hands first."

Ollie takes two plates of pancakes from the warming oven, sets them on the table, smoothes butter across the cakes, and pours thick dark syrup over Morene's.

"That's the last of the molasses, so don't waste any."

"We don't have more?"

"No, and we don't have sugar. I can't make cookies until Daddy comes home, but we still have canned apples for tomorrow's biscuits."

"I like cookies."

"I know you do." Ollie flops her pancake, and adds more butter. "Did you remember that your grandma's coming today to stay with you and baby Syble while I gather corn?"

Morene smiles and claps her hands. "Grandma brings chicken and cake."

Ollie grabs Morene's arm. "Listen, Grandma can't bring chicken and cake every time she comes, so don't ask for it. She has to have money to buy stuff for making cake."

"Not chicken. She's got chickens in her yard."

"If she kills all her chickens for you, she won't get any eggs. Don't ask her to bring anything. All right?"

A sad look covers Morene's face. She nods. "All right."

When Mama arrives, Ollie checks on the sleeping baby, and then picks up her gloves. "Mama, I'll be gathering near the creek. If I don't get the corn soon those wild hogs will destroy it. The ears are small, but they're all we have."

Ollie is on her way out the door when her mama calls, "Be careful! Remember that snake you killed near the well. A copperhead would be hard to see among those stalks."

Ollie does not want to hear about a snake—thinking of one makes her shiver. She has killed three since Roy went away to work in the wheat harvest. Again, she wishes he were home, but knows the necessity of his going. The drought-stricken crops have not produced enough to supply them through the winter.

Staring at the devastation caused by another night of foraging hogs, she drives the wagon into the cornfield, jumps down, and starts grabbing the dry withered ears. With quick twists of her wrists, she breaks them from the stalks and throws them into the wagon. At Ollie's command, the well-trained mares move along the rows without veering right or left.

The sun is high in the sky when she stops to go feed the baby. At the bottom of the barn path, she hears crying and begins to run. Mama meets her at the door. "I was about ready to come looking for you. This baby is starving."

Ollie washes her hands, takes the baby, and sits in the rocker. Syble is so hungry that she pants when she stops nursing to breathe. "I shouldn't have stayed so long. I was trying to finish one of those long rows." Ollie wipes the sweat from the baby's face. "Mama, do you mind bringing me a drink? I rushed off this morning without a jug of water."

"I'll draw a fresh bucket."

"No, I'm too thirsty to wait. The putrid creek water might even taste good now."

Mama's slim body stands straight. Her forehead has such a frown that it appears to pull against the braids wound into a bun at the back of her head. "My goodness. Don't ever do such a thing. You could get dysentery or malaria."

Ollie grins and licks her dry lips. "I know better than to drink from a stagnant pool. I didn't see a trickling stream anywhere, and the ponds have cloudy skims on top. I would even be afraid to eat fish from there. If any are still alive, they probably have worms from the filth."

She shifts the baby around to hold her with the other arm. "Dung and animal prints are thick along the edge of the water. Most of the tracks are from pigs."

Ollie takes the blue enamel dipper from Mama's hand, gulps, takes a breath, and drinks more. She hands the dipper back and exhales. "I was as thirsty as Syble was hungry."

"Ollie, do you know who those hogs belong to?"

"No. Do you?"

"Your neighbor. The one that went to prison for stealing a cow. I'm sure he's the same one who took Roy's harness and cottonseed from your barn last year. Every spring, he turns an old boar, a sow, and a litter of pigs loose to forage on nearby farms. He'll start putting out feed to catch them in the fall. They're wild after running free. The garden you're watering and tending so carefully, they could destroy it in one night."

"What if I shoot one?"

Mama's lips form a tight line. "You have a right to defend yourself, but be careful. A boar's dangerous. So is the sow if you get near her pigs. If you have to shoot one, keep it to yourself."

Ollie sighs and leans her head against the rocker. "Don't tell Papa and get him upset, but a man was sneaking around here Friday night—no doubt the same *good neighbor* looking for something else to steal."

"I hope you pull the curtains before you undress. He might try to peep in a window."

"While Roy's gone, I sleep in a dress. I want to be ready for any emergency."

Mama looks out the window to check on Morene. "What were you saying about a prowler?"

"Rabbits have been getting in my garden. Friday night, I shot one from the back window, and then I heard someone running out front. I reloaded the gun and ran to the door in time to see a man disappear into the bushes. I shot after him, but if he was hit, he couldn't be hurt bad. He was too far away."

Mama shakes her head. "I wish you'd stay with us until Roy comes home."

"Now, the gun's loaded with buckshot. That neighbor knows I'll shoot to protect what's mine." She lays Syble on the pallet. "I have to get to work." She pats and gently rubs a calloused hand down the baby's back.

"You haven't eaten, and you're getting too thin. I saved you some chicken, and a piece of cake."

"Mama, you don't have to bring goodies for Morene every time you visit. These hard times hit your house too."

"I love seeing her little face when she peeps in the basket."

"You'll have her spoiled."

"I wish I could do more of it."

"Put the cake in the cabinet for later. I'll eat the chicken on the way."

A flock of crows takes flight as Ollie nears the cornfield. They rise like a black cloud and settle in the woods across the creek. *Hogs at night, crows during the day, another group of thieves stealing our crop. They've destroyed enough corn to feed the horses through most of the winter.*

Several times during the day, snorting sounds come from the woods across the creek. "Snort all you want. You won't feed on this corn tonight."

At quitting time, only a few good rows remain unpicked. Ollie would force her tired body to continue until every ear is in the wagon, but milk is leaking through her dress. She parks the wagonload of corn under the barn roof, turns the horses out to pasture, and runs up the path to her hungry baby.

Mama leaves for home and her own children. Ollie and Morene sit at the table with bowls of beans and cornbread. Morene stirs her food but eats very little. "I like chicken best."

"Yes, I know, but God blessed us with these beans. Some children don't have *anything* to eat."

Morene turns her head sideways, squints one eye, and stares at her mother.

"It would be bad if there was nothing in our house to eat. Don't you think?"

Morene nods her head and takes a big bite.

Morene finishes her serving, and Ollie removes the piece of cake from the cabinet.

"Grandma left cake for me!"

"God and Grandma are very good to you."

Her mouth full of cake, Morene nods.

Before daylight the next morning, Ollie hangs a lantern on a barn post, unloads corn into the crib, and milks the cow. When the girls wake, the horses are hitched to the empty wagon, the milk is strained and cooling inside the dug well, the garden plants glisten with fresh well water, and Ollie is taking hot biscuits from the oven.

A bonnet in her hand, Ollie leaves for the field shortly after Mama arrives. As expected, hogs have ruined most of the remaining corn. She walks through the trampled stalks with a tow sack and gathers a few ears that she will feed to her own hungry pig.

She drives the wagon into the shade of a big oak tree at the edge of the cotton field, and unhooks the horses. From the top of a tree stump, Ollie climbs on Bell's back and rides up the hill, leading Bess. Releasing the horses to graze, she trots down the path, pulls the cotton sack strap over her shoulder, and starts picking.

Late in the morning, aching from bending and dragging the heavy sack, Ollie stands upright and yawns. Eyes blurry, she starts to reach for cotton on the outside edge of the left row. A stalk moves. She stops, and blinks to focus.

A large rust-colored copperhead is raised, ready to strike. She eases the pistol from its holster, pulls back the hammer, aims and fires. The thick-bodied reptile jerks back and begins to roll, leaving blood smeared across the sandy soil.

Near sunset, Mama bathes the children while Ollie milks. Both girls are asleep before the plodding hooves of Mama's horse fade to silence. A few stars are visible, and a hint of pink lingers in the sky as Ollie dribbles the last dipperful of water on the garden.

Legs trembling, she steps up to enter the house. It has been a long day with only a little food, eaten in a rush. She locks the doors, pulls the curtains closed, drops her clothes on the floor, and climbs into the tub of water left from the children's bath.

Leaving her dirty clothes in a pile, and the bathtub to empty tomorrow morning, she starts for bed, but stops. If she does not eat, her milk will dry up. She returns to the kitchen; she cannot afford to buy canned milk for Syble.

Ollie sits at the table with a bowl of lukewarm beans and a piece of crusty cornbread. She eats, takes a deep breath and gulps a glass of buttermilk. It has been sitting on the cabinet a long time. With the last swallow, she shivers. It is too warm and extra sour. Yet it will help to make sweet milk for the baby.

After turning out the lamp, she checks to make sure every window screen is hooked. The air is hot and still. She rakes strands of damp hair away from Morene's forehead, and pulls back curtains near the bed to let in any possible breeze.

Roy's last letter is on the mantle, tucked under a tin box where she stores matches. Tired as she is, Ollie takes the envelope, holds the writing to her cheek, and goes to the kitchen to turn up the lamp. She sits to read it again:

Dear Ollie and girls,

I think the wheat harvest will be finished by the first of October. I was hoping it would last longer, because every dollar I earn will help us to buy supplies and pay on the mortgage.

Besides these wheat fields, the boss owns cattle and horses. I asked him if he would need a man to help with the roundup, building fence, or repairs around the ranch. I told him about working cattle for Uncle Jim, and that I've done rough carpentry work. He said he would keep me in mind.

I miss you and the girls, and think about you all the time. I'll work as long as they'll let me, but when it's over, I'll be home as quick as I can.

Hug the girls for me.

I love you,
Roy

Ollie folds the letter, turns down the lamp, and lays her head on the table. *Roy, you can't miss me as much as I miss you, and I don't want to worry you about all the trouble I'm having with animals, snakes, a prowler, and now we're running out of food. I know Mrs. Hart would give me credit, but there are always people in the store. My pride won't let me ask in front of them.*

Ollie blows out the lamp and looks into the night. The moon is a thin sliver. Countless stars sprinkle light into the darkness. The piercing squeal of pigs in the distance rises above the constant screeching of katydids.

What are they tearing up now? Probably the sweet potatoes. Next, they'll be in my garden. If Roy were home, I bet we'd be eating pork—and I could truly sleep.

A loaded shotgun stands in the corner at the head of her bed. Tucked under her pillow, the pistol helps to assure safety. Extra shells and bullets are under her mattress.

Gritting her teeth, she mutters, although she is the only one to hear. *It's too hot to close the windows, but neighbor, I won't hesitate to shoot anyone coming through a screen. If that was you in my yard last week, I hope the shotgun blast causes you to sleep on your stomach through the winter.*

She crawls onto rough flour-sack sheets and closes her eyes. *God, You must have a reason for allowing this drought and depression. I know we're not forgotten. I thank You for my two babies, for a hard-working husband, for saving me from the snake, and for . . .* She is asleep before she can continue her thanks and ask for the many blessings they need.

Chapter 15
Ask and It Shall Be Given

Bronnie is playing 'Pat a Cake' with the girls when Ollie leaves for the field. Their giggles fade as she walks along the path. She gazes at broken stalks and pig manure littering the cornfield.

"At least, pigs don't eat cotton," she speaks to the demolished corn stalks. "There's no meat in my house, and I've fattened someone else's bacon. My little girl asks for cookies, and I have no supplies to make them. This is the second year of drought. How long will this go on?"

A large black crow descends to a treetop near the path. He flaps his wings and caws as if scolding. Immediately, she remembers the story of Elijah where God sent ravens to feed him. "Lord, I know You care for us. Help me to be strong and remember."

She unties the heavy wagon sheet. Cotton underneath is as dry as when she left it. With Papa's gun on her hip, and the sack trailing, she starts to work.

The sun gets hotter as the morning progresses. Ollie stops for water only when her thirst is strong. Time is precious while she has someone to watch the girls.

Nature tells her when it is time to feed the baby. Afraid Syble might be crying for her, she runs most of the way up the hill. Laughter drifts through open windows.

Morene comes running to the door. "Mama, look! Syble can

crawl."

Bronnie rolls a ball across a blanket spread on the floor. Syble crawls to it, sticks the ball to her mouth and starts sucking on it.

Ollie frowns, and then forces a smile.

"Aren't you happy that she can crawl?" Bronnie asks.

"I'm glad she's developing like normal, but she'll be much harder to take care of now. Before, I could put her on a quilt, and she would stay. How can I take her outside while I work? She'll be eating dirt before I turn around. The only time I'll be able to get anything done is while she's sleeping." Ollie reaches for the bar of soap and dips her hands in the wash pan.

"Mama sent cookies—Morene's eaten most of them already—and she sent potatoes, too. Do you want me to peel and fry them while you nurse the baby?"

"Yes. If you don't mind. I need to get back to the field as soon as Syble's finished. I have so little time, and a lot more work."

Ollie takes two cold biscuits from the warming oven and pours herself a glass of buttermilk. "I'll have this while I sit with the baby. I'll leave when she falls asleep."

That afternoon the pigs are noisier than she has ever heard. The brush cracks and snaps as they root about, grunting and squealing. It is nearing time for Ollie to leave when the robust sow trots into the clearing and enters the creek. Ollie estimates her weight at near three hundred pounds. Six pigs, half her size, follow to drink, splash, and wallow. It is not long before they cross to the bank where Roy buried the sweet potato roots.

Ollie wishes for the shotgun. A pistol will only injure one, and that big sow might attack. She continues picking, with the row leading her closer and closer to the grunting thieves.

She stops to straighten her aching back. The sow is standing directly in front of her. "Are you trying to protect your babies from me? Do you think I have food in this sack? If I turn to leave, are you going to chase me?"

They stand staring at each other while the young pigs burrow through the potato vines. Ollie slides the sack strap from her shoulder, takes the pistol from its holster, points it and yells, "Get! Shoo! Shoo pig!"

The sow shakes her head, and blows muddy slime from her snout.

Ollie yells louder.

The animal snorts and steps closer.

"God, please direct this bullet. I won't have a chance if she attacks."

With great care, Ollie aims at the sow's left eye, pulls back the hammer, and squeezes the trigger. The sow squeals, staggers, and runs for the woods, slinging blood as she goes. Her pigs follow.

Ollie drags her sack between the next two rows of unpicked cotton and works back until she is even with the wagon. She weighs her sack, records the weight, dumps the cotton, and ties the wagon sheet over the collection, before starting toward the house. The cotton is not as fluffy as in years past. Dry weather hardened the bolls before they fully matured, compacting the inside and making it difficult to get the cotton out.

The grass is dead and brown on the hills. In the meadow, dry streamers of orange-tinted sage grass wave in a soft breeze. Bitterweeds spread flowers in yellow profusion across a low section behind the barn. *Lord, I wonder why You didn't make the sage and bitterweeds into something good for the cattle to eat.*

The cow and horses are grazing close to the creek. The cow looks up from her munching, sees Ollie walking, and bellows to her calf. Her udder swings from side to side as she trots along a worn path. The calf, fastened inside a small pen beside the barn, answers.

Feeling liquid heavy in her own breasts, Ollie knows the cow is ready to be relieved of her milk. "You'll have to wait your turn, old gal. My baby comes first."

Ollie sits in the rocker holding Syble close. "Bronnie, did you and Morene eat supper?"

"Morene did, but I'll wait until I get home." Bronnie turns to Ollie. "I don't want to be too late getting home. Can you finish nursing Syble after you take care of the animals? I have the pail scalded and ready, but I'm afraid to milk your cow. She lowers her head and paws the ground every time I get near her."

"She doesn't like strangers. I'm glad you didn't get in the pen with her. Those horns could hurt you. Jersey's give rich milk, but they can be temperamental."

Ollie hands the baby to Bronnie. "Maybe she won't cry if you walk around with her. I'll be back to the house as soon as I can."

From one chore to the next, Ollie rushes to finish. She does not want her young sister riding home after dark. Leading Bronnie's horse with one hand and carrying a pail of milk with the other, she walks up the path.

Morene and Syble play with the ball on a pallet quilt, but as soon as Ollie walks inside, Syble whines and reaches for her. "Bronnie will you carry her outside and walk until I get the milk strained and put in the well?'

"I didn't realize playing was such hard work." She walks out the door, bouncing Syble on her hip.

After Bronnie leaves for home, Ollie takes the girls inside and sits Syble on the quilt. Immediately, the baby starts crying. "I know what you want, baby girl, but I have to wash your fat little body."

She dumps the water bucket into a washtub and mixes in water from the teakettle until it is the right warmth for the baby's bath. "Morene, get your nightgown and a clean pair of underpants from the drawer. You can take a bath with Syble."

Ollie stoops to wash the baby. Muscles in her back quiver from bending in the cotton patch. "Morene, why don't you pretend that Syble's your girl baby? You can take the rag and wash her tummy, and legs."

Morene giggles as she rubs the washcloth over her sister's chubby stomach. Syble giggles, but they change to screams when Morene flops the cloth onto her head and the soapy water runs into her eyes.

Ollie wraps Syble in a towel, dries, and dresses her in a nightgown while Morene continues to play in the water. "Morene, take my hand and step out of the tub. Now, dry yourself, put on your gown, and crawl into bed with your baby doll."

When both girls are asleep, Ollie goes outside to draw water, and haul it to the garden. The plants are wilted, despite the drenching of well water they get every morning and evening. Drawing the first two buckets, she pauses to rub sore fingers, pricked by the hard, dry tips of cotton boles, on the shoulder that has strained all day against a sack strap.

The next day is another scorcher. Ollie does not see the pigs, but squeals ring from the woods. Following a long hard day, she looks across the field. *If Bronnie can come back one more day, I believe I can get it all picked.*

She trudges up the hill with the thought chanting inside her head: *One more day. One more day.* She opens the kitchen door and announces, "Bronnie, with you watching the girls for me, I'll be able to finish tomorrow."

"I can't be here tomorrow. I'm going to town with Mama and Papa to get new shoes. School starts next week."

Ollie draws in a quick breath. "I didn't know you weren't coming tomorrow, and that school starts next week. How will I pick the rest of the cotton without someone to watch the girls?"

"I don't know. Maybe Mama can come Monday or Tuesday."

Ollie shakes her head. "I'll have to figure out something. I was counting on selling the cotton so I can buy enough supplies to last until Roy gets home."

After putting the milk in the dug well, Ollie brings Bronnie's horse to the house and ties the reins loosely to a small tree. "I really appreciate your coming to help, and I hope you get some nice things at town."

Long after both girls are asleep, Ollie still struggles to think of a way to gather the rest of the cotton without putting her children in danger. Bowing her head, she utters a simple prayer, "God, please send an answer, or an angel to help me."

She stands and glances at the clock. It is nine-fifteen. She bathes in the cool bath water left from the girls, slips into a clean dress, and makes the nightly ritual of checking every window and pulling back the curtains. Soon, she is asleep with the loaded shotgun standing in its usual place at the head of her bed.

Ollie wakes as morning light filters into the bedroom. It is not as warm as the past week has been. She draws the curtains together, unloads the gun and puts the shells on the mantle before going into the kitchen to prepare the milk pail.

The girls are still asleep when she returns from putting the strained milk in the dug well and retrieving the cooled jar. The flour is getting low. So is the cornmeal. She noticed when she made bread yesterday. *Maybe they will last another week. If I could get the rest of the cotton picked and taken to the gin, I wouldn't have to ask Mrs. Hart for credit.*

She looks in the coffee tin and shakes the last spoonful into the peculator. Taking a deep breath, she draws in the aroma and remembers mornings when she and Roy shared hopes and dreams over morning coffee.

While biscuits are cooking, Ollie makes gravy, and scrambles two of the eggs Mama brought. She places butter and applesauce on the table before going to change and nurse the baby.

Morene sits up in bed. "I smell breakfast. I'm hungry."

"Wash your hands and face. I'll sit at the table with you while I feed Syble. She can eat a little of my egg with gravy and biscuit."

Ollie has the dishes washed and the girls dressed when a buggy pulls into the yard. "Who can that be?" She looks through the window. Roy's parents step down. Both carry baskets. Ollie picks up the baby and walks outside.

Morene runs onto the porch. "Ma! Pa! What's in the baskets?"

Ollie frowns. "Morene, it's not nice to ask such questions."

Mr. Glenn chuckles. "She has a healthy curiosity. Come here, pretty girl, and I'll show you what's inside this one."

"Cookies! Mama, Pa brought me cookies. I like cookies."

He pats her shoulder. "Ma knew that. She got up early this morning to bake those for you. Did you eat breakfast?"

"Yes. Egg and biscuits."

"Good, then you can have a cookie."

Ma sets her basket on the porch and reaches for Syble. "I've been hungering to see these babies. It was after nine last night when I decided I couldn't wait another day. I woke Bart to tell him I wanted to come visit you today."

"I'm glad you did." Ollie motions with a wide sweep of one arm. "Come inside."

"Take the baby until I get up the steps." She hands Syble to Ollie, takes hold of the post, and with a little grunt places her left foot firmly on the step before bringing up the right. She follows the same procedure to get on the porch. "I'm a little sore; we dug late potatoes yesterday. Bending gets harder every year."

Pa sets his basket on the porch. "Ollie, have you harvested your late garden?"

"No. I've been trying to gather crops while Mama and Bronnie could watch the girls. I might finish in one long day, but I'm worried it'll rain before Mama can come back next week."

"We brought some Irish potatoes, and a few sweet ones."

"Thank you. A neighbor's hogs have been rooting in our sweet potatoes. I can't take the girls to the cotton field because of those hogs. The old sow acted as if she was going to attack me. When I couldn't run her off, I shot her. It scared her enough that she crossed the creek with the pigs following her squeals."

"Have they been in the corn?"

"Yes, they destroyed a lot of it before I could get it gathered."

He frowns. "Girl, you ought to be having roast pork."

"I'm sure we would, if Roy were home."

Mrs. Glenn is in the rocking chair with Syble sitting on her knees. "Giddy-up-horsey, giddy-up." The baby giggles each time Grandma bounces. "Ollie, get your cotton sack. I'm too old to pick, but we can watch the girls. We've got all day to play with them, and I brought food, so you don't have to worry about cooking dinner."

Ollie wrings her hands. "I hate to run off when you came to visit."

Mr. Glenn drops into a straight back chair. "Take advantage of an opportunity. When Ma woke me last night, she felt certain you and the girls needed us. I don't argue with a woman's intuition." He grins and takes a brown twist of tobacco from his pocket. "She can rock the baby, while I sit on the porch and help Morene put together a little cedar doll I've been whittling."

"If you're sure you don't mind, then I'll go to work. I finished feeding Syble a few minutes ago, so she should be all right until I come in at dinner." Ollie puts on a long-sleeved shirt, straps the pistol around her waist, and starts for the field.

It does not look like the pigs have been back to dig in the sweet potatoes. Ollie picks cotton as fast as she can grab it. *What luck that Mr. and Mrs. Glenn came today.* Then she remembers Ma saying it was past nine last night when she decided they should visit today. *It was nine-fifteen when I finished praying. They are the answer to my prayer.* She looks toward heaven. "Thank You, God."

The sun is in the middle of the sky when Ollie stops. *I wonder what Mrs. Glenn put in her picnic basket. I am so hungry—I could eat almost anything.*

Mr. Glenn sits on the edge of the porch, bouncing Syble on one knee. Morene jumps up from beside him and comes running to meet Ollie. "Mama, look what Pa made for me. It's a doll, and it jumps when I pull this string."

"How nice. Did you tell him 'thank you'?"

Morene goes running back. "Thank you, Pa."

Syble is crying and reaching. Ollie takes her and goes inside. "My fat little baby is starving again."

She starts nursing the baby as she walks into the kitchen where Ma is taking a pan of hot biscuits from the oven. "My, it smells better than Thanksgiving in here. You shouldn't have gone to so much trouble."

"I can tell by the looks of you that you've been working too hard, and eating too little while nursing a baby. You need a good meal."

"Is that ham and sweet potatoes I smell?"

"Yes. One of our pigs kept rooting out of the pen. Bart butchered it early. He figured it was better for us to eat it while it was small than for one of the neighbors to shoot it."

"I can hardly wait to taste it. I caught the scent when I was coming up the hill, and quickened my pace."

"Take a piece. You can chew while the baby eats."

When they sit at the table, Ollie can hardly believe all the good food. They have corn, new potatoes cooked with green beans, sweet potatoes, ham, and hot biscuits with peach pie for dessert.

"Your garden must have got rain when ours didn't. The dry weather took everything in our early garden."

"No, we didn't get rain. I canned the beans and corn two years ago."

Ma passes the bread. "I wish I'd brought you some flour. You don't have much left in the bin after I made these biscuits."

"I plan to get supplies when I sell the cotton. Mrs. Hart would give me credit, but I hate to ask. Customers are always in the store listening."

Pa tilts his head a little to the side. "Girl, there is no shame in asking for credit. The only shame is if you don't repay it."

Ollie looks down at her plate. "It's better than going hungry, but I haven't got to that point yet."

He clears his throat. "When do you think you'll have the cotton ready to sell?"

"I got a late start this morning, but if I pick until dark, I might be able to get it all today."

"Oh." He rubs his chin.

Ollie has been worrying all morning about how to get the cotton to the gin. In a gush of words, she blurts her thoughts. "Can you stay the night? You and Mrs. Glenn can sleep in the full bed, and I'll sleep with Morene on the cot. If you'll stay the night and take the cotton to the gin for me, I'll really appreciate it. I hate to ask, but it will be almost impossible for me to take it with these two little ones."

"Ma, what do you think?"

"We didn't ask anyone to milk the cow, or to feed and water

chickens and pigs. I can stay with Ollie and watch the girls while you go home and do the farm chores. You can come back and take the cotton to the gin in the morning."

"I'll do it, if you'll save me a biscuit from breakfast. I'm a poor cook."

"We'll gladly save breakfast for you." Ollie gets up from the table. "Mrs. Glenn, if you'll leave the dishes, I'll wash them when I come in from the field. I need to get back to picking. If I hurry, I might get it done earlier."

"Don't you want to have pie before you go?"

"If there's any left, I'll have some when I come in to feed the baby."

Ollie trots to the field and begins working faster than she has ever worked before. It is late when she finishes the last row and weighs-up. She lashes down the heavy canvas sheet over the fluffy contents of the wagon before running back to the house.

She bursts into the kitchen, "It's finished. All the cotton's in the wagon."

Ma, dozing in the rocker, jumps and rubs her eyes. Syble wakes and starts to cry. Ollie picks up the baby. "Where's Morene?"

Mrs. Glenn is still blinking, to get awake. "Morene—she went to the barn with her grandpa to hitch the horses. Did you say it's all picked?"

"Yes, it's all in the wagon. Ready to be ginned."

"Then I'll go on home with Bart, since you don't need me to watch the girls. I've enjoyed playing with them, but I'm exhausted. Reckon I'm getting old?" She laughs and shakes her head. "I had fifteen of my own, raised twelve until they were grown, and don't ever remember being this tired."

"I truly appreciate your help. As soon as the cotton's sold, I can get supplies, especially flour and sugar to make cookies for Morene."

The next day, Mr. Glenn returns from the gin with the cottonseed in the back of the wagon. He steps down, hands Morene a candy bar, and Ollie a check for the cotton.

Morene hugs, thanks him for the candy, and hugs him again before tearing away the wrapper.

"Mr. Glenn, thank you so much. I can't tell you how grateful I am to you and Ma for helping me." Tears sting Ollie's eyes; she swallows, determined not to cry. "Maybe I'm a little too proud sometimes. You see, I grew up with the storekeeper's daughter. She went away to nursing school and has never known what it's like to live on a farm and worry about money." She stops to clear her throat. "Anyway, I couldn't ask her mama for credit."

He nods his head and turns away to spit tobacco juice. "I understand girl. I understand." He slaps her on the back before stepping up into the wagon. "I'll leave these seed in your corncrib. Remember, we're glad to help anytime." He waves and drives toward the barn. "Bring those babies and come visit. I promise to feed you good."

Chapter 16
Gathering

Saturday morning, Ollie walks into the community store, her head held high and proud. She can pay for what she needs. Syble is on her left hip, leaving her right hand free to gather supplies. Morene walks behind with little hands plunged deep inside the pockets of her yellow dress.

Ollie looks back. "Remember to act like a big girl if you want candy." A yellow ribbon jiggles above Morene's bobbed hair as she nods to her mother.

Onto the counter, Ollie piles the basic provisions she will need until Roy comes home, plus sugar, cocoa, and cinnamon. "Do you have any pink flannel? It'll be cold soon, and I want to make warm nightgowns for the girls."

"Does it have to be pink? I doubt there is enough left for two little gowns. I'll cut the price if you can use what's left of the pink and make one from the red. Let me show it to you." Mrs. Hart walks toward the fabric table. "I haven't seen you for a while. Is Roy still in North Dakota?"

"He stayed longer to help with the cattle roundup. The wheat harvest is finished. He wrote that it's getting cold in the northern states."

"I know you'll be glad to have him home again. He was lucky to find a job. Times are hard. I've never seen so many people wanting charge accounts." Mrs. Hart shakes her head. "Some of them feel such shame at asking that they can't look me in the eye. A hungry child is most pathetic. It breaks my heart to see them, and it'll get worse if next year is as dry as this one."

Ollie jiggles the baby on her hip. "If it wasn't for Mama, Bronnie, and Roy's parents watching the girls while I worked, I might be asking for credit. Roy's pa hauled the cotton to the gin for me. I hope it's not a problem for you to cash the check."

Mrs. Hart shakes her head. "I wouldn't hesitate a moment to help you with anything you need."

Ollie looks around for Morene. She still has her hands in her pockets, but her big blue eyes examine everything in sight. "I hope next year is better. I've hauled water from the well to my garden twice a day for almost two months. It's still dry, but if we could get one good rain, I believe it would produce before frost."

Looking over the top of her glasses, Mrs. Hart clicks her tongue. "If it does, keep an eye on it. Your neighbor was in here yesterday, commenting on how green those plants are in this dry weather. She laughed and said she was hungry for a mess of fresh peas."

Ollie squints and grits her teeth. "The hogs they turned loose in the spring have destroyed at least a wagon-load of our corn, tore up my sweet potatoes, and I shot at a prowler one night—I'm pretty sure it was her husband. I won't hesitate to shoot her fat rear if I catch it in my garden."

Mrs. Hart grins. "He was in to see the doctor a while back. He said it was an accident, that she shot him instead of a stray dog bothering their chickens." She looks around to make sure no one else is in the store. "We figured some farmer caught him stealing chickens, although it was probably your birdshot the doctor dug out of his hip."

"Pass the word if you get a chance." Ollie returns her smile. "Now my shotgun's loaded with buckshot. No one better follow a hunting dog across my yard in the dark."

"Ollie, be careful. That bunch has always been scavengers."

"Exactly like those hogs." Ollie turns to Morene. "Go look in the candy case and decide which candy you want. We better get home before thieves take something else."

When they approach the house, Ollie sees hoof prints in the dry, dead grass beneath a tree. She drives the team into the yard and stops near the kitchen door where she can see the garden. "Those thieves have been grabbing our potatoes, and they're not ready for harvest. I bet they heard us coming in this rattling wagon, or they would have gotten them all. The vines they pulled haven't even wilted, and the ground is still moist on the roots."

Morene stands and jerks the sucker from her mouth. "Was it rabbits?"

"No. It was a varmint worse than a rabbit. It was a lazy, thieving human."

Morene's ribbon waves as she shakes her head. "I don't like humans." She turns her head to the side. "What do they look like?"

Ollie releases her breath in a long sigh, and through clenched teeth utters, "Snakes in the grass."

"I don't like human snakes."

Ollie wraps the lines around the brake and turns again to Morene. "Climb out the back. I'll carry Syble inside. She can finish her nap on the pallet. I want you to sit beside her and play quietly while I unload the wagon, and take the horses to the barn for some corn."

"No! Mama, no! The snakes might come get us."

Ollie sees the fear in her eyes. "What snakes?"

"The human snakes. The ones that got our baby potatoes."

Ollie gives her a sympathizing smile. "Those weren't real snakes. I called them snakes because they sneak around and take things that don't belong to them. Humans are people."

Morene's wide, astonished eyes question as she alternates between looking at Ollie and the empty space in the garden. "But you said—"

Ollie walks to the back of the wagon and jumps down. She wraps her arms around the frightened child holding tight to the sideboard. "Honey, I didn't explain very well. Someone too lazy to plant and carry water for their own garden came while we were gone and took our little potatoes. They'll not come around while we're home. They don't want us, only our garden things that we've worked hard to grow."

"I don't like lazy snake people."

Ollie lifts her to the ground, and unlocks the kitchen door. "Be quiet, so you don't wake the baby while I move her to the quilt." Morene sits beside Syble, continuing to lick her red candy sucker.

Leaving the horses in the barn to eat, Ollie walks to the garden and picks up one of the uprooted plants. It hangs limp and wilted across her hand. Soil, that was still moist when she came home, is now dry and falling from the roots. Ollie yells toward the woods. "If I catch you here again, you'll have more than birdshot in your—" She sees Morene at the window and whispers, "It will be buckshot next time."

Morene is asleep beside Syble when Ollie finishes unloading supplies. Ollie removes the sucker from her hand and places it in a covered dish.

The girls rest while Ollie prepares lunch and makes a batch of cookies. She is taking the last pan from the oven when giggles trickle from the next room. The baby is kissing Morene, and at the same time licking the sticky remains of red candy from her sister's face.

Ollie lifts the baby. "Morene, go wash your face and hands. Our food is ready, and I made cookies for dessert."

"Cookies! Cookies!"

The baby, trying to copy her sister, bounces in Ollie's arms and drools out, "Coo, coo."

"She's trying to say it, Mama. Listen." Morene stands in front of the baby. "Cookie. Cọo—kie."

"Morene, get in your chair. You can teach her this afternoon while you play with her in the wagon. We're going down by the creek. I want to dig sweet potatoes, if the pigs haven't got all of them."

The girls giggle through lunch, and continue as Ollie sweeps the wagon bed, places a folded quilt near the front, and eight half-bushel baskets at the back. "Morene, find some toys for you and the baby to play with while you're inside the wagon. I'm going to the barn to get the horses."

With the loaded pistol on her hip, Ollie is ready to leave when she remembers Papa's warning about watching for the old boar hog. *I've never seen him, or the sow since I shot her in the eye, and the young pigs are cowardly without their mama.* She has the door key in her hand, but glances toward the wagon before turning it. Two smiling faces stare at her. Roy's words come to mind: "Don't take chances. You have two babies with you alone to look out for them." Knowing the pistol would only injure the big hog, she goes into the house and comes back with the shotgun wrapped in a blanket.

Nearing the creek, Ollie sees that pigs have been busy, but one side of the patch looks undisturbed. She parks the wagon in the shade, ties the horses to a tree, listens, but does not hear anything except crows and the girls' laughter.

Three times before leaving the girls, she warns Morene to call if she sees or hears a pig. With two baskets, a shovel, a hoe, the shotgun and shells, Ollie walks to the vines. Her ears are keen for any unusual sounds as she digs, and her eyes keep a sharp lookout for snakes.

Not seeing any snakes or pigs, she works faster and faster, plunging the shovel into the sandy loam and lifting. Her efforts quickly produce two baskets of potatoes. She drags them up the bank and gets more baskets.

Excited at finding so many of the big orange-colored roots, Ollie works at a frenzied pace. Pulling more baskets to the top of the ridge, she starts down. Hearing a grunt, she looks in the direction of the creek. Coming toward her at a trot is the biggest boar hog she has ever seen. She pulls a shell from her pocket and runs for the shotgun.

Grabbing the blanket, she gives it a yank, unrolling the gun. Dropping in the shell, she looks up. He is about fifty feet away, advancing slower now. She raises the gun, aims at a spot between his eyes, and is about to pull the trigger when Morene screams, "Mama, a pig."

Ollie's left foot is positioned on a stick that is unsteady on the side of the bank. When Morene screams, Ollie jerks, and the stick rolls. While sliding down the incline, she tries to aim at the hog. The shotgun roars. The hog squeals and runs toward the woods.

Still on the ground, Ollie reloads the gun and looks toward the girls to see if they are in danger. Frightened by the blast, both children scream, but there are no hogs in sight. After calming her little ones, Ollie pulls the wagon close to the baskets, loads six half-bushels, dumps the seventh, and returns to fill it with the others she has dug.

She squints, shading her eyes with a hand, and stares at the woods, looking for the old boar. With the loaded shotgun in hand, she follows his tracks toward the creek. Near the water's edge, she finds two splotches of fresh blood. "Good, you old thief. I hope my buckshot keeps you in the woods tonight. I'll be back tomorrow."

"What, Mama?"

She smiles at Morene. "We ran that old pig into the woods."

"Will he come back?"

"If he does, I'll shoot him again." She glances toward the baby. Syble is sucking one of the dirty potatoes. "Morene, take that away from her. Hurry, wipe her mouth with a rag from inside her bag."

Ollie heaves the last basket into the wagon, steps up, grabs the baby and the wet rag. Morene, unable to get the squirming baby to open her clenched jaws, steps away. Despite cries, Ollie pries open Syble's mouth, swabs it, pours water on a clean diaper, and repeats the process. "Morene, don't let her put dirty things in her mouth."

When the wagon is under the barn shed, and the horses are in the pasture, Ollie takes the girls and the shotgun to the house. She hangs the big gun over the mantle.

Gently stroking Morene on the back, Ollie smiles down at

her. "You were a good helper to watch the baby today and to tell me when a big pig was coming. Daddy will be proud of you and proud that we got all those potatoes. Maybe we can get more tomorrow."

"And Daddy will bring me a present?"

"Yes, he will. Now, let's bathe the baby and eat supper. You can play in the bath while I nurse Syble."

Soon both girls are asleep in their beds. Ollie takes the milk pail and rushes to the barn. The sun has slipped behind distant hills when she places the milk in the dug well and starts drawing water for the garden from the drilled well near the house.

Knowing tomorrow is Sunday, Ollie lies awake worrying. If she leaves to go to church, neighbors may raid the garden and hogs the sweet potatoes. *Lord, you know we need those vegetable to feed us through the winter.*

Before dawn, she wakes from a nightmare: large hogs with long tusk and slobbering mouths trying to jump into the wagon with her crying babies. Heart pounding, she sits and wipes a strand of damp hair from her face.

Although more nervous than thirsty, Ollie goes to the kitchen for a drink. The water in the bucket is warm; one sip is enough. Standing beside the window, her eyes scan the yard, staring at every bush for something or someone that could be lurking. Near the garden, a small animal inches toward the peas. She squints for better focus. Before she can go for a gun, a large owl glides in, grabs the animal and flaps away. *There goes our rabbit stew.*

By early morning light, Ollie dumps yesterday's harvest of sweet potatoes into a corner of the corncrib. After they dry, she will pack them in the baskets and store them under the hay to keep for winter.

When breakfast is cooked, she wakes the girls, dresses, and feeds them. They laugh and squeal as Ollie ties their bonnets and lifts them into the wagon. Bouncing along the path going toward the creek, Ollie smiles. *This is the beginning of a nice day.*

Before leaving the wagon-bed, she looks over the area. Nothing has bothered the patch overnight. She steps down, ties the horses to a tree, slips a shell in the shotgun and places it on the blanket. One more look toward the woods and she starts to dig.

With two more baskets ready to load in the wagon, Ollie leans on her shovel to rest. No birds are chirping, and no animals can be heard in the distance, not even a leaf is fluttering. The girls have stopped giggling. They sit staring at her. *Here I am on a Sunday morning, missing church, and putting my babies in danger—It's almost like teasing the Devil.* She loads everything in the wagon and leaves for the house.

"Morene, there are only two cookies left from yesterday. I'll bake some with chocolate if you'll keep the baby on a quilt in the yard, and not let her eat grass and dirt while I water the garden."

Morene nods eagerly. "Cookies! Baby, we're gonna get more cookies."

Ollie drizzles water into small trenches she has dug close to the plants. *I hope this soaks to the roots.*

"Mama, can I take Syble inside to get the cookies?"

"I'm afraid you'll drop her. She's almost as big as you."

"I'm strong." Morene gathers the fat baby onto her stomach and waddles across the yard to the kitchen door.

Ollie grins and continues watering. When the last row is wet, she sits on the wash bench and leans against the back of the house to marvel at the green plants bordered by a parched yard and acres of yellowed pasture.

A wagon comes rattling down the road and stops. She takes the pistol from its holster and waits. Footsteps approach. Her neighbor is almost to the garden, with a hoe in his hand, when Morene yells, "No, Baby. No."

He whirls to see Ollie with her gun drawn. "Hey, there, I didn't see you behind the wash tub. I wanted to get a closer look at these nice green vegetables."

"With a hoe in your hand?"

"Put your gun away, little lady, I just came to admire. Why, after all your hard work, I wouldn't take anything from this garden."

"Get out of my yard. I shot your backside once. Do you want another dose?"

He scowls and side-steps toward the road. "I'm leaving."

Ollie's voice gets louder. "You thought you'd steal more potatoes while I was at church, didn't you?"

Walking backward, he shakes his head.

"I'm getting real tired of you. I could send you on your way to Hell, pretty quick." The safety lock on the gun clicks.

He turns, almost falls, and stumbles for several feet trying to regain his balance as he runs to the wagon. He is soon out of sight.

"Mama, who was that man?"

"He's the thieving snake that took our potatoes."

The little girl stands with a puzzled look on her face. "Human snake?"

"That's him."   Ollie picks up the baby and goes to her rocker. "Morene, come sit beside me and I'll tell you a Bible story. Maybe, I need one too. I was certainly tempted to shoot a thief this morning."

Chapter 17
The Tempest

October is still hot, especially in a small kitchen with a wood-burning cook stove. Ollie's girls giggle and play on a pallet quilt while she works. Cookies, promised to Morene for helping with the baby, are in the oven. Ollie adds more wood to the firebox. Thunder rumbles. *I hope that means rain.*

She steps to the window. The sky has a green tint, and a dark cloud is moving in from the west. She whispers, "It's too bad Roy didn't have time to build us a new storm cellar before he went away to work. The old one is falling in, and it's probably a snake den."

Lightning zigzags across the sky and thunder explodes. A blast of wind hits the house, rattling windows and flapping curtains. Ollie runs to lock the doors so the storm will not shake them open.

"Morene, we're going to play a hiding game. Scoot the baby's quilt under my bed. Take Syble and crawl under there on top of it. Hurry, while I get these windows closed."

"What are we hiding from?"

Ollie's voice is loud and firm. "Do what I said." She runs to close the damper on the cook stove and remove the half-done cookies. *Why didn't I notice the storm before I added more wood? If it blows the house over, this hot fire will set everything to blazing.* She grabs a dipper of water, opens the firebox, and slings the water inside. Smoke, steam, and ashes erupt in a cloud before she can slam the door.

Water has scarcely left the dipper before a wave of panic seizes her. *What if the cold water causes the cast-iron stove to crack?* She has no more time to worry about the stove—another blast of wind shakes the little two-room house.

Ollie dives under the bed where her babies huddle. Hail pelts the wood shingles on the west, and instantly bangs against the tin roof over the kitchen. "This will ruin our garden."

"No, Mama. It stopped."

All is still and quiet, except Morene. "Can I get out? I don't like it here."

Ollie hugs the girls and prays. She knows what the silence means: a tornado is close.

"Mama, what's that noise? It hurts my ears."

Ollie prays louder, squeezing the girls tighter as the roaring increases and the house trembles.

Morene squeals, "I can't breathe."

Washtubs and buckets bang, clatter, and tumble across the yard. With a terrible tearing and screeching sound, a piece of tin rips from the kitchen roof. The roaring fades, replaced by sheets of rain whipping against the house.

Ollie releases the girls and crawls from underneath the bed. Water pours through the ceiling over the kitchen door. "Lord, thank You for saving us." She has an urge to touch everything around her, but dreads looking outside.

"Morene, keep the baby in here. I'll bring you a cookie if they're not wet." She asserts the next words loud and firm. "Do *not* go to the kitchen."

Through the pouring rain, Ollie can barely see the barn is still standing. "Lord, thank You."

The cookies left on top of the warming oven are half-done, but not wet with rain. She moves them to a small table in the front room. "Morene, take one at a time, and remember only give the baby tiny, tiny pieces so she won't choke."

The wind has stopped, but rain continues slow and easy. Through the window, Ollie sees one of her washtubs leaning against a fence. No tin is missing from the barn. The hail was small and did not last long enough to destroy the garden, but the pea vines are twisted and bruised.

With the broom in her hand, she opens the kitchen door, and sweeps out water. Syble starts to cry. Ollie glances at the clock; it is past naptime for the girls. She takes the baby in her arms and sits in the rocker to nurse. "Morene, get your doll and lay down on the pallet. You've been a good girl to help me today."

Morene smiles and follows instructions. Soon, she is asleep.

Putting the sleeping baby down beside her sister, Ollie goes outside to look for the piece of missing roof. *The way that storm was blowing, the tin could be miles away. Please, Lord, help me find it. I don't have any to replace it.*

She looks around the barn. The tin is not there. The cow and horses are nowhere in sight. She assumes the animals took refuge in the woods. When she turns toward the creek, she notices a line of twisted timber. *I hope they weren't under those trees.*

Ollie considers going down by the creek to look for the animals, but the big hog she shot could be in those woods. *With buckshot in him, he'll be meaner than ever.*

She treks through the wet pasture without finding the tin. Disappointed, Ollie heads toward the house. The drizzle has stopped. Sun peeps through intermittent clouds, dappling trees and fields, sparkling wherever it touches clinging raindrops.

Her shoes are soaked. Her wet dress clings to her legs. *I have to find that tin.*

Wiping a strand of hair away from her forehead, she squints one eye, shades the other with her hand, and scans the hillsides. A bright flash stabs clear to her brain. She blinks until sight returns, and stares toward the location of the beam. The tin is stuck among the limbs of a tree.

How will I get it down? How will I get it home? How will I get it on the roof by myself?

Ollie goes into the barn and grabs some ears of corn. Whistling and calling for the horses, she walks outside. They come running from a section of woods unharmed by the storm. While they eat corn from the manger, she slips bridles over their heads.

She hitches the team to the wagon, loads a ladder, a rope, a hoe, and runs to check on the sleeping girls before turning the team toward the flashing treetop. Ollie drives the wagon to the opposite side of the tree, away from the tin, pulls the brake and wraps the lines around the handle. As an extra precaution, she ties the horses to a small tree.

Looking down at her skirt, she bends, grabs the hem, pulls it between her legs and ties it at the waist with her belt. *I look like a big baby in bloomers, but I can't let a dress-tail hinder getting that tin.* Ollie coils and fastens the long rope around her middle, stands in the wagon bed and places the hoe securely in the branches where it will not fall, then grabs a low-hanging limb and swings up.

Moving the hoe as she goes, Ollie climbs branches until she can push against the tin with the hoe, but it will not fall. Next, she unwinds the rope, makes a loop in one end and throws it over the tin, draws the loop back with the hoe, and drapes the loose end through the loop before tying it to the hoe. Through an opening in the branches, she hurls the awkward garden tool, hoping it will go up and over without tangling in branches—it travels exactly as she intended.

After climbing down, Ollie takes the end of the rope, walks as far away from the tree as the rope will reach, and begins pulling. The tin curls into a cylinder, but she is not strong enough to pull it from the tree.

She unties the horses, and moves the wagon to where she can tie the rope to the rear axle. *This may cause the tin to bend or break, but it's no good in those branches.* She does not want the mares to jerk the metal, so she stands close to one side of them, clicks her tongue and speaks softly, "Get up, easy now. Easy, girls." They start forward with a slow gentle pull. "Come on, come on, girls."

The rope stretches tight. The branches bend until the metal rests at the peak of the arched limbs.

Now what do I do? The horses will run away when that metal comes clanging to the ground.

She unhooks the horses from the wagon and ties them to a tree, crawls under the wagon, arranges the hoe handle evenly across the rope, and pulls down with all her strength. The curled metal rolls from the tree, and crashes against the wagon wheels.

The frightened horses jump, neigh, pull against the tie lines, and almost uproot the small tree. Ollie runs to them. "Whoa, girls! Whoa!" She pets and rubs the mares until they are calm, then loads the tin onto the wagon.

Nearing the house, she spots a horse in the yard and hears Eldridge calling.

"My goodness, Ollie, I was about to panic when I couldn't find you. I'm guessing the storm took that piece of roof from your kitchen. Is everything else all right?"

"As far as I can tell. Did it do any damage up there?"

"Nothing I know about, except it scared Mama half to death. She saw the funnel cloud coming this way. She asked me to come check on you and the girls. I saw them through the window, asleep on a quilt."

"I'm glad you came. I need help to get this on the house."

"I don't know a thing about fixing a roof."

"I do. Roy and I put this one on before we moved in the house. The wind bent this piece, but I think we can straighten it enough so it will shed water."

Within an hour, they have the tin nailed in place. Ollie places a can of tar inside an old feed bucket and sets it on top of the stove. "Eldridge, you don't have to wait. When the tar gets warm, I can patch those holes by myself."

"No! What if you fell?"

"You should have seen me in the top of that big tree, trying to unlodge the tin, or yesterday down by the creek, shooting at a boar hog." She smiles. "But I thank you."

"Ollie, that wasn't very smart. What if you'd fell and hurt yourself, with the girls here alone?"

She looks at the ground. "I know, but I didn't have anyone to help. I was careful climbing the tree. The real danger was yesterday; I had nightmares over that."

"What happened?"

"I got excited at finding so many sweet potatoes, and almost forgot to watch for danger. Then, I heard a loud grunt. Coming toward me at a trot was the biggest hog I've ever seen. I ran for the shotgun and dropped in a shell. Aiming at a spot between his eyes, I was about to pull the trigger when Morene yelled.

"My left foot was on a stick on the side of the bank. Morene screamed, I jerked, and the stick rolled. I slid, but tried to keep my aim on the hog. When the gun roared, he squealed, and ran into the woods."

"Did you hit him?"

"He was so close." She takes a deep breath. "He would have been hard to miss, but the fall spoiled my aim. After I calmed the girls, and myself, I walked down to the water's edge and found splotches of fresh blood."

"Goodness sakes, I bet you don't go back again until Roy gets home."

She sighs. "I went this morning and dug a few more sweet potatoes. A lot more are still in the ground. I would have got them all, but—"

He moves a step closer to look straight into her eyes. "But what?"

She shrugs. "A weird feeling came over me, a sensation that something bad was about to happen. I took it as a warning, threw the tools in the wagon and left."

Eldridge frowns. "What made you feel that way?"

She turns her face away. "I'm still trying to figure it out. Weeks ago, Papa warned me to watch for the neighbor's big boar hog. It's been running loose all summer. I'm sure I only nicked and scared it yesterday when I shot. I knew that, if that hog came back, he'd be meaner than ever. Before Roy left, he told me he didn't want me digging those potatoes until frost drives snakes into hibernation. I don't know what made me feel so strange, maybe my conscience was bothering me because I skipped church."

She pauses, pushes hair away from her face, before turning back to stare into his inquiring eyes. "I truly believe I was given a warning. The world around me got deathly quiet. Even the girls sat motionless and stared at me. It seemed as if everything was frozen—like the outside silence before that tornado went over."

"Well, I'm glad you were smart enough to back away, but why did you go in the first place, when Roy told you not to?"

"With those pigs running loose, there won't be any potatoes by frost. I have to save everything I can to hold us through hard times. This depression could last for years."

"Big Sister, it seems you've met with more than one narrow escape this weekend." He leans against the well post and frowns. "My advice is—don't be too proud to ask for help, and don't skip church next Sunday: You need to stay on the good side of your guardian angel."

Chapter 18
Fire and Frost

The weather turns cold following the Sunday afternoon storm. Wind howls out of the north, sweeping dust and leaves across the yard. Dead weeds, yanked from the earth, tumble in gusts that send them bouncing and gathering loose grass.

Ollie looks at the garden through the kitchen window. The plants appear greener than ever before. Night is fast approaching and the girls are hungry, but she hates to turn away. The vines wave green leaves, half-grown peas, and white blooms trying to tighten against the cold.

She shakes her head. *Nature is unsympathetic. An early frost will kill those tender plants. Tomorrow, I expect to see them wilted against the ground.*

Ollie shivers and turns from the window. Into the cook-stove, she adds more wood than necessary to heat the kettle and warm supper. The heat should make the small kitchen feel secure and comfortable, but for some reason Ollie senses danger.

She drags the rocker near the stove. "Morene, bring the baby in here where it's warm. You can rock her while I put food on the table. I should have asked Eldridge to clean the chimney while he was here."

"Why do you want the chimney cleaned?"

"To wipe out creosote, or anything that might blaze up when we build a fire. Your daddy cleans it every year before the weather turns cold."

"Can Daddy come home to get the stuff out, and bring my present?"

"Not yet. Maybe soon."

The girls, enlivened by a late nap, continue to giggle and play long after supper.

Ollie yawns. This has been a stressful day. She kneels on the hearth, and looks up the soot-black passage. Moonlit sky is visible through stringy cobwebs. The burlap bag, Roy stuffed in the chimney top to reduce dust and eliminate barn swallows, is gone. *I don't have to worry about climbing on the roof again. Roy said, if he wasn't home before cold weather, to ask Eldridge to climb up there and remove it, but the storm pulled it out.*

Morene wraps an arm around her mama's neck, touching her cheek. Ollie flinches. "Honey, your hand is cold. Jump in bed and wrap in the blanket. I'll put Syble in with you."

Ollie looks inside the chimney again. "Most of the time we burned dry oak. There shouldn't be enough creosote in there to flame."

"Mama, what did you say?"

"Nothing important. Get in your bed. You can play 'peek-a-boo' until I get a warm fire going in the fireplace."

The girls, dressed in their nightgowns, giggle and tumble while Ollie builds a fire with kindling and a few small sticks of dry wood. She tucks the covers around Morene, picks up Syble, and sits to rock and nurse the baby.

Flames flicker and her eyelids flutter as she recalls events of the day. She shifts the baby in her arms, and rubs her eyes. She has heard stories of women falling asleep and dropping their babies.

Ollie places the sleeping baby in bed, adds more wood to the fire and sits in the kitchen to write a letter to Roy. A roaring noise wakes her. Raising her head from the table, she slaps both hands to her face and tries to separate reality from a nightmare. Red-orange flames lick the fireplace walls and roar up the chimney.

Once, as a child, she stood watching as a neighbor's house burned from a chimney fire. It seemed mere seconds after the roof started to blaze until it caved in. She runs to grab the girls, wraps a quilt around them, and rushes out the door.

Wind whips the trailing quilt around Ollie legs. She can barely keep her balance as she hurries away from the house. Vaguely aware of Morene's screams and Syble's cries, Ollie concentrates on praying. She sets the girls on the ground, kneels, and tucks the quilt around them. "Please, Lord, keep our house from burning."

Flames, shooting from the top of the chimney, light the yard as if they were the sun at midday. Powerful gusts from the west sweep the blazes east, away from the wood shingles and over the kitchen's tin roof. At last, the roaring diminishes. Flames dwindle and draw their lashing tongues back inside the chimney. The yard turns dark, with only stars and a partial moon for illumination.

Ollie gathers her babies and returns to the quiet house where a warm and gentle fire crackles softly over red coals.

"Mama, I don't like big fire."

"Neither do I, but it's gone now. Don't worry. It won't come back. Go to sleep. Jesus is watching over us."

"And our angels. Mama, did they help make the fire go away?"

"Yes, honey. I'm sure they did."

She tucks the shivering girls under quilts and rubs their backs until they fall asleep.

Ollie returns to her letter at the kitchen table. Thinking over events of the day, she writes underneath the date, "This is a day that the Lord has made. We will rejoice and be glad in it." (Psalm 118:24).

She scrapes ashes over the coals left in the fireplace, turns out the lamp, changes into her nightdress, and crawls into bed. She does not forget to give thanks for God's blessings.

Winds are still blowing in the morning, but not at gale force. No frost is on the garden; the sky is blue with bright sunshine. *Lord, please hold the frost until I get the peas canned.*

Within a few days, green grass, brought on by Sunday's rain, is shining across the hills and meadows. Leaves on the potato plants are still a healthy emerald color, proof that potatoes are still growing.

"Morene, look. The pea hulls are turning purple. Tomorrow, we'll pick and shell some for dinner."

Every morning since the storm, Ollie looks from the window to the garden. Days continue to be warm with cold nights, but no frost.

On Friday, clouds roll in to block the sun. As the day progresses, it gets colder.

"Morene, I want you to stay inside and play with the baby while I pick all the peas that are big enough. I'll keep them inside tonight and shell them tomorrow."

Morene opens her mouth to speak, but Ollie continues, "We'll make your cookies when I get the peas inside." Morene smiles, and runs to play.

Ollie is pleased to stack three bushels of peas in one corner of the kitchen. Some of the hulls are still green. They will be hard to shell, but the peas will be good to eat.

"Stop pinching the cookies, Morene. Finish your supper, then you and Syble can nibble cookies. Remember, only give her little bites so she doesn't get choked."

Morene crams a bite of potato in her mouth, and mumbles, "Okay, Mama."

"I'm going to stack wood around the washpot, and fill it with water for washing diapers in the morning." Ollie plans to light a fire under the pot before breakfast. It won't take long to finish the washing before she shells the peas."

When Ollie comes inside, Morene, tired because she missed her nap to help bake cookies, has fallen asleep on the pallet quilt. Syble continues to babble and play with the rag dolls. Ollie washes her little helpers face and hands with a warm cloth and carries her to bed, then lifts the baby.

"After going to sleep so early, your sister will be making noise at the crack of dawn. She'll wake you to play with her, so as soon as you nurse, we'll go to bed." Within an hour, they are both asleep.

Ollie wakes in the night and goes to the water bucket for a drink. The water is cold. So is the house. She looks out the window and wonders if the glitter is frost on the yard.

About to put the dipper down, she hears pigs grunting. Five of them come uphill on the barn path, trotting along as if they are at home. Ollie gets the shotgun, quietly raises the window closest to the garden, and places a stick under it before unhooking the screen.

They head straight for the potatoes, rooting and pawing at

the dirt. Ollie chooses the biggest one, sets a bead on it, and pulls the trigger. It flops amid the plants, squealing and kicking at the air. Before she can reload, the others disappear into the woods. The one in the garden stops moving. Moments later, Ollie plunges a sharp knife into the pig's neck, dark liquid gushes onto the ground.

She calms the girls, frightened by the shotgun blast, and pats their backs until they are asleep again. Ollie dresses in warm clothes, lights the lantern, and returns to look at the pig.

She ponders how to move it, and decides she'll have to get one of the horses to drag it from the garden. Taking a small tin of matches from her jacket pocket, she lights the wood surrounding the washpot. Bell, standing by the corral gate, neighs as Ollie approaches in the moonlight. "Did the shotgun wake you too? I need your help to drag a pig out of the garden. It's a big sucker, nice and fat from eating our corn and sweet potatoes."

Ollie removes a singletree from the front of the breaking plow, fastens the pig's back legs to it, and gets Bell to pull the fat, floppy pig upon a wide flat rock near the house. She returns to the barn to hitch both horses to the wagon.

A large wood box made for curing meat is in the corncrib. Inside is a sack of sugar-cure. Roy bought it in the spring, at a reduced price because the hog-killing season was over. Ollie puts them in the wagon, and drives the team up beside the tree where she plans to hang the pig.

Water in the big black pot boils while Ollie sharpens her knives and ties the horses to a tree where hot water cannot splash on them. She dips and pours buckets of the scalding liquid over the pig, covers it with burlap bags and pours more on top. She refills the pot with water for scalding the other side of the pig.

Ollie has watched Roy and Papa remove the hair before, but this is the first time she has tried it. Pushing aside one of the scalding hot sacks, she drags the knife across the pig, until it looks almost as smooth as Roy's face after he uses a straight razor. When both sides are scraped smooth, she gets Bell to drag it under a big tree.

She throws the ropes over a large limb, and ties them to the singletree attached to the pig's back legs. With gentle urging, Bell pulls until the pig hangs nose-down from the limb.

Ollie grits her teeth, and grips the knife to cut a slit the length of the fat belly. Within minutes steam rises into the night air from warm entrails deposited in a washtub, and the red-brown glob of liver shakes like gelatin when she drops it in a dishpan. With her sharpest knife, she cuts the flesh around its neck and tries to saw through bones to remove the head, but gives up on the task until later. She cannot hold the hanging pig still enough to put adequate pressure on the saw.

While the pig drains, Ollie tosses several pans of cold water into the belly cavity, pats it dry with a clean rag, slices away large slabs of the middle, and puts them in the curing box. The slabs are kept for bacon. She separates the excess fat to render into lard.

To keep the meat clean while she cuts it, she drags the wagon sideboards to the tree and places them under the pig before backing the horse to lower the carcass. She removes the jowls, saws off the head and places it in the tub with the entrails. Next, she saws off the feet, hocks and ribs, and then cuts away the tenderloin, shoulders, and hams.

Her hands are raw and burning from rubbing the sugar-cure over each piece. When the meat is coated with the curing mixture and inside the box, she fastens the lid, hooks Bell to the wagon alongside Bess, and they pull it to the barn. The heavy box remains in the wagon, under the shed. Bell and Bess lumber into the pasture.

Ollie dumps and dries the wash pot, empties the pan of fat into it along with a can of lard from the house, and builds up the fire underneath. The liver, tenderloin and lean scraps she takes into the house and cuts into small pieces. She fries, and packs them into quart jars, covers the meat with hot lard, tightens the lids, and puts the jars in the cooker for canning. Between frying meat, and washing and packing jars, Ollie runs outside every few minutes to stir the pot of bubbling fat.

The fire has died to nothing but red coals when she stirs the pot for the last time and goes inside the house. The eastern sky is beginning to pale with a slight tint of pink. She locks the door and heads for her bed.

Ollie wakes to Syble's hungry cries. She picks her up and stumbles to the rocker.

Morene has dressed herself. Tiny pearl buttons, mismatched with the correct buttonholes, pucker the front of her pink dress. "Are you sick, Mama?"

"No, honey, I'm not sick. One of those mean pigs got in our garden, and I shot him. I was awake most of the night cutting meat. This morning, with our biscuits, we're having pork. I left some soaking in salt-water. Have you been awake long?"

She shrugs. "I tried to keep Syble quiet, but she wanted to get in your bed."

Ollie smiles. "She wanted to get her breakfast. I'll cook ours when she's finished nursing."

Morene remains at the table for a long time. "I like fried pork. It's good like Grandma's chicken. Can you shoot more pigs?"

Ollie chuckles. "I'd like to, but I doubt they'll come back. The shotgun blast scared them into the woods. They're probably a long way from here by now."

Looking out the window, Ollie sees the pasture below the barn—white with frost. "Morene, are you going to help me shell peas this morning? I think the vines will be dead after last night. No more peas. The fields, below the barn, look frozen."

She nods, "I'll help. I like peas."

"First, I want you to keep the baby inside where it's warm while I bury the pig waste. Take good care of her and we'll make a cake while she naps this afternoon."

Morene claps her hands. "Cake with a chocolate top?"

"If that's what you want."

After building another fire under the washpot to melt the lard, Ollie sloshes warmed soapy water over the sideboards, scrubs them with an old broom, and stands them against the house to dry. Then, she digs a deep hole at one corner of the garden, drags over the heavy tub of pig waste, dumps it, sprinkles on lime, packs dirt over the pit, and places flat rocks on top to prevent animals from digging inside.

After dipping the melted lard into clean cans, she sets them on the wash bench to cool, and removes the crisp pieces of fat for crumbling into cornbread batter. Dipping every tablespoon of grease from the pot, she wipes it with a rag, rubs the inside with soap, adds a bucket of water, scrubs, rinses, and leaves clear water over the coals to warm. The pot must be thoroughly clean before she can wash baby clothes, but the laundry chore will wait until tomorrow.

It is almost twelve before she is finished outside. She puts the cooker, filled with jars of meat, over the fire to start the canning process. While it heats, she shells enough peas for the mid-day meal, puts them on to cook along with a pan of cornbread and a cake for Morene to frost.

The noon meal is late, but so was breakfast. Morene lingers over a plate of fried tenderloin while Ollie makes the cake frosting. "Can I spread it on the cake?"

"When it cools some, if you'll be careful not to drop any on the floor."

"I'll not drop it."

Ollie washes dishes while Morene spreads the warm chocolate over the cake. She licks the spoon often when she thinks her mama is not looking, and even shares a few licks with her sister who hangs onto a chair beside her. Ollie ignores the conduct. She will teach manners at another time. This cake is Morene's reward.

Before milking time, canned meat and jars of peas sit cooling under flour sack towels. When Ollie goes to bring in the cans of lard, the pea vines are still alive and waving in the sun. Only a few potato vines on the west side of the patch are wilted.

Ollie leans against the wash-bench and looks at the sky. *Lord, I know Your angels are watching over us. First, You kept our house from burning. I rarely get up in the night to drink water, but last night I was thirsty in time to see the pigs come to the garden. They came on a night when it was cold enough for the meat not to spoil, and angel wings must have fanned the heat from the washpot across the garden so the plants would not freeze. I couldn't have planned it so well. Thank You, God.*

Chapter 19
Homecoming

Each morning Ollie checks for frost, but the garden grows two more weeks before she wakes to see ice crystals sparkling on the plants. Yesterday, she picked and shelled the last of the peas. This morning, after sun dried away the frost, she plowed up the potatoes and the wilted pea vines.

Ollie bends over the tilled rows, gathering bucket after bucket of red-skinned potatoes, and spreading them across the wagon bed to dry. When she has picked up all she can find—almost nine bushels—she drags the pea and potato vines to the pigpen.

Morene sits on a quilt nibbling and feeding Syble more of Morene's most frequent reward for watching the baby—cookies. Morene tries to pull Syble up and get her to walk, but the baby's chubby legs always sag back to the quilt. Ollie laughs at the sight. "Morene, I guess your sister is too fat and lazy. She won't even try to walk."

The runt pig that Roy brought home has now grown into a fat hog. Ollie fed it acorns from trees around the yard, table scraps, and lately more of the corn nubbins to sweeten the meat before butchering time. Eagerly, it chomps on the tiny potato buds clinging to the roots, and limp immature peas wilted by frost.

Many times, Ollie has worried about how to save the potatoes so they will last through the winter. The last three years, Roy stored them in the storm cellar, but the overhead timbers have rotted and the top has caved in. She remembers hearing a conversation at the store about burying root crops in a hole lined with hay. She knows they will rot if water soaks around them, but she has a plan.

Playing has left the girls tired and hungry. They are nodding before finishing lunch, and fall asleep quickly. The quilt looks inviting, but Ollie has work to complete before nightfall.

Where the garden's edge slopes sharply to the east, she digs a hole two feet deep, and over half the length and width of the wagon bed. During four years of living here, she has gathered many flat rocks from the creek and fields to put around flowerbeds. One by one, she transfers them to the hole, spacing the thickest ones close together on the north and around the outside edges. In the middle, she aligns thinner rocks about an inch apart, creating small canals from north to south. If water gets inside, it can drain between the rocks and down the hill.

Three weeks ago, she cut several tall saplings with a hatchet, and laid them on the barn roof to dry. She cuts the poles to the desired size, places them side-by-side across the rocks, and shovels dirt over the ends to hold them in place, before placing a border of larger rocks around the hole.

Ollie tucks a small piece of screen wire, leftover from the windows, under the rocks on the south side, folds it up, and secures it with a large rock. She hopes the screen will keep spiders and small animals outside. South of the screen, a narrow trench forms a drain with small flat rocks on the bottom and sides, and larger ones across the top.

She pulls the largest turnips, removes the greens, and places them root side down between the saplings on the south side of the hole. Since Roy has been gone, she has kept the grass cut from around the wells with Papa's scythe. Some she fed to the animals, the rest she piled near the garden. The pile has evolved into a small haystack. She gathers an armload of it to cover the poles.

Onions that have been drying under the house are placed on the north side of the hay, before pouring in buckets of potatoes. She covers the vegetables with lime Papa gave her to keep bugs from under the house. She hopes it will keep away mice and rats, as well. Next, she spreads plenty of dry grass over the vegetables.

A partial roll of tarpaper, found in the attic, is cut to cover the grass and prevent rain from seeping through. On the east side of the cache, she removes rocks to make a gate, refills the cavity with grass, props an oak board against it, and pushes rocks close to hold the sideboard in place until she is ready to slide it out and remove vegetables.

After shoveling dirt on top of the tarpaper, Ollie stands back to look at her work. *A hard rain will wash away dirt, run under the tarpaper, wet the hay, and rot the potatoes.* She frowns and sighs wearily. *I have to do more.*

She goes inside and gets a long, sturdy butcher knife. Choosing a low section of the yard where moss and soft grass sprang up behind the rain, she uses the knife to cut enough squares of sod to cover the pit. She hitches the team, loads the chunks of grass-covered earth into the wagon, and hauls them back to roof the underground chamber. Standing to study her accomplishment, she smiles.

After supper, Ollie stoops to runs her hand across the front of the full jars sitting in one corner of the kitchen. Twenty-one quarts of peas await winter. They took a lot of work.

She remembers carrying water to keep the garden growing—one bucket each for twenty rows, twice a day for at least sixty days. *That's over two thousand buckets of water, but we have turnips, potatoes and peas to last through the winter, along with the applesauce canned earlier. What could I have done more worthwhile? My family won't starve.* "Thank You, Lord, for the water, the energy, and the rewards."

Morene comes into the kitchen. "I didn't hear what you said, Mama."

Ollie smiles at her. "I was thanking God for the peas and potatoes that grew in our garden."

She frowns, looking puzzled. "Why do you thank God?"

"Because He helps us with all good things."

"Oh." She runs back to play with the baby.

With the girls giggling in the next room, Ollie looks out the window at the stars shining in a clear sky. She whispers, "Lord, please bring Roy home safely. It's been nearly two weeks since we've got a letter. Surely he's on his way home."

Ollie puts more wood in the fireplace, and gets the girls ready for bed. Morene pulls a chair close to the rocker as Ollie sits to nurse the baby. "Mama, tell me the story of baby Moses and his big sister."

"You've heard that many times. Tonight I want to tell you about Moses after he grew to be a man."

Morene nods, squeezes her doll, and leans back in the chair to listen.

"God told Moses to lead the Israelite people out of Egypt. He wanted them to go to a special land He promised to give them."

Morene jumps from her chair and runs to the window. "I hear a wagon. Maybe it's Daddy."

"Our wagon's in the barn. It's probably the man who took some of our potatoes. Jump in your bed while I put the baby down."

Syble is not finished nursing and starts to cry. Morene tries to quiet her but is not having any luck. The wagon stops in the yard. Ollie slips a shell in the shotgun and blows out the lamp.

"Ollie! It's me—Roy. Put away the gun. I'm home."

Morene runs to the door. "Daddy! Daddy!" She fumbles with the lock. "I can't get it open."

Ollie pushes her hand away and clicks the bolt.

Morene jumps into his arms. "I knew it was you. I knew it."

Ollie gives him a quick kiss before going to get the screaming baby. "It's a good thing you called to me. When I heard a wagon, I was getting ready to shoot our no-good neighbor."

"I figured you would have a loaded gun."

"Daddy, I've been a good girl. Huh, Mama?"

"Yes. She has been a very good girl."

"Mama wrote in her letters about how well you take care of little Syble. You deserve a special present. Let me put you down and I'll get it from my satchel."

From his brown canvas travel case, he takes a paper bag with a blue ribbon tied around it. Morene squeals when he hands it to her. She plops on the floor and gently pulls at the ribbon. "Will it break if I drop it? I can't get the ribbon loose. Help me, Mama."

Ollie smiles, and bends to untie the knotted ribbon.

Morene reaches inside the bag and removes a silver-colored bird. "It's a mockingbird, like in Mama's song. Will it sing?"

Roy chuckles. "It will if you help it. There is a hole in the end of each tail feather. Each feather makes a different sound. Blow softly and move your mouth across the feathers."

She blows, and the toy hums like a harmonica. "Daddy, it *does* sing! Like a real bird."

"Do you like it?"

She nods her head. "Yes, I like it."

"Tomorrow you can practice in the yard. I bet you'll make all the birds jealous." He reaches into the bag, takes out a package, and hands it to Ollie. "It's not what I would have liked to buy you, but we don't know what we'll need our money for before this depression is over." He smiles as she fumbles with the string. "Yours will break, so don't dump it on the floor."

Ollie takes a small round picture with a domed glass cover from the paper. The print behind the glass depicts a towering building. "This must be a fancy church, maybe somewhere in the Holy Land." She turns it in her hands. "Moving the picture seems to make it more real—as if I could walk into that church and see Jesus teaching." She smiles, looking, and turning the work of art. "This is beautiful. Thank you." She looks around the room. "Where should I hang it?"

"Maybe over the fireplace."

Ollie laughs. "Over or under the shotgun?"

He grins. "You have a point. How about between the south windows, over our little table?"

"That's a good place. I'll hang it in the morning."

Roy is cuddling Syble in the crook of his arm. "Now it's

your turn, little one." He hands her a rubber doll. She sticks its hand in her mouth and begins to chew.

Morene giggles. "Daddy, it looks like her. It has the same fat tummy."

Roy kisses Syble and hands her to Ollie. He picks Morene up, tosses her into the air, and hugs her tight. "Jump into bed and get a good night's sleep. Tomorrow, you can teach all the birds how to sing pretty. I have to take Pa's team and wagon to the barn. Ma has it loaded with things she thought we could use."

Both girls are asleep before Roy comes inside. "It's so good to be home with you and the girls, and I can hardly wait to see the farm in the daylight."

The next morning while Ollie cooks breakfast, Roy goes to milk and feed the animals. The girls are still sleeping when Ollie takes the biscuits from the oven. She covers them with a towel and walks down to meet him.

The empty milk pail hangs on a hook while Roy pets the horses. "Ollie, have you noticed; Bess looks like she's going to have a colt? Did she get out while I was gone?"

"About two weeks after you left, a black stallion jumped in our pasture and chased her away. I was afraid he might have killed her. He was a mean scoundrel. When I came down to milk, he chased me into the loft, pawed at the steps, and stretched his neck trying to bite me. No one knew where he came from. Mama said someone finally shot him because people were afraid to let children outside."

"You didn't write me about a stallion."

"Mama said I shouldn't worry you while you were so far away."

"It would have done that, but I don't want you keeping things from me."

"Bess came limping home with bite marks and several bad bruises where he kicked her. At first, I thought her jaw might be broken."

"Well, it looks like she's all right now, and she'll have a colt by next summer."

"I've suspected, for a while." Ollie shakes her head and lays a hand on his shoulder. "I don't want a frisky colt around here with the girls so young."

"Neither do I. We'll sell it as soon as it's old enough to wean."

She sighs. "Good. The way you love horses, I was afraid you'd want to keep it. I've heard too many horrible stories about children being kicked. A colt's hooves are like deadly weapons controlled by a baby."

He pauses to look at her. "You knew that little Johnson boy who was kicked, didn't you?"

She nods. "Let's discuss something cheerful."

He grabs her in a tight hug. "Cheerful is being home with my wife and babies."

Her head against his shoulder, she whispers, "I've missed you so much."

"Hey, I noticed meat in the curing box, but our pig's still in the pen. Also, when I was getting hay for the cow, I stuck the pitchfork into a basket of sweet potatoes. I think there were a lot of things you didn't want to worry me about."

She pulls away and lowers her head. "Many times I wanted to cry on your shoulder and tell you of frightening things: shooting at a prowler, falling in the dug well, a big copperhead in the barn path and one in my cotton row, the horses running away, shooting a sow and a wild boar, the tornado, and the chimney fire." She takes a deep breath.

"I knew Mama was right about things worrying you, and I was safe by the time I sat down to write, so were the girls. Besides, it's easier to tell a story than to write it." She smiles and reaches to hug him. "I'm so glad you're back with us."

"Me too." He holds her close.

"By the way, I didn't find any snakes in the sweet potato patch." She grins. "I think the hogs rooted them out before I got there."

Chapter 20
Whoever Listens

Roy and Ollie unload pumpkins from his pa's wagon. Morene, in the yard with her silver-colored bird-shaped whistle, watches. Roy ties Bell to the back of the wagon, and drives onto the dusty road.

"Mama, why's Daddy taking Bell? I don't want him to sell her like the calf!" The little girl's face puckers to cry. She clenches her fists and stomps her feet, trying to defy tears.

"He won't sell the mare. He'll ride her home, after he takes Pa his wagon and team." Ollie sets a pumpkin on the step, and wraps her arms around her three year old.

"Honey, the horses work for us, and the cow gives us milk, so we have to keep them. A calf does nothing but eat. We couldn't afford to feed it through the winter. The man that bought her has plenty of feed. Someday she'll grow into a cow and give milk for his little girls."

She wipes at her eyes. "Why didn't we go with Daddy to see Pa and Ma?"

"We'll go soon. Your daddy has business to take care of today."

Morene frowns. "What's business?"

Ollie pauses in the doorway with one of the pumpkins on her hip. "Business is things he has to do, like go to the bank and pay the banker some money for our farm, and go to the store to buy sugar for making your cookies."

"Oh." She smiles, her eyes still shining with tears. "Do *you* have business?"

Ollie grins. "Yes, I have to can these pumpkins. Do you want to help?"

"No. I have business teaching songs to the birds."

"All right. Stay in the backyard where I can see you from the window."

Roy gets home before the last half of the red sun slips behind the mountain. He leaves Bell in the yard and comes inside. A sack of sugar is across one arm; he holds Morene with the other. He lays the sugar on the cabinet, and sets his squirming daughter on the floor. Dropping into a chair, Roy motions for Morene to sit on his knee. "It smells good in here."

Ollie wipes her hands on an apron splotched with pumpkin. "I've canned seven quarts of pumpkin, and made a pie for supper." She pauses to look at his face before placing a hand on his shoulder. "Are you feeling all right? Is something wrong? You look so downcast."

Morene slides from his knee and runs to the kitchen door.

"Wait, honey." Ollie reaches for a jacket. "Put this on before you go out. You can only play for a short time. It'll be dark soon." She closes the door behind the child. "Now, Roy, tell me what's wrong."

He frowns and shakes his head. "On that big farm in North Dakota, we had plenty to eat and lots of work to do, with very little news from the rest of the country, except letters from home. Other wives and parents must have felt like you, and didn't want to worry us with bad news—or maybe I didn't listen well enough. Anyway, I had no idea the depression was so severe."

"What do you mean?"

"Since I left North Dakota, you, our girls, and my folks are the only people I've noticed with smiles. Near the bank, a young man was begging for food. While I was in the store getting your sack of sugar, a family with several children stopped." He swallows hard and looks down before continuing.

"The man and woman came inside and asked if anyone could afford to take a child. The bank took their farm; they had nowhere to go, and no way to feed the children. I looked outside and saw the kids lined up beside the wagon. The biggest girl was holding a baby. It was the saddest thing I've ever seen. Those kids stood as if waiting for a firing squad. I wanted to take them all, but I knew we wouldn't have enough to feed them through the winter."

"Oh, how sad." Ollie pulls a chair close to the table and sits across from him. "We have to make good use of every morsel of food God gives us. We don't know how long this will last."

He nods in agreement. "When Pa and I got back from the bank, Ma gave me a bag of goodies for Morene. I think it was fried chicken and cookies. Don't tell her about it, because I handed it to the oldest boy and told him to share with his brother and sisters."

"We would be in a sad shape ourselves, if you hadn't gone away to work."

"I know. As much I hated to be away, I'm glad I went." He leans forward, props his elbows on his knees, and massages his temples. "I'll probably have to do the same next year."

"I understand. We'll do what we have to do."

That night, as the rosy-faced little girls sleep, Roy and Ollie relax in front of the fire. They talk about the months they were apart and discuss plans for the future. The moon is high in the sky before the conversation lulls.

The burning wood shifts and crumbles into red coals. Roy stands and hooks his thumbs around his overall straps. "Early in the morning, I'm going squirrel hunting."

She leans back in the rocker and looks at him. "According to Papa, wild game is getting scarce. Men are hunting to feed their families. I've seen several hunters near our creek."

"Well, maybe I'll find some walnuts and hickory nuts. If I do, I'll go back and gather them in the afternoon. Thanksgiving and Christmas will be here soon. Wealthier people in town will want nuts for pies and cakes."

"I think you'll be lucky to find any of those, unless the tree is in a remote area. Hungry people are taking anything they find that's good to eat."

The fruit and vegetables Ollie canned, vegetables stored in her makeshift cellar, and the fish and game Roy brings home, help them to survive another winter. By April, despite a doctor's warning that she must have surgery before she can carry another baby to full term, Ollie is almost five months pregnant and has no more problems than she did with the girls.

Roy needs a mule to help him clear land. He buys one for a low price—no one else would bid on it. It has a wild attitude and a split tongue. The former owner said the mule got his head tangled in a barbed wire fence. A strip of the tongue often hangs out the side of his mouth, drooling slobbers.

Ollie and Morene watch from the yard as Roy turns him loose in the barnyard. The mule lays back his ears and runs around the lot, kicking at the sky, the barn, and the fence posts.

"Mama, I'm gonna call him Muley, but I don't like him."

"I feel the same way."

Roy comes up the path, shaking his head. "I need a strong mule for clearing land. I got him for almost nothing, but he's not gentle like the mules I used to own. Although he's big enough to move a mountain, working with this one will be like dealing with the devil."

"Roy, I'm afraid for you to be around such a scary animal. He's so big, he could go over or through any fence we've got— or over you, if he takes a notion."

"In the morning, I'll build a high fence to keep him separate from the horses and cow. Morene, don't go near the fence where the mule stays. He's a mean animal. He'll bite or kick you if he can. The same goes for you, Ollie."

One beautiful day while the girls nap, Ollie goes to look for poke greens. Yellow dandelions dot the yard, buds on the rose bush are beginning to unfurl glossy red petals, and the peach trees Roy planted four years ago are loaded with glorious pink blooms.

Ollie walks around the yard, to the barn, and circles the cow and horse lot. She has almost enough greens to cook, but a large clump in the pasture that Roy fenced off for his new mule catches her eye. It will make plenty for a pot of poke sallet.

She looks for the mule. He is nowhere in sight. On warm afternoons, the animals usually graze in shaded areas near the creek.

Ollie drops her sack over the top wire and is about to climb through when a voice says, "Don't."

She turns to see who spoke. No one is in sight.

"Roy, where are you hiding?" The only answer she gets is a

swift gust of wind whistling through nearby trees. She is embarrassed, even though she is alone.

Ollie climbs through the fence, walks to the greens and begins to break the tender shoots and leaves. She releases the last handful into the sack and glances toward the creek. The mule, ears laid back and hoofs pounding the path, is coming fast.

She drops the bag, and runs. His drumming hooves get louder. Ollie dives under the bottom wire and rolls away from the fence. She trembles on the ground while the mule whirls, kicking his back feet high in the air, slinging his head, and stringing slobbers from the split tongue.

Afraid the irate mule may try to jump the fence, Ollie attempts to stand. A terrible pain rips through her insides, sending her to her knees. *The baby! I've hurt the baby!*

She remembers hearing the voice, and part of a passage from Proverbs that her grandma often quoted: "The complacency of fools will destroy them; but whoever listens will dwell safely." *Why didn't I listen?*

Roy, coming from the field, sees her stumbling across the yard and runs to help her inside. The baby is born that afternoon. It never takes a breath.

Roy wraps the tiny infant in a blanket, puts it in a wooden box, and buries it in the orchard under a blossoming peach tree.

Overwhelmed by guilt, Ollie can barely contain her grief. She wonders if she killed the baby in her attempt to get away from the mule, or would it have died anyway? Trying to concentrate on something other than the loss, she works harder than ever.

For months, Ollie shies away from people, even family

members, other than Roy and her girls. She avoids church, family gatherings, and the community store. Someone always tries to talk about the baby.

Roy insists she have the surgery, even though crops were poor and they earned very little profit.

"Roy, it's risky to spend our money for something we don't have to get done. I think we should wait longer, maybe another year. We might not have enough money left to buy seed and fertilizer for planting crops in the spring."

"If the need is there, we'll borrow from the bank."

"But we still owe money on the mortgage."

"We'll borrow, or I'll go away to work. This is a necessity."

They visit the doctor and make the surgery appointment. The doctor tells her it is a simple procedure. "You won't have to stay in the hospital long."

The night before going to the hospital, Ollie dreams that the nurse puts a hot water bottle on her feet and burns them. She wakes with her heart pounding. Since agreeing to go, she has worried about being put to sleep, and has made every excuse imaginable to postpone it. *Roy will laugh at me. Anyway, why would they put a hot water bottle on my feet?* She cannot bring herself to tell Roy the details of the dream.

Early the next morning, they leave Morene and Syble with Ollie's mama. The wind is blowing cold, and snowflakes whirl as if dancing in the currents of air. Roy and Ollie wear heavy wool coats, and she has a scarf tied around her head. He has the flaps from inside his cap pulled down over his ears. Roy wraps a saddle blanket around Ollie's feet and tucks a quilt around her legs.

"Roy, I want to go home. I'm uneasy about this."

"You'll be fine. The doctor said it's a simple thing. I'll bring you home in a few days."

"I know what he said, but I'm still afraid. A bad dream scared me last night."

"You want more babies, don't you?"

"You know I do."

Roy puts an arm around her, and pulls her close. "I know you're worried. You tossed and turned all night, but the operation is scheduled. It'll be over in a few hours."

When they arrive at the hospital, a nurse takes Ollie to a small room and gives her a gown to put on. The closer it gets to the time of surgery, the more Ollie frets about the hot water bottle. *I should tell them not to put one on my feet.* The nurse comes back into the room, and Ollie starts to tell her, "While I'm asleep, don't—"

"Don't you worry. I'll take good care of you."

"But I want to—"

"Yes, you need to go before surgery." She points toward a doorway. "The lavatory is behind the door."

"But I—"

"Hurry along. The doctor will be ready soon."

When Ollie leaves the bathroom, the nurse, ready to roll her into the operating room, starts talking immediately. "I hope you followed instructions, and didn't eat or drink anything this morning. If you have food or liquid in your stomach, the anesthetic will make you sick."

"I didn't eat of drink anything, but I want to tell you something."

"I've helped with dozens of these operations. You don't have anything to worry about. Scoot onto the table and lie still.

The doctor's ready."

The doctor steps to her side. He has a white cloth in one hand and a bottle of something in the other. From the bottle, he douses liquid onto the cloth. "Ollie, when I put this over your nose, I want you to count to ten."

The sweet scent of ether is strong. "First, I want to say something."

He flops the cloth over her nose. In a panic, she takes a deep breath and mumbles, "I, I—"

Ollie wakes with burning pain in her feet. Frantic, she pulls at one then the other, but cannot move either foot. The sheet, stretched tight over her, is tucked under the mattress. "Nurse! Nurse!" No one comes to help. She wiggles and twists until at last her feet no longer touch the bottle, although she can still feel the heat.

Ollie keeps calling until a nurse finally comes into the room.

"What's wrong? You should be asleep."

"The hot water bottle has burned my feet. They feel like they're blistered."

"I'm sure they're not. You're just waking from the anesthetic."

"I'm wide awake, and my feet are burning."

"I'll give you something for pain."

"No! Bring a cold water bottle to put on my feet."

"Let me look at your feet." The nurse pulls the bed covers from the end of the bed and removes the red rubber container. "This bottle is not hot enough to burn you. You must have chill blains."

Ollie raises her head to look at the nurse. "I have good leather shoes. My feet were never frozen—I've never had chill blains. You burned my feet with a hot water bottle. I want to see the doctor. Untie me. I'm awake; I won't fall off the bed."

"The doctor is with another patient. When he's finished, I'll tell him you want to see him." The nurse walks from the room, leaving Ollie struggling with the restraints.

Ollie watches the wall clock ticking away for almost an hour before she frees herself of the long sheet wrapped around her and pulled tight underneath the mattress. While suffering through the night with blistered feet, Ollie berates herself for not listening to the voice in her dream, and the voice that spoke to her before she went into the mule pasture.

When the doctor finally comes to the room, he insists the hot water bottle did not burn her. "My diagnosis is that you have chill blains from not wearing proper shoes."

"It's not true. My feet were fine when I came into this hospital." Despite Ollie's protests, it is a case of his word against hers. She has no money for a lawyer.

She worries about how they will make another mortgage payment. Was surgery really necessary, or did they waste money so desperately needed to save the farm from foreclosure? In the following weeks, while she limps with pain, Ollie vows that she will never again ignore a warning spirit.

Chapter 21
Tenacity

Ollie watches through the kitchen window as Roy walks over the farm. He sits on a stump at the edge of the woods where he cleared new ground and tosses pebbles into the field. Ollie remembers snowy days when he burned brush piles, windy days when he pulled stumps with the mules, and hot dusty days when they prayed for rain.

When Franklin Roosevelt was inaugurated for U.S. president earlier in 1933, many people expected the economy to improve immediately. Yet, the devastation that spread across the South by floods along the Mississippi River in 1927, the stock market crash in 1929, the drought in 1930, and the failed banking system has not vanished.

After selling the corn crop, a yearling calf, and the hog they were fattening for meat, Roy and Ollie do not have enough money to make the mortgage payment. They feel certain the banker will take their farm for nonpayment.

Roy walks into the pasture, pets the mares, hops up on Bell's back and rides her toward the creek without a saddle or bridle. He pauses at the ditch where he shot and buried the split-tongued mule that chased Ollie and caused her to lose a baby. He disappears into the woods beside the creek where, over the years, he has caught stringer after stringer of fish. At last, he kneels in the orchard he planted and pulls weeds from around a tiny grave.

When he comes to the house, he has a bunch of small turnips

in one hand. Ollie goes out to meet him and stands silent as he releases the long slender well bucket to go clanging through clay tiles. It gurgles; he draws it up, and hangs it on a giant nail protruding from a post. Cold water drizzles from the leaking bottom seal as they scrub dirt from the purple and white roots.

"There'll be some fine turnips soon. I thought we might as well eat a few before that banker takes the place." Roy leans against the well post. "Ollie, we've given this a good try. We would have made it on this farm if the economy hadn't turned sour. Now we'll have to try something else."

She nods, but a lump in her throat keeps her from speaking.

He spits a stream of tobacco juice into the grass. "After they take this place, if you'll stay with your folks until I find a job, I'll send for you and the girls as soon as I can."

She swallows, and dries her hands on her apron. "Where will you go?"

"I've already checked on jobs everywhere around here. Roosevelt has that big project starting in Tennessee. I'm gonna try that first."

"That's an electrical project. You don't know anything about electricity."

"They'll need all kinds of laborers, from carpenters to ditch diggers. There's bound to be a job for me."

"Should I start packing our things?"

"We don't have much to take. Tomorrow, I'm going to talk to the banker. He'll tell me when we have to leave."

"Is your pa going to the bank with you?"

"I didn't ask him. It would only make him feel bad that he can't help. I'll go by myself."

The next morning, as usual, Roy and Ollie wake early to take care of farm chores. Roy pushes away from the breakfast table without a word, unties Bell from the well post and leaves for the bank. As he rides away, Bess whinnies from the pasture.

Ollie watches the mare prancing around the barn, calling for Bell. Her silver-gray mane and tail glisten in the sun. *Those mares are like part of the family. I'll hate to lose them almost as much as the farm.*

Looking at the garden, Ollie wonders if she will have enough time for the potatoes to mature. She takes a bucket from behind the house, picks the purple-hull peas, and grapples enough of the new potatoes for supper.

Watching the girls skip around the yard, Ollie sits on the porch shelling peas and wiping stray tears on her sleeve. Leaving the shelled peas in a pan of water, she walks with the girls to the orchard to pick the remaining fall apples and leave a bouquet of late roses on the little grave.

When Morene and Syble start squealing "Daddy's home," Ollie has peas, cornbread, boiled new potatoes, turnips, greens, and apple pie ready for the evening meal. She pulls a chair away from the table and sits, waiting for the bad news.

Roy leaves Bell grazing in the yard and comes rushing through the kitchen door. "Ollie, we don't have to leave! Anyway, not yet."

"What?" She jumps up with hope in her heart.

"Wait a minute." He takes two red suckers from his pocket. "Girls, sit on the rug and eat these while I talk to your mama."

Hands stuffed deep in her pockets, Ollie trembles while the words, "We don't have to leave!" echo inside her head.

He grabs her in a tight hug. "We don't have to move."

"Say it again."

"It's true."   He releases her enough to let her catch her breath. "I told the banker that I didn't have all the money for the payment, and that I guess he'll need to come and repossess the place."

Roy hugs her again before backing away to take off his good jacket and hang it over a chair.

"Come on! Tell me the rest of it."

His mouth forms a grin, but his forehead wrinkles into a frown as he looks at the floor. "That rich banker shook his head. His fat jaws jiggled, and at that moment, I hated him. I just knew he was going to take our home."

Ollie slaps her leg. "Well, what did he say?"

"He heaved a big sigh, sat down in his swivel chair, and said, 'Roy, I don't need another farm. Pay what you can. Maybe the coming year will be better. I'll add the rest of this year's payment and interest onto the balance for next year. These hard times can't last forever.'"

"Oh, thank Heaven."

"He told me to save enough that my family wouldn't starve through the winter. So, I kept enough to buy us another pig."

"Where can we get one this close to butchering time?"

"Pa said if I'll butcher two for him, he'll let me have one for half price."

"Did you tell him you'd do it?"

"The weather's a mite warm for hog killing, and I plan on going to Tennessee as soon as I can."

"I'll do it."

"No. Hog killing is not woman's work. Besides, you have the girls to care for."

She raises her chin. "Not woman's work! Who do you think

killed and dressed that meat you ate after you came home from working up north?"

"That was different. Now we're talking about three full-grown hogs. I don't want you to try it. You could get hurt, and then who would take care of the girls?"

"I should do it, to show you that I can."

Roy grins. "You think so?"

She returns the grin. "You know that I could."

He frowns and turns to go. "We'll work something out. Right now, I need to get Bell some feed and turn her into the pasture. Something sure smells good in here. I'm ready for food." He stops and hands her his good hat. "Will you hang up my Sunday hat and coat? The girls might get sticky candy on that jacket."

Ollie smiles at him. "Hurry. There's apple pie in the warming oven."

"Good! I'll be back by the time you get it on the table."

Through the window, Ollie can see the mare trotting behind Roy as he runs to the barn.

Later, he lingers at the supper table, smoking his pipe and telling Ollie every detail of his day. "At the store, there was talk about the weather turning cooler next week."

Ollie, stacking the dishes, stops abruptly and wipes her hands on a dishrag. "What if I leave the girls at Mama's, then you and I can spend the night with your folks and get up before daylight to light a fire under the water we'll need for scalding. We can get two hogs processed before the day starts to get warm. I'll take care of the last one by myself when the weather gets colder."

He clears his throat. When he speaks, his voice is deep.

"Ollie, I'm leaving for Tennessee as soon as I get a few things done around here. Getting work is more important than butchering hogs. If I wait, I might not find a job."

Ollie turns to put plates in a pan of water that has been warming on the stove. "You're right. We can make it without meat if we have to. I read somewhere that dried beans are almost as good for people as lean meat." She looks over her shoulder.

Roy takes the pipe from his mouth and wrinkles his forehead. "Maybe so, but fried beans for breakfast with biscuits and gravy does not sound good."

"Don't make too much fun. You may be trying it before this depression is over."

"I'd eat them every meal if I knew that would save our farm."

Three days later, Ollie leaves Roy at his parents' house. His pa will take Roy to catch a bus heading for Knoxville, Tennessee. Through her tears, Ollie can barely see the road, and she has the same empty feeling in her chest as when he went to North Dakota looking for work.

On the way home, Ollie stops to borrow her papa's pistol. She straps it on her hip before leaving his yard. She will wear it every day while outside, and leave it and the loaded shotgun at the head of her bed every night until Roy comes home.

Within a short time, the weather turns cold. As Ollie tosses the last of the salt pork into a pot of beans, she thinks about the hogs Roy's pa wanted killed. *I could have done it by myself.*

One afternoon, Eldridge opens the kitchen door and calls, "Hey, Sis." Before she answers, he takes the dipper from a bucket sitting on a nearby washstand, drinks, and gasps. "I emptied my water jug hours ago."

Ollie sets a dishpan of water on the cook-stove and opens the damper. "Are you as hungry as you were thirsty?"

"Just about, but I gotta get home. I need to borrow your wagon to haul wood. Papa took his to help someone on the other side of the mountain. I don't know when he'll be back."

She nods toward the open door. "Okay, but why'd you bring both mules? I don't mind you taking the mares."

"Mama said for me not to leave you afoot in this valley. If need be, you can ride a horse with the girls, but they're too small to walk and too heavy to carry."

She frowns. "Mama worries."

"I wish you lived closer, so we could check on you and the girls every day."

"I take care of things."

"Do you need help with anything before I go?"

"I've already milked and fed the animals, but if you hear of anyone that has a butchering hog for sale at a decent price, I'd like to buy one."

"I'll ask around, but it may be a day or two before I get all that wood hauled." He hugs the girls and backs out the door.

The mares kick up their heels and run from the log barn with silver tails soaring as her young brother leads his mules to the wagon, but the Jersey cow continues grazing outside her calf's pen. Within minutes, wagon wheels mark the dry yard and leave tracks in the dust where he pulls onto the road.

Ollie turns to gaze around the two-room house, built for a sharecropper. Her rocker, a small table, the fireplace, and two double beds fill the front room. Patchwork quilts cover flour-sack sheets, and striped cotton mattresses made at the community Work Center. Her girls play under their bed—never on top—beautiful quilts are treasures and hard to wash. Jars of canned fruit and garden vegetables sit neatly beneath Ollie's bedstead.

"Girls, wash up and put nightgowns on. You skipped your naps, and I don't want you falling asleep under there."

She tucks them in, locks doors, pulls curtains, and stretches across her quilt to rest before lighting a lamp to read her husband's letter again. Fully dressed, she falls asleep.

The room is dark when Ollie wakes to the sound of a cow's frantic bawling. The pistol, that she wears all day while Roy is working away from home, remains on her hip. She grabs the loaded shotgun, drops extra shells in her pocket, and slips out into the cool autumn night.

Ollie crouches beside the well. Shadowy forms of two men are in the calf pen. She aims the shotgun at a tree limb hanging over their heads and shoots. Tree bark splinters. Men tumble over the fence and run.

She reloads and fires after them. A howl of pain echoes across the valley. Moments later, hoof beats resonate from a hard roadbed and fade into the distance. She grits her teeth, loads another round, and whispers, "One scoundrel will have regrets."

Ollie slips toward the barn, her heart pounding as if it could break through her ribs. Through the fence, moonlight illuminates the calf on the ground with legs tied. Separated from her baby by thick oak boards, the cow runs back and forth, blowing, bawling, and stirring up the stink of fresh manure.

On her way to the gate, through the unlit barn, Ollie steps with caution. Snakes and spiders might hide beside the dirt path, or another thief could wait in a stall. Musty scents of leather harness and hay mix with sweet feed, but her sensitive nose does not detect the sweaty odor of a man or the rotten-egg stench from a disturbed snake.

Before going into bright moonlight, she stops to stare at the brushy timber. Dust, stirred by the angry cow, tickles her nose, and mosquitoes hum. Convinced that the thieves have fled, she places the shotgun on the ground, and unties the helpless animal.

When the calf jumps up, Ollie sees a shiny knife blade. With a shiver, she glances toward the woods, picks up the knife, and turns to the cow. "They were gonna kill it here. Seconds more and your baby would have been dead."

She rushes through the barn and toward the house. Her heart leaps. The kitchen door stands wide open.

To avoid the crunchy path, she runs through wilted grass, and drops the knife and shotgun in shadows near the well. Gripping the pistol, she inches around the house, but drawn curtains conceal everything inside.

Her back to the wall, she stands near the open door, listening. The only sound within is the loud ticking of the old clock. If a man is waiting, he will grab her the moment she steps in. The clock tick, tick, ticks.

Minutes pass as she tries to convince herself that she did not close the door. Gun ready, she stands on the ground, peeps around the door, steps up, and inside. She checks everywhere an adult could hide, and finds no stranger.

Seeing her girls asleep, Ollie returns to the moonlit yard for the shotgun and knife. When back inside, behind locked doors, she breathes in the clean scent of soap, and gives thanks for the safety inside her small home.

She slumps into a ladder-back chair beside a rough oak table to examine the knife. It has no marks of identification. Holding it in the light, she whispers, "What a trade. I have a sharp knife, and someone has buckshot in his behind."

Chapter 22
A Long Lonesome Winter

Hearing the sound of an approaching wagon, Ollie looks out the window. Eldridge stops in the yard and comes inside. "Mama sent more eggs and three pieces of meat left from breakfast. She said tell you to eat one of them: don't save your share for the girls."

"Why would she say that?"

He raises his chin. "Because she knows how you are."

"Mama knows, 'cause that's how *she* is. I bet she didn't eat any this morning so she could send this to me."

Eldridge shrugs. "Maybe so, I'm only passing along what she said." He bends to hug the girls. "Are you behaving?"

They nod. "We're good."

"I'm glad." He pats their backs. "I've gotta be going. I have a lot of wood to stack. Sis, thanks for letting me use your wagon."

"Sure, anytime you need it. Did you hear of anyone that has a hog for sale?"

"I've been hauling wood, but I'll ask around when I get a chance. Somebody's bound to have one they want to sell."

Ollie reaches for her jacket. "I'll walk out with you." She turns to the girls. "Mama sent some meat. You can each have one piece. Sit at the table to eat it."

Once outside, she tells Eldridge about the men trying to steal the calf. "Ask Mama to call the sheriff and report it. I couldn't see them well enough to identify them, but I believe they were my sorry neighbors. Also, ask Mrs. Hart if the doctor has removed buckshot from anyone within the last few days."

   "I'll bet they were snooping around and saw the wagon tracks going out, with none coming back in, and figured you were gone. Maybe you shot one of them."

   "They were leaving as fast as they could, but one of them yelled like he was hit."

   When she goes inside the girls have finished eating their meat. They stand watching as Ollie puts the last piece inside a cold biscuit. They turn sideways, and look at her with smiles.

   Ollie removes a tiny taste of the fat and puts it in her mouth before cutting the sandwich in half. "Sit close to the table, so crumbs don't fall in the floor." They grab for the biscuit halves. "Eat slow. I'll get you some milk."

   The next morning Ollie fries eggs for the girls, but not for herself. She knows that chickens do not lay many eggs in the winter. She eats a biscuit with gravy.

   Several days later, she gets a letter from Roy. She rips it open and reads:

Dear Ollie and Girls,

I found a job working as an unskilled laborer. The skilled work will not start until they begin building. Now, we're getting the building site ready. It's hard work, but I'm glad to have it. The boss said they should have work here for years.

If things continue to go well, I plan to work until spring planting season. We get off two days for Christmas. I can hardly stand the thought of being away from you, but two days is not enough time to make the long trip home.

I hope your papa or Eldridge was able to find a hog for butchering. You need meat this winter.

Write me all the news. Tell the girls I will send them presents for Christmas.

I love you,
Roy

Morene and Syble dance around, laughing and squealing, "presents, presents." "Mama, when is Christmas? What will he send us? Can't he come home too?"

Ollie answers their questions, but cannot help feeling sad.

Eldridge has not heard of anyone with a pig for sale, but promises to continue looking. Ollie makes biscuits and gravy for breakfast, eggs for the girls when Mama and Papa have extra. Morene and Syble drink milk with meals. Ollie hates milk.

Every day Ollie cooks cornbread, beans or peas, and fried potatoes. Before the first hard freeze, she cooked turnip and mustard greens often, but they froze in November. So the girls will not get sick from lack of vitamins, Ollie makes vegetable soup with canned tomatoes, and desserts from canned fruit.

The girls are growing and seem to be healthy, but a rash is developing on Ollie's hands and arms. She gets tired with very little exertion and has stopped eating the green tops sprouting from the turnips stored in the cellar. She thinks they are causing her to have stomachaches.

Ollie stops going to church because of the frequent stomach problems, and is so depressed that she wants to cry all the time. She does her best to hide the tears from the girls, but irritability causes her to shout at them often.

"Morene, peep out the window and see who's outside. I heard a horse."

"It's Grandma!"

Morene opens the door and wraps one arm around her grandma. Syble does the same on the other side. Ollie sits on the edge of the bed.

"Ollie, what's wrong? Are you sick?"

"I've been feeling bad for a while now. Every day I get a little weaker. The girls have been taking care of me instead of the other way around. It's all I can do to milk the cow and cook a little food." Ollie bites her lip. Tears roll down her cheeks. "Mama, what am I gonna do? What's wrong with me?"

The older woman takes Ollie's hand in her own and looks at it carefully. "When was the last time you ate any meat, and green vegetables?"

"I don't have any meat, and it's winter. The greens died with that hard freeze."

"What about milk?"

"I give that to the girls. Once in a while, I drink buttermilk."

"Ollie, I think you have pellagra. Dr. Hart said a lot of people are having it."

"No. That's what homeless people get. I have food."

"Yes, but not the right kind. The doctor said people have to eat meat, greens, and dairy products to get the right kind of vitamins."

"I'm too tired to talk about it now. Will you watch the girls while I rest a bit?" Before Mama can answer, Ollie lies over on the bed and is instantly asleep.

When Ollie wakes and walks into the kitchen, Morene and Syble are eating. Ollie blinks. "I didn't mean to go to sleep. I only wanted to rest a few minutes."

"Sit down at the table. I brought eggs, butter and a piece of pork shoulder. The girls helped me fix lunch, and we have a plate ready for you."

Ollie slides into the chair Mama pulls out for her. "Oh, Mama. That's too much food for me. Cut this meat in half and save it for the girls. I don't want them to get sick. The milk, too.

I don't like it, and the girls need it."

"That's why you're sick. Eat that meat, and drink the milk. Hold your nose if you have to, but drink it."

Ollie smiles a weak smile. "All right, but I can't eat those greens. I've been having trouble with my stomach."

"That is another symptom of pellagra. Eat the greens."

Ollie props herself up on one elbow and eats slowly.

"This evening, when I get home, I'm going to call Dr. Hart and ask him if there is something he can give you to take for this."

"Don't get it if it costs very much. I should be fine in a few days. Roy left me some money, but I'm saving it to buy a butchering hog."

"Yes, you need one. I'll send Robert out looking." Mama stands watching as Ollie picks at her food. "I want you and the girls to come home with me and stay until you get well."

"No. I can't leave. Those thieves would kill the calf and the cow. The girls can go spend the night, but I have to stay here."

"I hate to leave you here when you're feeling so bad. I'll tend to the animals before I go, bring in vegetables from the cellar, and wood for the fireplace and cookstove, but I wish you would come with me."

"I can't leave; they'd steal everything we have."

"I wish the sheriff would catch them in the act."

"So do I, but that's unlikely. It's a greater possibility that someone will shoot them." Ollie pushes her plate aside and lies over on her right arm. "Sometimes I think I'd like to be the one to do that."

Mama shakes her head. "Ollie, I can hardly stand to leave you here alone."

"I'll be fine, and the girls will enjoy some time away from me."

Early the next morning, Mama returns to take care of the animals. She brings Ollie a ham-and-egg biscuit from home and a bottle of medicine from the doctor. "Dr. Hart said take one of these pills three times a day with your meals. Also, he said people that can't get medicine or proper food often die with pellagra. Others end up in jail or the insane asylum. The disease works on your nerves."

"Mama, I don't think I have pellagra. I have plenty of food to eat."

"Not the right kind." Mama slaps her hand on the table. "You'd better listen to me. You have those little girls to take care of. They need a loving mother, not someone half crazy because she doesn't get enough vitamins and protein."

Ollie looks down and picks at one of the scaly sores on her arm. "Was that medicine expensive?"

"No. No charge at all. He gave me this big bottle. Take these like you're supposed to, and maybe you'll be well by the time Roy comes home."

Ollie straightens to look out the window at Syble and Morene playing in the yard. "Did Papa know of anyone who has hogs for sale?"

"He mentioned someone over in Happy Valley. He'll check on it today."

Late Saturday afternoon, Papa and Mama drive into the yard. Morene and Syble hurriedly pull on jackets and rush to greet them.

"Grandpa, what's in that big box?"

"Pork. It's hams and bacon for frying and eating."

Morene licks her lips. "I like fried pork."

Ollie grabs a well-worn jacket from a nail on the wall and hurries out the door. In her haste, she trips and falls on one knee.

Within seconds, Papa is off the wagon seat and at her side. "How bad is it?"

Ollie, now in a sitting position, is holding her knee with both hands while trying to wipe tears on her sleeve. "It's all right. I wasn't watching where I was going. I'm all right, truly I am."

"Then stop crying, girl. Let me help you. We brought you a hog. It's time for gettin' happy." He helps her to her feet and looks at the knee. "Bend it."

Ollie bends her knee several times and takes a step. "It's fine." She smiles, and wipes at the tears. "Tell me about the hog."

"I brought it home yesterday. This morning, with the help of Earl and Eldridge, we butchered and rubbed parts of it with sugar-cure. Your mama canned the tenderloin, sausage, and part of the liver for you. We'll bring it tomorrow when the jars are cool. We ate fresh liver with onions and gravy for lunch, but she saved a bowl of it for you."

Ollie sniffs, wiping her eyes again. "Thank you for doing all that."

Papa clears his throat. "Remember what I told you when you were a kid? 'Dry those tears or go to the house.'"

Ollie laughs.

Morene and Syble have been standing back with wide, sad eyes. Now, they begin to laugh and repeat, "Dry those tears."

Papa leaves in the wagon taking the box of meat to the corncrib to finish curing.

Mama lifts the tail of Ollie dress and gently rubs the bruised knee. "Can you walk over and open the door so I can carry that pan inside?"

Ollie limps, and grimaces as she steps onto the doorstep.

"Go wrap a cold, wet towel around it. I don't think you cracked any bones." Mama sets a pan on the table before going to call the girls. "Morene, Syble, it's getting late and cold. You have to come inside now."

Mama puts a stick of wood in the fireplace, and some split wood in the cook stove's firebox. When Papa comes in from the barn, she has a scalded pail ready for him to milk the cow.

"I don't expect the girls will want much liver, but you need it, Ollie. They can have candied sweet potatoes, green beans, biscuits, and gravy. It's all ready to eat, but I'll put it in the warming oven until your papa gets back."

"Mama, I would have helped with the hog, if I'd known."

"You didn't need to help." Mama lays a hand on Ollie's shoulder. "You look a little better today, but you are still very sick. It has never been your nature to cry. Fight—yes. Cry— no. The lack of niacin in your body has messed up your nerves. Make sure you take that medicine like the doctor ordered, drink milk, and eat plenty of meat with your vegetables."

Ollie continues to get better, but it takes months before she regains her normal energy. A few days before Christmas, a package comes in the mail. On the outside, Roy has marked, "Do Not Open until Christmas Eve."

By the time they open it, the package is shabby from handling by little hands. Inside are three boxes marked with names. The girls' packages read, "Do not open until Christmas morning." The note on Ollie's box instructs her to wait until the girls are asleep on Christmas Eve.

Certain that the children are sleeping; she opens her package. Two boxes fall out. One is marked "Ollie, open in the morning." The other is marked "Open now." She rips at the paper. Inside, she finds warm socks, peppermint sticks, chocolate drops, hair ribbons, and a note:

Dear Ollie,

Hang up one sock from each little pair; stick the other inside along with candy and the ribbons.

Love,

Roy

Ollie cannot get the socks to hang over the fireplace: She lays them across the foot of the girls' bed. On the hearth, she places two apples and two oranges that she asked Papa to buy as Santa presents. She sits in her rocker to finish the hem on one of the red print dresses that she is making them for Christmas.

Moving a little closer to the lamp, she adjusts a dress over her lap, and sighs. *It's a good thing I allowed for growing room when I cut these. I've been trying to sew them since October.*

Ollie looks down at her hands. The sores are healing, and she is beginning to feel better since taking the medicine. She sighs again and looks at her bed. It's so inviting.

She shakes her head to help push away the need to crawl under the quilts. *I have to finish this. Tomorrow is Christmas.* Blinking away sleep, she sticks the threaded needle into the material.

Chapter 23
Big Cat

On the first clear day in January, Ollie dresses the girls in warm clothes and goes to the store. Money left after paying Papa for the hog, will stock her cabinet before the weather turns colder accompanied by snow and ice.

The girls laugh and talk with people inside the store. One old man peels and halves an apple, and gives it to the girls. He holds Syble on his knee while she eats. Morene politely tells him she is too big to sit on his knee, and goes to sit on a bench near the stove.

Ollie places a box of shotgun shells on the counter beside flour, sugar, coffee, cocoa, vanilla, and cinnamon. Syble slides to the floor and goes to sit beside her sister. The old man stands and leans against the counter. Lifting the box of shells, he says, "Do you think you'll need these to keep thieves away from all those good things you're planning to bake?"

Ollie laughs. "I never know when I might have to shoot a varmint."

He sets the shells down. "I've heard that you wear a pistol on your hip while Roy's gone. Is that true?

She lifts the tail of her jacket, exposing the gun. "It is."

"Do you know how to use it?"

She frowns. "I wouldn't bother lugging it around if I didn't." Ollie goes to get a box of salt.

"Well, you might think about toting a bigger gun for a few

days. This morning, someone spotted a panther near the road to your place."

She catches her breath, but does not look in his direction. Some men think it's funny to frighten a woman. "I'll keep an eye out."

"I'm not joshing. Don't let these little ones get far from the house. There's not much wild game around anymore. Wolves and big cats are coming onto farms for calves and chickens. A panther could easily drag off a child that size."

Ollie turns to face him. "Thanks for telling me. I'll watch them even closer."

After loading the supplies, she helps the girls into the wagon, and hurries home. When Morene and Syble fall asleep for naps, Ollie goes to the barn. With web wire, she builds a fence across the middle of the stall.

In late afternoon, she milks the cow, lets the calf suck, and fastens the calf behind the web wire in the same stall with its mother. "Jersey, I begged Roy to cut off your horns, but now I'm glad he didn't. You may have to use them to defend yourself and your baby."

Ollie takes the milk to the house, strains it into a gallon jar, and sets it in a box that Roy built near the well. The enclosure does not have a hinged lid. It is covered with heavy oak boards nailed together with short pieces underneath that prevent it from slipping. Hooks on the ends can latch it down, but they fit tight and are hard to open and close. Ollie only uses them during times of high wind. In summer, the box holds garden tools, a paddle for stirring the washpot, and makes an excellent spot to sit and watch the girls play. When the weather is cold, it is a good place to keep the milk cool, close to the warm kitchen.

Many mornings milk has to thaw before pouring; even the yellow cream, at the top of the jar, is laced with ice crystals. During a hard freeze, Ollie puts the milk inside the house to prevent it from freezing and breaking the jar. Sometimes, Ollie mixes sugar and vanilla with cream and lets it freeze in a pie tin for the girls to scrape out with spoons while sitting in front of the fireplace, but tonight the weather is not cold enough for a solid freeze.

"Morene, I'll put more wood on the fire when I get in from the barn. I don't want you and Syble getting cold, so put on your sweaters. Don't go outside for any reason. That man at the store said a giant cat was on our road this morning."

Morene's forehead wrinkles. "A giant cat!"

"Yes. Big enough to bite your arm off. You girls can't go outside without me until it has time to leave."

Syble, sitting on the braided rug, begins to rub her arm, but does not say anything.

Morene runs to Ollie's side and looks up at her face. "Where will it go?"

"Another county, maybe."

"What's a county?"

"A long way off. I'll explain when I get inside. I've got to bring our meat from the barn so the cat can't eat it tonight." Ollie rushes out the door and down the path.

From the corncrib she grabs several ears of corn, tosses them into the trough, and starts pulling away shucks. The hard ears hitting rough boards is like the clanging of a dinner bell to the horses. They race across the pasture and under the tin roof. The dry grain cracks and pops as they crunch with big yellow teeth.

Ollie climbs the ladder to the barn loft, unwinds the wire

that holds one ham and takes it to the house. She goes back three times for the second ham, a shoulder, and a slab of bacon.

She wants to get the partially used shoulder and side of bacon, but her legs are weak and the sun is starting to set. Dumping the bacon into the curing box, still in the loft from when Papa hung the meat, she secures the latch with wire and pushes the box into a corner.

She stuffs the shoulder into a feed sack, and lowers it with a rope like the other pieces. When she gets to the kitchen door, she is perspiring inside her jacket, and sits on the step to rest and cool before going into the warm house.

The wind spins leaves across the yard and whistles through the trees. The horses prance around the lot with noses in the air and tails flailing as if they were swishing at horseflies. It is January—there have been no flies since October. They sense danger.

Most evenings, they walk or graze slowly to the creek for a drink after eating. Tonight, they keep sniffing at the dry watering trough. Ollie does not draw water to fill it unless an animal is penned in the lot. The corn has made them thirsty, but for some reason they do not want to go to the creek.

Ollie flexes her tired back before standing. A shrill scream echoes across the valley. The mares run from the lot and race across the pasture to the top of the hill, but do not go into the woods.

Morene opens the door. "Mama, what was that noise?"

"It was that big cat I told you about." She heaves the sack of meat inside, closes and locks the door. "Sit on the rug while I get some firewood from the front porch. Once I get the wood, we can't open the doors anymore until morning."

Syble whines, "I'm scared."

Morene hugs her. "Don't worry. Mama will shoot if he tries to come in here."

Syble, still clinging to Morene, whines. "Will you shoot it, Mama?"

"It can't get in the house, but I'd shoot if it tried." Ollie stacks extra wood in the wood box and puts an armload into the fireplace. "Girls, we're gonna eat cold cornbread and milk for supper. I'm too tired to cook."

Ollie adds wood to the fireplace several times during the night and looks out windows for movement in the yard. Sleep does not come easy. Early in the morning, a scratching noise wakes her.

Easing out of bed, she takes the loaded shotgun and tiptoes to the kitchen. Through the window, she watches a big black cat scoot the lid off the box holding the milk. He licks at the jug, gnaws at the top, tries to lift the jar out of the box with his teeth, and drops it. Then his entire head is inside the box. *He's probably lapping up milk from the broken jar.*

Ollie considers opening the door to shoot while the panther is busy getting the milk, but each time she touches the lock she has visions of falling, like when the stick rolled under her foot as she aimed at that big hog. As she ponders—the cat disappears around the house. She moves to the kitchen window in time to see it go into the barn.

Ollie raises the window a couple of inches. She can hear the calf bawling and the cow snorting and kicking. "I'm sorry, Jersey, you'll have to save your baby this time."

Listening for several minutes is more than Ollie can stand. She steps outside, aims her gun at a board underneath the overhanging tin roof of the barn. A loud noise, like something landing hard, thunders across the yard. She pulls the trigger. Buckshot slams into the barn seconds before the panther rushes outside and across the field.

The calf is still bawling, but the cow moos soft and low, trying to calm and comfort the baby. Morene and Syble are screaming, "Mama! Mama!"

Ollie rubs their backs and sings a lullaby until they sleep.

In the morning, before going to milk, Ollie cooks breakfast and wakes the girls to eat. "You'll have to stay in the house today. That cat came around last night, broke the milk jug and drank the milk, went to the barn, and scared the cow and calf."

Morene and Syble stand with wide frightened eyes. Morene asks, "Did it hurt the calf and mama cow?"

"I don't think so, because the cow's been bawling like she does when she wants to be milked. She'd be bawling all the time if she or her baby were hurt."

Syble shakes her head. "Poor baby calf. I bet it's scared."

"Girls, that cat might return. I don't think it will, but I'm not sure. So you can't go out for any reason."

"Not even to go to the outhouse?"

"That's right, Morene. You'll have to use the chamber pot, like at night."

Syble takes hold of Ollie's hand. "What if the cat tries to bite you?"

"I'm taking both guns. Don't worry. I'll be fine." Ollie motions toward the rug. "Go play with your dolls until I come back."

Ollie hooks the milk pail over her arm, and has the shotgun cocked and ready to fire when she steps into the barn. The cow moos a soft greeting, telling Ollie that no strangers are inside the barn.

The calf stretches her neck and bawls a loud rattling complaint, but not because she is hungry. One of the cow's milk teats hangs wrinkled and flabby. The other three stand outstretched from her bag, tight and shining.

"Well, Little Daisy, I see you've already reached through the fence and gulped your breakfast."

The meat-curing box is in the floor at the base of the ladder. *That must have been the loud noise before I shot.* The wood has deep claw marks on the top and sides. Corners and edges have teeth marks. A crack runs down one side. "If that cat hadn't got scared, he would have enjoyed a meal of bacon."

Ollie climbs into the loft. A new hole, rimmed with fresh splinters, penetrates a board on the side next to the house. She smiles. "It's close to the roof, so it shouldn't let in any rain— simply another air hole."

She milks the cow and turns her out to pasture. Jersey heads straight for the creek. If the cat were nearby, a cow would not go there.

Ollie gets a few ears of corn and whistles for the mares. They race from the woods. She pets their necks before letting the calf out into her pen.

Now, I have to get up to the house and figure out a place to put that pork. Ollie never builds a big fire in the fireplace before going to milk, so the living room is cool. She pushes the feed sacks holding the meat underneath her bed.

"Girls, we'll work and play in the kitchen today. Our meat is cured and smoked, but I don't want it to get too warm. We won't keep a fire in the living room."

Morene asks, "Can we cook while we're in here?"

The girls are eager to make a sweet dessert with some of the things Ollie bought at the store yesterday. They decide on cinnamon cake. "That is your Uncle Eldridge's favorite. He may catch the scent and come down to help us eat it."

Morene giggles, "Can we open the window so the smell can get out and go up the hill to Grandma's?"

"No. I was only teasing. That's too far away, but maybe they'll come visit us."

The mailman's buggy horse has a little bell on its harness. Morene and Syble hear it jingling. "Can we go meet the mailman, Mama? We'll watch for the big cat. Please."

"All right, but Morene, hold your sister's hand. Don't let her get too close to the wheel."

Through the window, Ollie watches the girls looking all around, even up in the trees, for the cat. They giggle and jump when the mailman gets near. Excited voices tell him about the big cat drinking the milk and trying to eat the calf.

He appears to enjoy the conversation as much as the girls. He always holds the mail until he is ready to go before handing it to them. Sometimes, he gives them an apple or a peppermint stick to share.

Ollie is about ready to go out and get the letter he is holding before he hands it to Morene along with a stick of candy.

The girls come running in the front door. "Mama, the mailman said it's a letter from Daddy! Open it! Open it!" They jump up and down. "Maybe he can come home!" They scramble to sit on the rug and divide the candy while Ollie opens the letter.

Dear Ollie and girls,

I've never spent such a lonesome Christmas. We are too far from town to walk, but the few of us left on this crew piled in a truck on Christmas Eve and went into Knoxville. I walked around looking in store windows. When I got cold, I went into a church where they were having a Christmas program. Seeing the kids made me even more lonesome, but the women served good coffee and cookies.

The church maintains a room that was almost full of things they sell like a second-hand store or donate to homeless people. I asked the preacher if they might have some warm gloves and long-underwear. He said the store wasn't open, but he dug around and found some in my size. He sold them both for a quarter. That made the trip worthwhile. The underwear looks like new and feels good-and-warm under my overalls when I'm working outside. The gloves are fur-lined leather, a little fancy for working, but they're warm.

The last week has been colder, with the sky spitting snow. Some of the workers didn't come back after the holiday. I think the big bosses got worried the rest of us would leave because of the bad weather. This week they've been giving us hot soup and coffee three times a day.

I'll try to be home for Easter.

Love,
Roy

"Mama, when is Easter?" Morene asks.

"About three months away. It's almost Easter when the grass turns green and flowers start blooming."

She runs to look out the window. "I don't see any flowers."

"We'll have snow first. It's winter now, but Daddy will come home in the spring."

"When Easter flowers bloom?"

"Yes. When Easter flowers bloom."

Chapter 24
Snow

Ollie walks toward the house. The sun is setting and the clouds are uncommonly beautiful. She opens the kitchen door and calls, "Girls, come look at the pretty striped sky. The clouds feather out like a giant bird's wing."

They run to the door and step outside. "O-o-oh, it's pretty."

"The sunset makes the clouds pink, but when they are layered like that it means winds are blowing high in the sky. If the clouds drop close to the ground, and cold wind blows over them, we could get snow."

"Tonight?" Morene asks.

"Maybe, but I hope not. It's hard for animals to find anything to eat in the snow, and we don't have much hay in the barn." She gives them each a gentle push. "Get back inside. We're letting in a lot of cold air."

Ollie fills the wood boxes, stacks extra sticks on the hearth, and draws water to fill all the big jars and buckets in the house, just in case it snows. It is much easier to hang onto a well rope and bring in wood when the rope, steps, and porches are dry.

"Girls, our supper will be a little late, but you ate hot rolls and butter this afternoon. Are you too hungry to wait for cornbread muffins to go with our soup?"

"No. We like muffins." Morene answers for them both. "Can we make cookies while the oven is hot?" They stare at her with pleading eyes.

"My goodness, we'll all be fat by the time your daddy comes home." She pauses to look at the girls. "I planned on us having the rest of those buttered rolls with apple butter for our dessert." Ollie cannot bear the disappointed looks.

"Those rolls will still be good tomorrow. So, why not? We have the stuff to make cookies." They laugh and hug each other.

While the sweet scent of muffins and cookies fill the house, Ollie looks around the kitchen. "Girls, anyone would think we're expecting a crowd for supper. Today I made a big pot of pinto beans, and a pot of vegetable soup. We have enough food to last for three or four days if we keep it hot, so it doesn't sour. I was hoping Papa and Mama would come eat with us, but they didn't. Maybe they'll come tomorrow. With what we have fixed, some fried potatoes, and a pie, we can have a feast."

The girls are peeking into the oven and do not hear her.

Instead of taking the wood she has stored in the box, Ollie goes onto the porch to choose a big log that will burn through the night. Wind tugs at the door and whips her dress tail. Clouds hanging thick and low scatter a few snowflakes into the lamplight coming through the window.

The log in the fireplace is still fluttering with gentle orange flames when Ollie wakes the next morning. Windowpanes reveal a Christmas card image of winter. Snow covers the yard, laying high against the north side of every bush and tree, and giant flakes are still falling from low-hanging clouds.

Ollie pokes at the burning log and adds small sticks to increase blazes and warm the room before the girls get up. The cookstove's firebox still has coals that quickly ignite kindling and sticks of wood. Within a short time, breakfast is on the table, and yesterday's soup and beans are boiling to keep them from spoiling.

Ollie cautions the girls to stay inside while she goes to milk and tend the animals. "Morene, I've let the fire burn down. I don't think it will pop, but if a coal bounces out, take that little shovel and lift it back onto the rock hearth."

Morene nods. "I'll watch for one."

The calf bawls, as if promped by Ollie's arrival to the barn. This is a sturdy one. She will be old enough to wean by the time spring grass starts coming up, and will bring a good price if they have to sell her.

In addition to hay, Ollie gives her a little of the cow's ground feed. "Daisy, you can have more milk tonight, but this morning I'm keeping most of it for my girls. I plan to make snow ice-cream with last night's milk."

Ollie is glad that she filled the watering tub the night before. She turns out the cow, gives the calf extra hay and leaves her in the stall. "I know you'll make a mess in here, but I hate to put you out in this weather."

Careful not to tilt the bucket, Ollie hurries to the house. After straining the milk and swapping it with the jar in the box beside the well, she takes a dishpan and goes outside to gather snow.

Once inside, she lets each girl make a snowball while she puts sticks of damp hickory over the coals in the firebox. "Girls, do you want to smoke your snowball before you eat it."

"Smoke it? Their faces show confusion.

"Yes, I'll open the firebox door enough to let out a little smoke. If you hold your snowball in the smoke, it will taste like hickory."

They giggle and run to the stove.

"Careful. One at a time. Not too close, Syble. You don't want to burn your hand."

Making lots of slurping noises, they suck the liquid from the snowballs while Ollie rakes the heavy cream from the top of the milk jar into the mound left in the pan. She adds sugar and vanilla flavoring. "If you'll let me toss those snowballs outside, you can stir the ice cream."

"All right." They hand her the dripping balls in exchange for spoons.

She sets the pan in the floor and sits watching them stir, giggle, and taste the mixture. Outside, the dark sky seems to have no limit to the blitz of white flakes coming down. Ollie's footprints along the path are completely covered and the barn is barely visible.

Yesterday, she brought in potatoes, turnips, and onions from the new cellar she and Roy dug. She looks at the basket that holds them in the corner. *Today, with all this snow, it would take a lot of hard digging just to get the cellar door open.*

"Girls, eat a little more, then I'll pour the rest in a pie tin and set it out to keep frozen. In here, it's melting fast."

In late afternoon when Ollie goes to milk, snow is still coming down hard and fast. It almost covers the top of her galoshes when she steps into the yard. Before letting the cow inside, she gives corn to the mares, draws water for the calf, shovels manure from the stall, puts hay in the manger, and fastens the calf behind the web wire gate.

The hungry cow rushes to lick ground feed from the trough and is munching hay before Ollie finishes milking.

"Jersey, couldn't you find anything to eat with all that snow on the ground? I'll give you extra feed before I leave, and I'm gonna let you stay in here tonight—this is a bad storm. I'll fasten Daisy behind the wire with the water tub, but you'll still have to go to the creek when you get thirsty."

Ollie plods up the hill with the milk pail, opens the kitchen door and scoots the milk inside. "Morene, bring me that empty water bucket. I want to fill it before I come inside." With extra water pushed inside next to the milk, she scrapes snow from the step with a garden hoe, and stomps clumps from her rubber overshoes before going inside to pull them off.

The wood boxes need refilled before dark, after that chore, she builds up fires in the fireplace and cookstove, and puts soup and beans on to boil again. "I'm glad we don't have weather like this all the time, like winters in the north."

"Morene, you and Syble can eat while I take care of the milk. I'm pouring soup into your bowls. Come on to the table while it's warm. I'll eat later."

Ollie pulls on the overshoes and goes to exchange a jug of fresh warm milk for a cold one left in the box. Returning with the towel-wrapped jar and open pan of ice cream, she steps onto the rock doorstep.

Her foot slips, ice cream flies into the yard, Ollie and the milk fall into the snow. When she tries to stand, a terrible pain runs through her back. The milk jug lies beside her, unharmed.

She rolls over and crawls to the step. "Morene, open the door."

Both girls rush out, trying to help, but they are not strong enough. "Girls, go inside. You'll hurt me more if you pull on me. Hold the door open and I'll crawl into the kitchen."

Morene picks up the milk, sets it inside the door, and follows Syble into the kitchen.

Ollie crawls through the doorway and lies flat on the floor. The girls cry, and pat her face and arms.

"Syble, Morene, both of you hush. I'll be fine. I just need to lay here and rest for a little while. Did you finish your supper?"

They nod. "Uh-huh."

"Then you can be big girls and wash your dishes. Cold water is fine."

While the girls are distracted with the dishes, Ollie scoots into the living room and onto the braided rag-rug. Soon they come rushing to her side. "Mama, what can we do now?" Morene asks.

"Lock the doors and put the milk underneath the kitchen window." Morene does not hesitate to follow instructions.

"Morene, do you remember us talking about how to turn off the stove damper?"

"It's that little thing that sticks out from the pipe. You said it's off when you turn it sideways."

"Good, you remembered. Now, I want you to go turn it off. You'll have to stand in a chair to reach it. My gloves are on the windowsill. Put them on. Be careful and don't fall or touch the stove. Syble, you sit here by me while she does that."

Ollie listens as the damper scrapes against the stovepipe. "What now, Mama?"

"I want you to climb on a chair and get a little bottle from the cabinet where I keep medicine. It has yellow and brown paper on the front. The biggest word on it starts with an 'A.' Remember? It's the first letter of your ABC's."

Morene returns with the aspirin bottle. "Is this the right one?"

"Yes, it is. You did good. Now will you bring me a little

water in the dipper?"

Ollie takes two of the aspirins with a sip of water. "Do you remember how to turn down the kitchen lamp and blow it out?"

"I turn the little wheel-like knob toward my belly, blow down the top of the globe, and don't breathe until my nose is turned away."

"That's right, but I want you girls to put your gowns on and be ready for bed when the lamp goes out."

Morene blows out the lamp. The room is dark except for the flames dancing over the split wood in the fireplace. "Mama, can you get in your bed now?"

Ollie hears a sob catch in Morene's throat.

"I think so. I probably pulled a muscle when I fell, and needed to let it relax and rest awhile. I'll crawl over to the bed, but you'll have to help me get out of these galoshes and my jacket."

Not wanting to frighten the girls, Ollie grits her teeth against the pain and crawls to the bed. She pulls herself up and sits while Morene unbuckles and pulls at the heavy overshoes. Each tug is like a hot knife stabbing against nerves and muscles.

Ollie sits on the edge of the bed with her arms straight while the girls slide the jacket off her shoulders and down her back. She draws in a quick breath; her heart beats fast. She hurts too much to stand, but they cannot slide the jacket off while she sits on the bed. Her arms are stuck.

She tries bending forward—the pain is too great. She pulls up on one arm—that is worse. Tears fill her eyes. She hopes the girls cannot see them in the flickering firelight.

"Morene, get in front of me and keep me from falling on my face." Ollie slides onto one knee. Syble pulls the sleeves off, one at a time.

Gritting her teeth again, she pulls herself upon the bed. Morene tucks the quilts around her mama and Syble, before going around the room pulling curtains closed as she has watched Ollie do so many nights. "Do you want me to put more wood on the fire so it won't burn out in the night?"

Ollie wants to say no, but she does not want a five-year-old trying to start a new fire in the morning. "Honey, do you think you're strong enough to toss one of the sticks behind that burning log?"

"I'm strong enough."

Ollie silently prays as she watches her lift a big stick, move into the right position, and toss it into the fireplace. "Now, do the same with a small stick?"

She chooses one about half the size of the first, and lobs it in. Morene smiles. "I can do it."

"Perfect. Now go wash your hands, and jump into bed. I certainly have two good helpers."

Ollie holds her breath against the pain and rolls over to lie flat, praying repeatedly that in the morning she will be able to take care of her girls.

The room is bright when Ollie wakes. She starts to roll out of bed, but feels the muscle tension. Slowly, she turns over and sits up.

Morene's wide serious eyes are watching. "Does your back still hurt?"

"Not as bad as last night." Ollie forces a smile. "You may need to take care of me for a few days, until it heals."

"I can do a lot of things, but I don't know how to cook and I can't milk the cow."

"Don't worry about that. We still have soup, beans, rolls, and corn muffins. We can eat those until they're gone. After that, if we need to, we'll get spoons and eat right out of the canning jars."

"But what about milking the cow?"

"I left the gate open so Jersey can come in and leave from the stall. The calf is behind a flimsy wire gate. I would't be surprised if she is not already out with her mama. We won't get any milk, but maybe the cow won't go dry."

Morene jumps up, goes to the fireplace, stokes the fire with the poker, and tosses some small sticks in close to the flames. "Mama, can I put kindling in the cookstove?"

"Come over here and let me lean on you. Maybe I can go in there with you."

With Morene's help, Ollie makes it to the kitchen. "Pull my rocker in here. I'm afraid I can't get up from a straight chair." She eases into the rocker and leans back. "Now you can stir up the coals and add kindling, but first pull back the curtains. I want to see how much snow we've got."

"Look, Mama. I never saw so much snow."

"I hope it didn't do this in Tennessee. Your daddy has to work outside."

"I wish Daddy was home."

"So do I." Ollie leans her head against the chair back. "Morene, you'll have to help me and Syble for a few days until I get better and this snow melts away. We're alone out here. Papa won't take the buggy or wagon out in snow this deep."

"I'll help."

"This snow may last for days, and we only have two buckets of water in here. We'll have to reuse the same dishes. Today, when we get thirsty, we'll need to drink that milk; it'll start to sour by tomorrow." She looks at Morene, standing next to her waiting for more instructions. Ollie smiles. "We'll make it fine, won't we?"

"We can save water by not washing our hands so much. We won't be outside to get them dirty." She looks toward the stove. "Can I start the fire now?"

All day, the sun shines bright with melting snow running off the roof like rain. Icicles, some of them two feet long, form where water drips from the roof. Bright red cardinals, a blue jay, and a dozen or more tiny black-and-gray snowbirds flutter over the yard and beneath the trees. The birds fascinate Syble. She names some of the more colorful ones and gives reports throughout the day on what they are doing.

Morene keeps wood burning in the fireplace and the cookstove. For breakfast, they eat crusty buttered rolls that she warms in the oven. They top them with apple butter—right out of the canning jar.

At lunch and supper, they eat warmed beans and soup that Morene keeps stirred throughout the day. The cookies are gone by mid-afternoon and the milk jug is half-empty.

Ollie's heart flutters each time her daughter climbs up in a chair to stir something on the stove or take a hot pan from the oven. Morene always wears the leather gloves to handle something hot, proceeds slow and careful, and seems to be enjoying her new rights. Syble is young enough that she accepts her sister's authority without resentment.

Ollie takes aspirins every three hours, keeps the rocker moving as much as she can without causing pain, and silently prays. When the cow and calf bawls or the horses nicker, she instinctively draws in a worried breath. Each deep breath causes a spasm in her back.

Late in the day, while the girls are watching birds from the kitchen window, Morene gasps, "Mama, the calf's in the lot with Jersey. It got out of the stall."

"I'm glad it did. Jersey will take care of it. Daisy's big enough now that she won't die from drinking too much milk."

"But how did she get out?"

"The horses probably pushed over the fence while trying to eat her hay. I knew that, after they ate their own and what I put out for the cow, they'd be stretching necks to get any left in the calf stall. They probably drank the water too, but melted snow is in the watering trough, and the cow will go to the creek if she gets thirsty enough."

"Mama, I can go to the barn and drag some hay into the manger."

"No, honey. You have enough work taking care of Syble and me. The animals will be fine now that the snow is melting."

Chapter 25
Easter Flowers and Baby Chicks

Morene and Syble run to the clothesline where Ollie is hanging dishtowels. "Mama, Daddy's coming home."

Ollie drapes a cloth over the line and takes a clothespin from her mouth. "What?"

"You said when flowers bloom. Look! Over there. Lots of them." Morene points to a patch of yellow.

"Honey, those are not Easter flowers. Those are dandelions. They're weeds. They usually bloom long before Easter."

"Oh." She turns her face down. "What do Easter flowers look like?"

"They're yellow, a little darker than dandelions. Some people call them buttercups, because the flower looks like a bell-shaped cup on a ruffled saucer. Instead of leaves, they have blades, like onions. Last year, only one bunch bloomed. It was on the south side of the porch, near the rosebush. Look and see if you can find some blades."

Morene yells, "We found some, but they're barely out of the ground."

Ollie hears her tell Syble, "We'll look at them every day to see when the blooms pop out. Then Daddy will come home." They jump up and run laughing with jackets spread out like wings.

Wind pops the laundry. Robins scurry across the yard,

searching for straw to build nests. Ollie watches the birds for a moment. *A farm is not complete without chickens. In May, Morene will turn six, and I still don't have a chicken house and pen.*

A roll of rusty web wire and some cedar posts have been leaning against the backside of the barn for a long time. The posts will work, and the wire will keep out dogs and coyotes. Raccoons and opossums can climb over any fence.

While the girls play, she walks down to take a look at the wire. Roy left a hammer and saw hanging in the barn, and a few odd-size pieces of lumber in the loft. *I won't need a big chicken house, but first I need a pen.*

The posts holding up the barn are spaced six feet apart. She measures six feet out from each of the first three posts, digs deep holes with the post hole-diggers, sets the poles and tamps them in with rocks. To avoid using more posts, she bends one end of the wire and nails it to the barn with long staples that reach through the boards and into the strong post on the other side.

She steps away to look. *I hate to use more posts, but if I don't brace those at the corners, they'll fold in from the pressure of wire pulling on them.* She positions braces, then stretches and staples wire to the first, second and third posts.

Last fall, Ollie and the girls found a heavy four-by-four post floating at the edge of the creek. It is perfect for hanging a gate. Before milking time, a narrow wood gate is swinging from the post to the barn; the other side is braced and has the wire attached.

The next day, after morning chores are finished, Ollie sees the neighbors go down the road. As soon as they are out of sight, she hitches the team to the wagon. *While those thieves are gone is a perfect time to visit Mama.*

The girls can hardly stand still while she ties clean sunbonnets to keep the stiff breeze away from sensitive ears. "Climb into the wagon. It's been a while since we've seen your grandma." Even the mares seem excited about going for a drive. They hold their heads as high as parade horses and walk at a brisk pace.

Ollie hears Morene whisper to Syble, "Maybe Grandma will have cake, but don't ask, or Mama will get mad."

Before Ollie can tie the horses, the girls are on the porch, hugging their grandma. Ollie walks up in time to hear her tell them, "I had a feeling you might come today. I made a chocolate cake, and put yeast rolls out to rise."

Ollie interrupts, "Mama, before we go inside I want to ask if you think Papa would mind if I take a couple of those old apple boxes he keeps stored in the barn loft?"

"We took several out and tossed them on a brush pile, but he hasn't burned it yet. What do you want them for?"

"I've built a chicken pen and was hoping to use the boxes for nests."

"You can nail them together. They'll be plenty good for that. Let's walk down and look. The girls can play with the kittens while we gather what you need."

Morene and Syble race ahead. The cows are grazing in the pasture and the mama cat should be out hunting at this time of day. The girls ease into the barn. Ollie's hears them talking to the kittens. She and Mama pause to listen. Ollie peeps at them through a knothole.

Syble rubs a kitten. "Morene, do you think Grandma would give me this one?"

"She might, but Mama won't let you have it. Sometimes, cats eat baby chickens. We better not ask for a cat until our chickens get big."

"We don't have chickens yet, and they don't eat the ones in Grandma's yard."

"We're gonna get some. That's why Mama built a pen, and I heard Grandma tell Mama that one of her cats killed a baby chick."

"Did she whip the cat?"

"Papa took it way off by the creek." Morene waves an arm as high as she can reach, and quickly jerks it down. "And he threw it in the woods. A wolf or panther probably ate it, 'cause it didn't come back."

"Oh, that kitty must have been so afraid."

Morene shrugs and leans closer to Syble's face. "What about the poor baby chick that the cat ate? Mama said people can't keep mean animals. Once, Daddy's mule chased Mama. He shot that mean mule before it could run and hurt somebody else."

Syble frowns and turns her head sideways to look at her sister. "Why did God make mean animals?"

Morene gently strokes the kitten she holds. "God only makes good things. Mean animals belong to the devil."

Remembering the incident with the mule, Ollie flinches, swallows and turns her face away from Mama. Quickly, they walk on to the brush pile where Papa has thrown the broken crates. "Mama, these will make good nests, and I can use those old pieces of lumber to extend the barn roof over the pen. Tin would be better, but when I cut off the rotten ends, these will shield the roost from a lot of rain."

"There's some old tin in the barn. Your papa has plans to dump it in that big ditch, but if you can use it, he won't have to haul it away."

"Good. Do you think Papa will mind if I borrow his tin snips to cut it to the right size?"

"You know he won't. He'll come down to help, if he has time."

"I'm excited about working on the pen. I think I have everything I need, except about twenty-five feet of chicken wire." She looks at Mama and grins. "That is if you'll still give me a setting hen and some fertile eggs."

"I have two hens trying to set. You can take your pick." She pauses, cups a hand behind her right ear, and turns it toward the barn.

Syble comes screaming toward them. "The kitten scratched me."

Morene yells, "She picked it up by its tail and hurt it."

Ollie stoops to look at the scratch. "We'll go to the house and wash it."

Mama takes a handkerchief from her apron pocket and wipes Syble's nose. "Ollie, I'll wash her arm and dab it with kerosene while you bring your wagon down and load those boxes and boards. As soon as we eat, I'll help you with the tin."

"The tin needs to be on the bottom with the boxes on top. I can get it by myself." She starts toward the wagon, but stops and turns to Syble. "You can't play with the kittens anymore if you can't be gentle. They're babies."

Syble buries her face in her grandma's apron and continues to cry as Ollie walks away.

The scent of fresh baked yeast bread drifts from the house.

Ollie's stomach growls. *I could eat a whole pan of those rolls with butter and Mama's blackberry jam.*

The girls, stuffed with rolls, ham, and cake, fall asleep on a pallet in the living room floor. Mama insists that they stay with her until Papa gets home. "They're too sleepy to sit on the wagon seat, and they might get cut with that rusty tin or get splinters from the boards if you put them in the wagon bed. They'll be fine staying here with me."

"All right. I have a lot of sawing to do this afternoon. I'll try to have the boards and tin cut before Papa gets home." She lays her hand on Mama's arm. "Thanks for everything, and for watching the girls."

When her parents arrive with the girls giggling in the back of Papa's wagon, Ollie's right hand is blistered from using the saw and tin snips. Papa glances around at the tin, the boards, and the supports she has cut and laid out in the order they need to be used.

He reaches for her hand. "My goodness, girl. Don't you have gloves?"

"I was wearing some, but they're rough leather and ill-fitting."

Papa shakes his head. "Anyone but you would have waited for help."

The western sky is turning orange when Papa stands to admire the little shed. "Who would have thought we could make such a nice building from old stuff I planned to throw away."

He walks around nodding his head and looking at the fence. "Mr. Smith has a good size roll of chicken wire that I've noticed standing at the edge of his garden. I'll try to trade him something for it. That and some chicks are all you need."

The girls, holding their grandma's hands, come down the path. "Grandma, look at the little house. Can we have a hen and baby chickens now?"

Mama smiles before answering. "I've been saving eggs, but you'll have to wait twenty-one days before they hatch. That's a long time."

Morene shrugs. "We can wait." Syble copies the action.

"Your mama needs to decide which hen she wants." Mama turns to face Ollie. "One hen is gentle, but last year she only raised one baby out of the dozen she started with. The other hen is aggressive. I've seen her jump on a cat and send it running. She won't let the girls near, but she'll protect her chicks."

"The girls don't need to play with them. I want a hen that will fight for her little ones. Out here she may have to battle rats and snakes."

The next morning, Ollie takes the ax and chops down some tall saplings growing at the edge of the yard. She strips the limbs and lays the long poles in the sun while she positions and nails two of the best apple boxes to the barn wall. They are low enough that Morene can see inside when she stands on her tiptoes. Each box will hold two nests. *By fall, I hope to have laying hens in these.*

From the saplings, Ollie builds a roost, with two poles going from ground to roof and three nailed across. She knows that as soon as the chicks are old enough to leave the nest, they will hop onto the lowest pole. When they are stronger, they will choose the highest rung. Before lunchtime, the girls have filled the nests with hay. They beg Ollie to go get the hen.

"No, Papa is going to try and get some chicken wire to enclose the pen. You'll have to be patient."

They frown and mumble. "Why do we need two kinds of wire?"

"I used that old stuff because I had it, and such a small piece wasn't good for much else. The pen will be stronger with chicken wire around it, and it can keep smaller animals from crawling through."

It is almost dark when Papa drives his team into the yard. Ollie and the girls rush to meet him.

Syble wrinkles her nose. "Grandpa, you stink."

He chuckles. "Your wire didn't come cheap. I shoveled manure from that old man's chicken house in exchange for it. That's why I'm so late, and why I smell so bad."

"Papa, supper's on the table. Come in and eat with us."

He shakes his head. "No, I need a bath in the worst way, and your mama's waiting on me to eat supper. Tonight, we'll put that hen in a coop. According to the almanac, tomorrow is the best day to set a hen. You can get her tomorrow, or wait a few days if that's more convenient."

"It won't take me long to staple that wire around the pen. Then, I'll come get her. The girls can hardly wait. They wanted to go today."

Ollie reaches out to take hold of his hand. "Will you accept a chicken dinner as payback?"

"Sounds good to me."

"Although we'll have to put it off until I raise some fryers."

"I can hang on a while." He winks, clicks the lines against the horses, and heads for home.

Ollie gets up early the next morning and rushes through the

morning chores. She gets the girls to stand on one end of the wire while she rolls it out, measures and cuts a piece to go around the pen. The remainder, she stores in the barn loft.

"Girls, should we go get the hen?"

"Yes! Yes!" They dance around the yard.

The next week is unusually warm. Ollie lets the girls play outside without jackets or bonnets. She is cooking lunch when they come scampering inside. "Mama, the hen's cackling and flying around the pen. Maybe a rat's trying to get her eggs."

Ollie runs to the pen with a garden hoe in her hand. A big black snake slides over the side of the nest and is about to go under the barn. She slams the hoe onto it. The hoe bounces. The snake whips its tail around and tries again to leave. Ollie hits it repeatedly, until she can drag it out and chop off its head.

Morene has a bewildered look on her face. "Why didn't you shoot it?"

"I knew I could kill it with the hoe, and there were too many things around that might cause a bullet to ricochet."

"To what?"

"Ricochet. That means reflect or bounce off. It's easy to miss a fast-moving snake. A bullet could have bounced off one of those rocks and come back to hit me or one of you girls."

She nods. "What's that big lump in the middle of the snake?"

"Probably one of the eggs it swallowed. I can hardly believe I didn't break it while I was chopping with the hoe."

"Get a knife and cut it out."

"It may be cracked, and I rather not touch that snake."

Syble's wide eyes stare at it. "Is he still alive with his head gone?"

"No. It's dead."

"Then cut the egg out before the baby chick dies. I'll get your gloves." She runs for the leather gloves in the corn crib."

Ollie reaches for the pocketknife she left on a rafter when she trimmed the sapling poles. She puts on gloves, cuts across the snake above the bulge and squeezes the snake below the lump. The egg rolls out on the ground.

Morene starts to pick it up, but backs away. "Oh, it has snake blood on it."

Ollie clears her throat, suppresses her own reluctance, and takes the egg to the horse trough where she dips out water to rinse it, wipes it on the grass, and then dries it with a handful of hay from one of the nests. "Maybe the hen will still take care of it." She returns it to the nest. Two weeks later, twelve baby chicks are peeping out from under the hen.

That night at supper, Morene tells Syble, "Daddy will be happy to see our chickens. He'll be home soon, because Easter flowers are almost ready."

Ollie looks up from her plate. "Morene, did you say the flowers are ready to bloom?"

"Yep." She nods and smiles. "The tops are yellow."

"Are you sure? It's still several days until Easter."

"I'm sure." She slides from her chair. "Come on, I'll show you."

"No, I believe you. It's chilly outside. We'll look tomorrow."

The next few days are cold and rainy. Ollie maintains wood burning in the fireplace and keeps the girls inside. She does not say anymore about flowers, but secretly hopes the blooms are not opening yet—Morene will be disappointed if they open before Roy can come home.

Roy's letters have become less frequent and in his last letter, he did not mention when he would be home. She tells herself that he is probably working longer hours since some of the workers left. Maybe he'll be home in a few days.

It is still cold on Saturday, and a strong wind is blowing. Ollie lets the girls dye eight boiled eggs in beet juice, and helps them bake and frost a spice cake.

The sun is shining on Sunday morning. Before Ollie can stop her, Morene runs onto the porch in her nightgown to check on the flowers. "Mama, they're blooming, like you said. It's Easter, and Daddy will be home today."

"Honey, we're a long way from Tennessee, and it's been raining. Daddy may not get home for a few more days."

Morene puts her hands on her hips, and looks up at Ollie. "He'll be home for Easter."

Ollie takes a deep breath and lets it out slowly. "Girls, keep your gowns on until after breakfast, and then you can put on the new dresses I made for you. I don't want you to get something on them before church."

"What if Daddy comes while we're at church?"

"He'll wait for us. He knows where we'll be."

"But I want to be here when he comes home."

"Morene, it was a long time ago when he said he would try to be home on Easter. He may still be working. It could be days or weeks before he gets home."

Ollie sees tears shining in her eyes before she turns away. "No! Daddy's coming home today."

Usually, Morene wants to play with other children after church; today she stands beside Ollie, and keeps telling Syble she can't go play because it's time to go home and see Daddy. Grandma asks if they are coming by to eat. Before Ollie can answer, Morene says, "No. We have to go home. We made a cake for Daddy."

That afternoon the girls take turns hiding and hunting the eggs until Syble has cracked all but one. Morene puts the good egg in a cabinet drawer. "Syble, you're not gonna ruin my last egg until I show it to Daddy." Ollie peels the seven cracked eggs, and serves them for supper with bowls of soup.

At bedtime, Morene puts on her gown, but insists she is not sleepy and wants to wait up for Daddy. Syble falls asleep quickly. Morene sits in bed, listening to Ollie tell one Bible story after another.

"Morene, I'm too tired for any more stories. I'm going to turn out the lamp, but if Daddy comes home in the night, I'll wake you."

All is quiet in the house except for the sputter of fireplace flames and Syble's soft breathing. Ollie, drifting into sleep, jumps with a gasp when Morene says, "Mama, I hear a horse trotting on the road. It's Daddy. I know it's him."

"I hope so, but be quiet until he calls. It might be someone else." She lays her hand on the pistol but does not lift it from the holster.

The horse stops in the yard. Heavy steps cross the porch to the door. "Ollie, it's Roy."

Morene squeals and runs to click open the lock. "Daddy! Daddy! I knew you'd come."

Chapter 26
Squirrel

The day is clear and warm. Dandelion fluff is already blowing in the early morning breeze. Roy comes inside with the milk pail and sets it on the cabinet. "Ollie, that's a nice job on the chicken pen. Did you build it by yourself?"

She grins. "Papa helped with the roof, and he cleaned out Mr. Smith's pen in exchange for wire. I knew you'd build us one when you got the time and money, but I got most of the material for this one from Papa's junk heap. It didn't cost anything except I promised him a chicken dinner."

"It looks good, and you've already got chickens. Maybe we can buy more hens."

"I'd like to have two or three dozen, but this is a start." She shakes her head. "Most people don't want to sell good laying hens."

He washes his hands and sits at the table. "I checked the fields. The ground's not ready to plow, but it's drying fast. There's not a speck of dew this morning. Why don't we take the girls and drive over the farm? We can picnic in the woods."

"That sounds good, but I'm afraid snakes might be out. It's awful warm today."

"The girls can take their dolls and stay in the wagon. They'll enjoy riding and seeing parts of the farm they've never seen before. That way, I can check on the fences and spend the day with my family."

"All right. I'll pack a lunch." She winks. "And the rest of your cinnamon cake."

They leave the yard with Roy and Ollie on the wagon seat. Morene holds onto the sideboard with one hand, a strap of Roy's overalls with the other. Standing behind Ollie, Syble clings to the seat.

Morene asks streams of questions about Tennessee and Roy's job. He answers, carefully describing things so she can understand.

"Daddy, someday when you go off to work, I want to go."

"Honey, you can't do that. Women and children are not allowed. The work is hard and dirty. The boarding houses where the men stay at night are not very clean either, but they don't cost much. They have mice and sometimes rats."

"Big rats?"

"Pretty big. Maybe someday we can all go on a trip to see things and stay in a nice place."

"When, Daddy? Can we go soon?"

"No. I have to plow the fields as soon as the ground gets dry. It may be a long while before we can afford a trip. It costs a lot of money to travel, but we can dream and plan. Sometimes the dream is more fun than the trip. "

"When I get big, I want to fly in an airplane and ride on a train like the pictures in Bronnie's books—and maybe ride in a boat, but I wanna learn to swim first."

Roy reaches around to hug her. "I bet you'll do all those things someday."

A few days later, Roy is breaking the fields for planting. Ollie has plants growing in buckets on the south side of the house ready for transfer to garden rows. She prepares the ground and plants the largest, but saves the small ones in case there is a late frost and she has to start over.

In previous years, Ollie worked as many hours as Roy— sometimes more, with sewing in the evenings. Lately she is tired all the time, and wonders if she could be getting pellagra again. It is too early to harvest garden vegetables, a little salt pork is all that is left from the pig and, despite the need, she cannot make herself drink sweet milk.

Roy has the fields ready to plant, after days of plowing. The wagon, parked near the kitchen door, is ready to go get seed and fertilizer.

"Roy, I've made a list of things I need from the store. Will you give Mrs. Hart this empty pill bottle and ask for a full one or a refill? They were the ones Dr.Hart gave me for pellagra."

He jerks his head toward her. "Do you think you have that again? We've been eating good meals."

"But not much meat, greens, and milk. The doctor said I should take the pills for a year or more to build my body back to normal. I only took the ones Mama brought to me. She said they're not expensive."

"I saw poke greens near the creek. I'll pick them if I get back in time this afternoon."

"Daddy, can I go with you?" Morene asks.

"Not this time. I have several places to go. It would be tiring for you."

"No, it won't. I don't need naps anymore. I'm old enough to go to school next year."

He raises his chin and looks at her. "I said no. I have business today."

Slowly, she walks away to play with her sister.

Ollie and the girls look around the yard and along the road, gathering poke greens. It does not take long to find enough for supper. By the time Ollie expects Roy to be home, she has finished the outside chores, parboiled the greens and fried them in bacon grease, made cornbread, beans, and candied sweet potatoes.

When sunset fades into darkness and the girls start to whine with hunger, Ollie calls them to the table. "Your daddy's running late getting everything done. I'll save him a plate of food, but we'll go ahead and eat."

After the girls are in bed, Ollie sits at the table, patching Roy's work clothes. With each pull of the needle, she prays— "Please, God, let him be all right."

It is almost midnight when the wagon rolls into the yard and stops near the kitchen door. Ollie rushes out in time to see Roy jump to the ground, stumble, stagger, and grab onto the well post to keep from falling. She runs to him. "Roy, what's wrong. Are you sick?"

She gasps at the scent of whiskey and backs away. "You're drunk! Drunk! Why, Roy?"

He slumps to the ground and leans his head against the post.

Moonlight illuminates a wagonload of supplies. Ollie unhitches the horses from the wagon, leads them to the barn, and turns them out to pasture. Returning to the house, she lights a lantern and unloads flour, sugar, and other items for the kitchen.

Setting the lantern on the step, she goes to Roy with a wet cloth to wash his face and wake him.

He pushes her. "Get away from me, you cheating bi—" He is asleep again.

Backing away to stare at him, she mutters. "That better not be what I thought you were trying to say." She takes the lantern, rolls down the wick, blows it out, and steps up into the doorway. As she turns to look again, an object comes flying through the air. Pain explodes inside her head. She grabs at shadows.

A throbbing headache greets Ollie when she wakes and tries to move. It pounds like a parade drum, so loud that it might split her eardrums. She reaches for a rock, a stick, anything. Only the bare wood floor meets her hands. Lying there, all is quiet except the tick of the clock and snoring.

She pushes up and scoots over to sit in the open doorway. A full moon brightens the yard. Roy, asleep in the grass, is snoring and mumbling. She remembers, but it cannot be. Why would Roy get drunk and lash out at her?

Reaching to touch a sore spot near her temple, she feels something thick and sticky. She lights a lamp, and takes Roy's small shaving mirror from a hook on the wall. Holding it close, she looks at a bloody knot above and a little to the side of her right eye. Bending over the wash pan and splashing cool water only makes it throb more.

On her way to a chair, her shoes crunch on shards of glass. She rests until dizziness subsides, before squatting to pick up broken pieces. The label from the pellagra medicine clings to one of the large chunks.

Roy moans and rolls over, a whiskey bottle in his left hand.

Holding to the door facing for balance, Ollie goes into the yard, pries the bottle from his grasp, and dumps the remaining liquid onto the ground. When safely inside, she closes and locks the door.

Her head hurts too much to lie flat, so she props herself up with two pillows against a quilt. Ollie cannot sleep or rest, more from the pain in her heart than the one in her head, and the question, "*Why?*" keeps running through her mind.

Before daylight, with the lantern and milk pail in hand, she goes to the barn. Roy is sitting at the table when she returns. He continues to sit and stare at her as she strains the milk and cooks breakfast. Finally, she turns to him and asks. "Roy, what upset you so much? Why did you hit me with that bottle?"

He gets up and goes to the barn.

Morene gasps when she walks into the kitchen and sees the knot on Ollie's head. "Mama! What happened?"

"I fell. It'll be all right. It's only a bruise."

"What made you fall? Did you trip?"

"I got a little dizzy and lost my balance. I'll be fine. Now go on and play."

Syble stares but lets her older sister do all the talking.

Morene keeps looking at Ollie's head as she turns to go. "Where's Daddy? Did he get home?"

"Yes, and he's already gone out to work."

Morene looks out the window. "Why didn't he eat breakfast?"

"How do you know he didn't eat?"

"All the biscuits are still in the pan. Is Daddy sick?"

"He has a headache, so you need to be quiet when he comes inside."

The girls are playing on the front porch and Ollie is cooking the noon meal when Roy comes to the house. He does not say a word, just goes to the warming oven, takes out a biscuit and fried egg left from breakfast, and walks out the door. Ollie has milked, fed the girls and put them to bed, before he comes again to the stove, takes food, and leaves for the barn.

The same ritual goes on for two days. Ollie answers one question after another from Morene. Finally, "Mama, does Daddy not love us anymore, or is he still sick?"

"He loves you. He'll always love *you*." She swallows and turns away.

Ollie needs to work in the garden, wash clothes, and do mending. She could force herself to go on with the work if she only had a headache, but the pain inside her heart is paralyzing. She sits in the rocker, looking around the tiny house. One Sunday dress hangs on a nail behind the door beside Roy's khakis and good jacket. Every-day dresses hang on another nail.

She remembers her friend Kay's warning: *If you marry a farmer, you'll have one or two decent dresses, a half dozen or more kids, you'll work from sunrise until sunset, and have work waiting the day that you die . . . .*

The next morning, rain drizzles over the fields. Roy stays in the barn. The girls eat, and then play dolls under their bed. It is midday when Ollie takes Roy's breakfast to the barn. He only glances up from the harness he is repairing.

"Roy, I have a right to know what this is about."

He spits a stream of tobacco juice near her feet. "Why do you think you have a right for me to even speak to you?"

Ollie jerks her head back. "I'm your wife."

"From what I heard at the store, you've been a Jezebel."

"A what!" She drops the plate. "Who dared to call me that?" She kicks the biscuit into a corner. "I've never been unfaithful! I've worked beside you, bore your children, took care of them and this farm while you were gone." She clenches her fists, and looks straight into his eyes. "And I've never been unfaithful to you." She turns around, almost falls, grabs her head, and stumbles outside, letting the rain fall on her face.

"You're getting wet." He reaches his arm out to her.

Pushing it away, she wants to scream but uncried tears clog her throat. She swallows, and several seconds pass before a deep angry voice asks, "Who told you such a lie? Tell me now!" She steps inside to face him.

"I don't know his name. He's a tall skinny guy. All I've ever heard him called is Squirrel."

"He's exactly that, and a liar. Who was I supposed to have cheated with?"

"He said he heard our neighbor's cousin's been slipping around here."

"That trash—a lowdown thief—you dared to think I'd stoop that low." She stares at him, eyes squinting, mouth drawn tight.

Leaning her head against a post, she exhales. "Ask Dr. Hart who was in to get a piece of buckshot removed. Two men tried to steal our calf, and I shot one of them. They left a knife behind. It's on the kitchen shelf. I asked Eldridge to have Mama report it, but the Sheriff never came around. Besides family, and a couple of hunters near the creek, those are the only men that I've seen on this place." She walks into the rain and up the path to the house.

Running a towel over her face and arms, and shaking her skirt, she stands beside the stove turning instinctively as her dress warms and dries. Combing fingers numbly through her hair, she touches the throbbing bruise and flinches.

Ollie remembers seeing him at the store—hunched

shoulders, skinny tucked-under buttocks, and guilty-grin. He looked more like an egg-sucking dog sneaking out of a henhouse, than a squirrel. At escaping punishment for evil deeds, he is squirrelly, and rumors say there have been many of those cases.

I can't think of a single person that would grieve for him. His own folks ran him off. She clenches her teeth. *I can't turn the other cheek like Mama would.*

She pulls a bonnet over her damp head, goes to the barn, and as Roy stands watching, hitches the team to the wagon.

"Where are you going?"

"To the store. I need my medicine."

"I'll go get it."

"You had a chance. All I got was the empty bottle thrown against my head. Watch the girls. They're playing in the house." She reaches and grabs the seat to pull herself into the wagon. Her jacket slides up exposing the pistol.

"Wait a minute," he yells. "Why are you wearing that gun?"

She slaps the lines against the horses.

The drizzle stops before she gets to the store and sun pops in and out around the clouds. With each whisper of breeze, thousands of raindrops shimmer on leaves and grass, reflecting multicolored prisms.

Horses at the hitching post stomp, snort and twitch their ears. She recognizes two that often travel the road in front of her house. They are thinner than most, but carry fancy saddles.

The door opens, jingling the bell. A variety of scents greet her—tobacco, apples, kerosene, and human bodies needing to bathe. A vision of two little girls and the fragrance of perfumed soap comes to mind.

Ollie turns her back to people inside, takes off her wet bonnet, lays it across the top of several ax handles standing in a nail keg near the entrance. Her hand slides under the damp jacket, touches the leather holster and moves away. Seconds pass while she fluffs her damp hair and stares at the keg's contents. Calmly, she removes a handle, runs her fingers over the smooth surface, and grips it tight.

Two gray-bearded men are playing checkers; others sit around talking and watching. The guy called Squirrel is leaning back on two legs of a cane-bottom chair, balanced with the fingers of his right hand on a counter. He glanced at Ollie and grinned before she turned away.

She walks behind him, and swings the broad piece of polished hickory hard against the underside of his right hand. He falls backward with only the floor to stop him. Cursing, he braces with his left hand to get up.

The handle is drawn back like a baseball bat. "Don't move or I'll crack your skull."

He swears again. "What are you doin', woman?"

"I'm here to defend my good name. I'll bash your head flat if you tell any more lies about me."

"I don't know what you're talkin' about."

The handle swishes above his head. He blinks and ducks.

"Lie to me again and I'll do it now. You twisted the truth way out of shape when you told Roy that Cousin's been slipping around while he was gone."

His whiney voice drawls, "That was jus' a joke. I was only kiddin'."

She grits her teeth and glares at him. "I'm not. Unless you want a stone bearing your name to decorate the cemetery, don't utter my name again." She steps back, still holding the weapon. He scrambles away and leaves the store, rubbing his arm and muttering.

Turning to the neighbor, she states, "The same goes for you and *Cousin*." She spits out the nickname as if it tastes rotten. "I keep a loaded gun handy. I trust that one of you still feels the effects of the welcome shot you received when trespassing on my property."

They stand and leave the store without a word. One walks with a distinct limp.

When the bell stops jingling, an old man playing checkers slaps his leg. "Ollie, it would've been nice if you'd come in two hours ago to clean out that scum."

"Scum is right."

Everyone nods.

Mrs. Hart has a worried frown. "Ollie, can I help you with something?"

"I need a bottle of niacin pills and two red suckers for my girls."

Mrs. Hart places the medicine on the counter, and lays her soft hand on top of Ollie's calloused fingers. "I worry about you almost as much as your mama." She lowers her voice to a whisper. "That bunch is wicked. They sneak around to do their dirty work. Watch carefully when Roy's away, and watch those little girls. I wouldn't put anything past that trash."

Ollie hears giggling when she nears the house after releasing the horses. It is good to regard happiness again.

Roy meets her outside. "I don't remember throwing a bottle. I wouldn't have if I'd been sober."

"That's not a good excuse."

"No." He bows his head. "I let that—that Squirrel make a fool of me."

She draws a deep breath and pushes past him. Ollie hands the candy to the girls. "Go play and eat these while I start supper.

She turns without a smile and tosses a stick of wood into the cookstove. "As soon as the water's hot, I'll scald the pail so you can go milk."

Gently, he places his hand on her arm. "Why did you put that gun on to go to the store?"

She exhales. "I took it to shoot a squirrel, but God changed my mind."

Chapter 27
Timing

Ollie is well enough to do essential farm chores, after taking niacin pills for several months, but no longer sews and reads before going to sleep at night. She falls into bed exhausted. Dr. Hart insists she keep taking the medicine, in addition to an iron tonic.

Morene's eager mind develops an endless stream of questions: "Mama, why are you sick all the time? When will you be well? You're not gonna die, are you?" Every answer prompts more questions. Mentally and physically drained by the end of the day, Ollie is ready for assistance when Roy comes in from the fields.

"Morene, ask your Daddy a few of those questions. My brain needs a rest."

Ollie is not only worried about her health, she worries about the girls'—they look pale, tire easily, and wake in the night crying with bad dreams. During the day, Syble runs and plays, but often has stomach upsets.

The doctor does not think the children have pellagra—they drink plenty of milk and do not have sores on their hands and arms. He suggests that they take iron tonic.

Ollie is certain that something else is wrong with her girls. Sorghum is rich in iron; they eat sorghum molasses at breakfast on buttered biscuits, and canned fruit and vegetables every day. If they do not have pellagra, seep-water may be polluting the well, or frequent mosquito bites could be making them sick. She questions her mama and sister Bertha for possible answers. They tell her not to worry so much—all children have stomachaches and bad dreams.

One Saturday while they are getting ready to go to the store, Syble grabs onto Roy's leg and slides to the floor. She is limp and breathing shallow when he picks her up and puts her on the bed.

Ollie runs to get a cold rag to wash her face. When she returns with the cloth, Syble has stopped breathing.

Roy holds Syble's nose, breathes into her mouth and keeps compressing her chest.

Stricken with panic, Ollie yells, "I'm going for the doctor." Crying and praying, she runs a half-mile down the road. Gasping for breath, she pauses at the creek. As if a higher power has touched her, she feels a calming influence. She turns around and runs home to find Roy rocking Syble—she is pale but breathing.

Within an hour, they have Syble in Dr. Hart's office. He asks questions, and listens to her heart and lungs. "Roy, Ollie, I think this spell was caused by worms. Often when an autopsy is performed on a child, they find worms in the lungs or blocking the airways. Sometimes, they even find them in the heart or brain."

He goes to a cabinet, takes out a brown bottle and hands it to Ollie. "Follow the written instructions. All of you have to take medicine, or you'll never get rid of them.

"On the morning after taking the medicine, wash all of your bedding, sun the pillows and any toys that can't be washed, and scrub the floors. I'm not suggesting that your home and bedding are not clean, only that you need to wash everything to help prevent reinfestation. Eggs from these parasites, like dust, can cling to anything in your house." He rubs his chin, pats Syble's back, and listens to her heart again.

"Watch this little one close for a few days and let me know if she has any more problems. Don't be surprised if they get worms again next summer. Probably eighty percent of Arkansas children have them, especially those that like to play outside in the dirt."

That night when the girls are asleep, Roy asks, "Ollie, what would you have done if you were alone with the girls when that happened to Syble?"

"I don't know. I think I would have tried to blow air into her lungs, like you did. But today, while you were working on her, and I stood watching my baby die, all I could think of was to run get the doctor."

"But it's three or four miles to the doctor's."

"I panicked. What mother wouldn't, thinking her baby is dying?"

Morene starts to school in the fall. Ollie and Syble walk with her to the main road to catch the school bus, and meet her in the afternoon. She likes riding the noisy bus with the straining gears, and is excited about learning. Most of all, she likes drawing and coloring. Every day she has a new picture to show the family.

When Syble gets home on the first morning after walking Morene to meet the bus, she sits on the porch crying and tells Ollie, "I want to go to school. I don't like staying home by myself."

"You're not alone. I'm here."

"But you're always working. I want someone to play with."

"When you get old enough, you can go to school, but for a while we'll have to keep each other company. Come in the kitchen. We'll make cookies. You can cut them out by yourself and put them on the pan. We'll sing songs while we work."

"I don't cut good like Morene, and I don't know the song words. She knows all the words."

"She didn't when she first started helping, but she learned. You will too. Come on." Ollie starts to sing as she steps toward the door. "Mary had a little frog."

Syble stomps her foot. "She didn't have a frog. She had a lamb."

Ollie nods at Syble and grins. "See, you do know the words. Sing with me. You can have a bite of cookie dough for every time you catch me singing the wrong word."

Syble wipes her eyes and smiles. "Is this a game?"

"Yes, and if I hear you say a wrong word, you have to give me one of your cookie bites."

All morning they sing and tell stories, while baking cookies and working together on the noonday meal. At naptime, Syble snuggles close to Ollie. "It's fun playing games and working with you. Can we do that tomorrow?"

"We can do that every day if you want. Now let's go to sleep. When you wake, it will be time to go get Morene."

In the spring of 1935, Ollie is sick every day. She cooks breakfast, but cannot stand the smell of eggs, and leaves them for Roy to fry while she sits on the porch sipping black coffee. Each morning, when Roy goes to plow, Ollie and Syble work in the garden, or go to the fields to hoe crops. Syble walks along the rows with a short hoe that Roy fixed for her. Sometimes she chops at weeds, sometimes she drags the hoe and listens to the many stories and nursery rhymes Ollie recites. In the afternoon, Ollie is too weary to do anything but nap with Syble.

Coyotes have taken up residence near the creek. They howl at night, and frighten the girls. Roy has seen them crossing the fields in the late afternoon and commented that one is larger and has a darker coat than most.

Ollie knows coyotes do not normally attack adults, but they might overpower a child. Afraid that she might not be awake in time to meet Morene at the school bus, Ollie tries skipping naps, but falls asleep while sewing. Roy suggests that she set the alarm clock and continue getting extra rest.

That fall, she helps with harvesting each morning, but can hardly stay awake until the lunch dishes are washed. After crop gathering is complete, Roy walks with Syble to take Morene to the bus and to meet her in the afternoon. While they are gone, Ollie sews on Christmas dresses and presents for the girls, and a shirt for Roy.

The new baby is due in December. Ollie worries that something might be wrong with it. Rarely was she sick during the months before Morene and Syble were born. She prays continuously for the baby.

On Christmas Eve, Roy takes the girls to stay with Bronnie and brings Mama back to be with Ollie. That night, a little girl is born. They name her Mary Ann. Mary is in honor of the Virgin Mary. Ann is from Ollie's middle name.

The new infant is not as big as Morene and Syble were at birth, but appears healthy. Roy sits rocking the baby, beside the bed. Ollie places her hand on his arm. "A healthy baby is the best of all Christmas gifts."

"I was relieved when the doctor handed me this little bundle. You were sick so much, I couldn't help but worry that something was wrong."

The older girls are thrilled with a new sister. Each time she cries, they run to her side. Since they quarrel over whose turn it is to hold her, Ollie rarely takes her away from them except when it is time for Ann to nurse.

In 1936, spring sunshine seems to bring better health, renewed hope, and enhanced energy. Roy and Ollie plant crops and a big garden. While Ollie hoes grass and weeds from the crops, Syble watches over her little sister on a quilt in the shade—swatting at flies or bees that come near, fanning when the baby perspires, and even changing wet diapers.

High spirits are stifled when hot summer winds blow across the crops. It looks like Roy will have to go away again after harvest. Dreading another long lonely winter, Ollie begins to hate the farm.

Syble is old enough to start school in the fall. On the first day, she is awake early to put on her new shoes and a dress made for this special occasion. Waiting until her sister is ready to go meet the bus, she walks back and forth through the house holding a yellow pencil sharpened with Roy's pocketknife, a red Big Chief tablet, and a lard bucket packed with cookies and a biscuit filled with bacon and egg.

Ollie glances toward the sleeping baby before following the older girls outside. "I want you to wear these bonnets. It'll be hot when you get off the bus."

Morene frowns. "Mama, no one else wears a bonnet. It's

hard to keep up with, it messes my hair, and boys yank it off. We're both tan. We won't sunburn."

"The teacher should stop those boys from pulling at your bonnets."

"She doesn't see them. They do it on the bus and the playground. And they're really mean to kids that tattle."

She hesitates. "All right, leave the bonnets here. Behave yourselves and come straight home when you get off the bus. Don't you dare stop to play in that creek. Snakes and animals come there for water."

"We won't." Morene picks up a long slender tree branch. "Syble, get a stick. We'll hit anything that comes close."

Ollie wants to call them back and keep them near where she can make sure they are safe, but knows she cannot. Her mouth quivers and her eyes blur as she waves and turns toward the house.

Hearing a crash, Ollie runs. Sitting on the floor, the baby is chewing on an embroidered scarf pulled from a small table. A broken snuff glass glitters across the room. "Well, little one, I can't leave you alone for even a few minutes." She bends, and swings the baby into the air. "One of your sisters must have left that glass on the table. I didn't know you were awake. Are you ready for breakfast?"

That afternoon, while Ann naps, Ollie mends one of Roy's work shirts and keeps a close eye on the hour. It is almost time for the older girls to get off the bus. As the clock ticks away minutes, she gets an increasing uneasy feeling that something is wrong.

She checks the baby. Ann sleeps soundly, her mouth twitching into smiles as she dreams. Ollie glances out the window. Nothing seems unusual, except her anxious fears.

Far in the distance, Ollie hears the school bus. Unable to reason away the anxiety, she lifts the shotgun from the rack above the fireplace, thrusts in a shell, and drops two more into her dress pocket. Quietly, she rushes out the door, and walks fast toward the bridge where the children will cross the creek.

Morene and Syble approach the bridge, carrying lunch pails and books, talking and giggling. The sticks they boldly walked away with that morning are nowhere in sight. They do not see Ollie advancing from the top of the hill; neither do the scruffy coyotes waiting in the thick brush with attention focused on the little girls.

Careful to walk on the grassy edge of the road where she will not kick a rock and alert the animals of her presence, Ollie quickens her pace. When she is within shooting range, she kneels on one knee, aims and fires. The largest coyote falls, the other yelps and disappears into the underbrush. The girls scream, drop schoolbooks, and grasp each other.

"Morene, Syble, grab your books and come on. I have to get back to the baby."

Grabbing books, they run past the dead coyote, but not without slowing to look at the sharp teeth in his gaping mouth. Morene is asking questions before she reaches Ollie. "Mama, how did you know the wolf was there?"

"I think it's a coyote, but it's bigger than most. It might be part wolf, or maybe it's related to a big dog."

"But how did you know to come with the gun?"

Ollie smiles and runs her hand around Morene's shoulder in a gentle caress. "I got a worried feeling. Maybe your guardian angels warned me. By the way, where are the sticks you were carrying this morning to fight off wild animals?"

The girls look at each other with wide-eyed stares. "We forgot to get them when we got off the bus."

Chapter 28
Time to Move On

Roy and Ollie never speak of it, yet she feels despair and sees it reflected in his eyes. Is there no end of struggling to pay bills and save enough to plant crops the following year? At the end of harvest, after Roy sells the last load of cotton, he comes home with a Victrola.

"Ollie, it's time we have some fun. Saturday night, Clarence and Mary Lou are coming over to listen to music with us."

Ollie turns on the Victrola and dances to the tunes while cleaning the house. Humming as she bakes cookies, makes punch with wild cherry juice, and gets a pot of coffee ready to set on the stove, she is as excited as Roy about having friends visit.

Mary Lou comes in the door with a plate of deviled eggs and one of muffins. "Turn it on. I'm ready to dance."

The girls, even little Ann, laugh and jump as the records go 'round. Roy's brother Coy and his wife Bronnie arrive. She sticks her head inside the house and calls, "Ollie, we came to cut a rug." With hearty laughter, her feet move in time with the music.

As the evening progresses, people keep coming. Some of them, Ollie has never met. They make themselves at home, dancing, singing, eating, and drinking punch and coffee. When Morene and Syble get tired, they scoot under a bed with blankets, pillows and their baby sister. It is not long until they are asleep; before the party ends, Ollie is wishing she could join them.

Ollie goes to the well to draw a fresh bucket of water. The yard is full of wagons, buggies, horses, and even a couple of cars. Beside the porch, a group of men pass around a whisky bottle. She pauses, considers telling them to leave, but they are not rowdy. *Maybe they will go on without trouble.*

It is past midnight before the crowd begins to dwindle, and nearly three before the last couple leaves. Roy falls into bed and is immediately asleep. Ollie puts clean sheets on the girls' bed where someone spilled punch. Then she drags the children from underneath, lifts, and tucks the clean bedding around them.

Sun is shining through east windows when the bawling cow wakes Ollie. She rolls over and swings her feet onto the floor. "Roy, you need to go milk while I cook breakfast."

Morene and Syble are as lively as on other mornings. They giggle, tease, and place Sunday clothes across their bed so they can quickly dress after they eat.

Roy puts the full milk pail on the cabinet and goes to sit on the porch. He yawns and rubs his eyes when Ollie opens the door to call him to the table. "Ollie, let's skip church this morning. I couldn't stay awake."

"How will that look to the girls? They've already laid out dresses. We have to go."

"I don't. Go ahead and take them if you want."

She stiffens, grips the door facing, and pauses to choose her words. "Roy, if this is what that Victrola's gonna do to our family, you need to get rid of it."

"I enjoyed having people over and laughing for a change.

We can't work all the time. Go on. Leave me be."

The door slams as she walks away. *He's not the only one who works. The devil works in various ways, but I'll not give in.*

Morene and Syble, sensing Ollie's anger and Roy's indifference, swap knowing glances. No one, except little Ann, speaks during breakfast.

Ollie takes the girls to church and goes to Mama's for the noon meal. *He can do without or cook for himself. He knows Mama usually asks us to eat Sunday dinner at her house.* It is late afternoon when they get home. Roy is asleep on the bed.

The next Saturday night, Ollie prepares a good supper for her family. They are about half-finished eating when people start arriving. Some bring snacks, some only bring appetites; a few men have whisky bottles or pint jars of homebrew tucked into pockets.

Ollie drags her rocker onto the porch and sits rocking Ann as the Victrola blasts out music. A few people have brought children who run loose through the yard and garden. Again, when Morene and Syble get tired, they retreat underneath the bed with their sister and two little girls Ollie does not know.

The next morning, the family can hardly eat breakfast for yawning. Ollie looks at Roy and the girls propped on their elbows, and starts laughing. "Roy, we can't do this week after week. You have to sell that machine."

Roy trades the Victrola for farm tools. Two weeks later, people are still arriving on Saturday night with plans to dance and listen to music. Most of them stay and visit for a while; others leave quickly to search for a party.

Monday, while Morene and Syble are at school and Ann is playing, Roy comes into the kitchen and stands near Ollie while she rolls out a piecrust. "We both know there's no work for me here. I've searched everywhere. If you think you and the girls can manage another winter without me, I'll go back to Tennessee and try to work until spring. Maybe I can save enough to pay off that mortgage. It's like a guillotine—always hanging over our heads, threatening to take the farm."

"I hate for you to be gone again at Christmas. The girls miss you so much."

"What about you?"

She wraps her arms around him, and swallows a sob. "You know I do." Without another word, they embrace, lost in their own thoughts. Ollie's eyes are shining when she steps away, but she manages a grin. "I bet you have white all over your back. I forgot about this flour." She dusts his shirt before they start planning for the months ahead.

Roy holds up his hands and counts off fingers for things that would worry Ollie if they were not taken care of. "I have enough wood split to last until summer. I've cleaned the chimney. Meat is hanging in the barn loft. The cellar is full of root crops, cabbage, and fall apples. The cow shouldn't freshen before I get back in the spring, and you're getting eggs from the new hens. Is there anything else?"

"Picking up supplies."

"Make out a list. We'll go to the store before school is out. You can get material for sewing the girls' Christmas presents, and I'll buy enough feed to last the cow."

Early the next morning, they stop to leave Morene and Syble at Mama's to catch the school bus. She declares that the baby should stay also, rather than chance getting an earache in the cold air. Ann giggles and snuggles into Grandma's arms.

Syble pulls on the pocket of Roy's overalls. "Daddy, can I miss school today and ride with you to Pa's?

"Missing one day of school won't hurt a smart first-grader like you." He lifts, hugs her tight, and sets her in the wagon. "Wrap yourself in that quilt. You don't want to get sick while I'm gone."

She cuddles her doll in the wagon bed, but talks and asks questions all the way to Ma and Pa Glenn's.

Mr. Glenn has his wagon and team ready to take Roy to the bus station. As soon as they eat the early lunch Mrs. Glenn has prepared, they get on the road: Roy beginning a long trip to Tennessee, Ollie and Syble going home.

Ollie expects Syble to sleep on the return trip, but she sits and talks until they are back at Mama's house. Remembering how Syble rarely talked before Morene started school, Ollie smiles at the little brown-haired girl with big blue eyes.

Mama meets Ollie at the door. "Will you and the girls stay and eat supper with us?"

"Thanks, but I want to take care of the animals, and be inside with the doors locked before dark."

"That's a good idea."

The second week after Roy leaves, Ollie wakes to the sound of the chickens squawking and flying about. She runs outside with the shotgun and fires it above the pen. Illuminated by moonlight, an animal scrambles over the wire, jumps to the ground and scampers toward the woods. She fires again. The creature jerks and rolls over.

The two older girls are sitting up in the bed when Ollie comes inside to get a lantern. Morene whispers, "Mama, what did you shoot?"

"I think it's a raccoon, but I need to get a light on it to make sure. It was in the chicken pen."

"Oh, I hope it didn't kill any."

"Raccoons are mean. I bet it got at least one."

"What will happen to the baby chicks if it killed the mama hen?"

"Stay in your beds and let me take a look before we worry about that." Ollie goes out the door with a lantern and the reloaded gun.

As Ollie expected, the baby chicks are all dead. The mama has a broken neck. She will not live long. The other chickens are squawking and flapping their wings on the top rung of the roost.

Ollie stares at the mama hen. "Girl, you did your best to fight for your babies, but you were no match for that big coon. I wish he'd got one of those hateful roosters instead of you, but you wouldn't fly away and leave your babies."

She lifts the fat hen. *God wouldn't want me to waste a good bird.* With a few twists of Ollie's wrist, the chicken is no longer in pain. Quickly, she skins and washes it.

The girls are asleep when she goes inside. She puts the meat on to boil, and sits near the lamp, but before opening her Bible, she glances at the girls. *I hope Morene and Syble don't think about that hen when I serve them dumplings tomorrow.*

It is a long cold winter, with two deep snows, and heavy rainstorms that blow so hard the water comes between the sheets of tin over the kitchen and leaks onto the floor. Ollie counts her blessings as she sweeps out the water. "It could be worse. At least our beds are dry."

Ollie knits long wool stockings and caps for Morene and

Syble to wear to school, but the girls hate them. Before she gets them on, Syble starts complaining that they itch. Sometimes when they get home from school, the stocking are rolled down around their ankles and the caps are in the lunch buckets.

One afternoon, the cold wind blowing especially hard, the girls come rushing inside with nothing on their heads.

Frowning, Ollie plunks her hands on her hips. "Girls, I'm not gonna feel sorry for you when you start crying with earaches. If you refuse to listen to me, you'll suffer the consequences."

Both girls wake crying in the night, their left ears hurting. Ollie uses sweet oil drops, and continually warms cloths by the fire to place over their ears. When they are still in pain, she takes an old pipe Roy left on the mantle, fills it with tobacco, lights it, and puffs warm smoke into their ears. Before morning, they fall asleep, but Ollie is sick from accidently inhaling smoke.

Early, one March morning, Ollie wakes to loud popping noises. At first, she thinks someone is shooting a gun. She jumps up and looks out a window in time to hear the noise again and see a large ice-covered limb from a nearby tree go crashing to the ground.

None of the trees are close enough to the house to drop limbs onto the roof. Through the hazy dawn, Ollie looks toward the barn. One big limb is lying beside the chicken house. Only a few small sticks are on top of the tin. "Please, Lord, let the cow and horses be in the barn and not in the woods."

Trees, especially along the road, lean, crack and fall from the weight of the frozen rain. She whispers, "I was isolated before. Now I'm trapped with my little girls. There is no way I can walk down that road, much less drive a team and wagon. If the whole road is like this, it will take months to clear. Watch over us, Lord. Keep me and my babies safe."

Ollie opens the kitchen door to go milk. The doorstep has a thick coating of ice; so does the path leading to the barn. "I'm glad I brought in water last night. I'm not going out and take a chance on hurting myself. The cow will have to manage the best way she can."

The frozen world fascinates the older girls. Morene pulls on long wool stockings. "Syble, hurry and get dressed. I want to skate on the yard while Mama cooks breakfast."

Ollie looks up from a pan of frying eggs. "Get rid of that thought. You're not leaving the house until this melts away. You might fall and break your arm, leg, or even your back, and I couldn't get you to a doctor. The road is full of downed trees and broken limbs."

In early afternoon, the sun emerges from behind the clouds and the melting ice comes down like rain. Since morning, the cow has been standing near the gate, bawling to be milked and fed. Ollie uses a broom handle to beat icicles from the roof overhanging the entryway, gets on her knees in the kitchen doorway to pound the ice from the doorstep with a hammer, and then sweeps chips from the step.

Warning the girls again not to go outside, Ollie cautiously moves from the doorstep onto the crunching grass, takes a hoe from beside the house to use as a cane, and walks to the barn with the milk pail.

The cow stands munching feed while Ollie milks, but the calf does not stop bawling until she stands beside her mama, gulping and dribbling white liquid from the corners of her mouth.

Should I leave the gate open? Tomorrow the ground could be slick again — better for the calf to get sick from too much milk than for me to fall and hurt myself. I have to take care of my girls. At the barn door, Ollie stands looking at the melting ice running off the roof, and the clear blue sky beyond. She turns, herds the calf into the pen, and watches as the cow slops through the muck to join the horses at the haystack.

Roy comes home in April. They rejoice at having money to pay off the mortgage, although they barely have enough left to pay for seed and fertilizer to start another crop. Disappointed in the fall harvest, they debate all winter on selling the farm and moving to a warmer climate.

In early spring, Roy lists the farm with a land agent. It is not long until he finds a buyer. They sell furniture, farm equipment, chickens, the cow, and almost everything they own, even some winter clothes.

Bell, Bess, and the wagon are the last things sold. Ollie and the older girls have tears in their eyes as the new owner drives away. Syble begs, "Daddy, why can't we take the horses with us to California?"

He spits tobacco juice into the grass. "They can't walk that far. They'd die on the side of the road and we'd have to leave them in the ditch." He kneels on one knee and smiles at her. "This way they'll be happy in a green pasture. Don't you think that's better?"

She nods and sniffs. "But I'll miss them."

Although he has never driven an automobile, Roy buys a truck and drives it home. The sun shines bright the morning they climb into the truck at Mama and Papa's. Roy, Ollie, and little Ann are in the truck's cab. Morene, Syble, Ollie's sister Bronnie, and Roy's friend Snake Ward sit in the bed of the truck, under a tarpaulin tied over the sideboards.

Ollie, Mama, and Bronnie are crying before the truck pulls out of the yard. Ollie cries again when they stop to say goodbye to Ma and Pa Glenn, but Roy maintains a smile until he drives onto the Soda Valley Road leaving his childhood home. Then he starts wiping his eyes.

He clears his throat and looks straight ahead. "Ollie, have you asked for your angels to watch out for us?"

She touches a flowered handkerchief to her eyes. "I prayed that they would be with us all."

- Title: Dark Secrets
- Author: Nancy Powell
- Price: $27.99
- Publisher: TotalRecall Publications, Inc.
- Format: HARDCOVER, 6.14" x 9.21"
- Number of pages in the finished book: 288
- 13-digit ISBN: 978-1-59095-585-7
- Month and day of publication: Nov: 2012
- Distribution arrangements: Ingram, Baker Taylor, Amazon.com, Barnes and Noble, etc.

Dark Secrets is the first book in a series based on the life of a farm girl born in 1908 when the United States was becoming a world leader, and farm families made up over half of the population. Conditions for the Negro had worsened, women rallied for the right to vote, and social change in music, dance, and fashion filtered into rural areas. This book shows prejudice faced by Negroes, Gypsies, Jews, and women of that era.

The book begins with Ollie trying to get home after receiving a head injury in an attack by two boys—the same boys that she thinks raped her friend and murdered a girl in a nearby community. She remains in a coma for five days, recalling vivid events of her first fifteen years.

Ollie is competitive and contends with schoolmates, and her older brother and sister, but is eager to help with younger siblings. With a gift for premonition and healing, her ambition is to be a nurse, but when her papa has to pay a promissory note signed for a friend, he cannot afford to send her away to school. With no money for schooling, she worries about becoming a spinster. Still, she rejects all the young men—until she meets Roy.

- Title: Listen For The Angels
- Author: Nancy Powell
- Price: $27.99
- Publisher: TotalRecall Publications, Inc.
- Format: HARDCOVER, 6.14" x 9.21"
- Number of pages in the finished book: 308
- 13-digit ISBN: 978-1-59095-591-8
- Month and day of publication: Apr 8, 2013
- Distribution arrangements: Ingram, Baker Taylor, Amazon.com, Barnes and Noble, etc.

Listen for the Angels, the third book in the Ollie's Angels Series, begins on the road to California where Ollie and Roy move with three young daughters in search of a prosperous life following struggles on an Arkansas farm during the Great Depression. Roy works at farm labor. Ollie joins him in the fields during cotton-picking season, and become infected with a disease that the newspapers call Sleeping Sickness. Several people have died from the illness, but doctors do not know the cause. Ollie's intuition tells her that mosquitoes cause it—she takes a quinine tonic and recovers. They move back to Arkansas, after hearing that Roy's ma has cancer.

They buy a small farm and continue the struggle toward the home of their dreams. Almost every year, Roy goes away to work in other states to earn money for the mortgage, to buy seed and fertilizer for crops, and to pay doctor bills.

In 1946, Roy and Ollie buy the farm of their dreams, but drought destroys crops. In 1950, Ollie is expecting her seventh child: at delivery, she discovers she has twin girls. After four of their eight children are grown, Roy and Ollie begin operation of a successful dairy farm.

About the Author

Nancy Powell has won several writing awards for short stories and poetry. Dark Secrets the first book in the Ollie's Angels Series (under the name Ollie's Angels) won first place in the 2010 Mainstream Novel category at the Oklahoma Writers Federation, Inc. (OWFI) Contest. Dark Secrets was also awarded the 2012 third quarter Grand Prize at the "Books Without Publishers" writing contest sponsored at www.UltimateHeroContest.com

Nancy Powell is married, the mother of two children, and seven grandchildren. She is a member of the Church of Christ, River Valley Writers of Fort Smith, Oklahoma Writers' Federation, Inc., and Round Table Poets. Nancy is a graduate of the University of Arkansas, Little Rock.

In addition to writing, Nancy loves gardening, sewing, and painting—this book's cover background is her interpretation, in oil paint, of the White Oak farm with Ollie holding her baby beside the cornfield—from Chapter 4. The title page picture is her depiction of the White Oak farm—from the story in Chapter 20.